Sometimes I'm so Smart
I Almost Feel Like a Real Person

Graham Parke

No Hope Media
www.nohopemedia.com

This is a work of fiction. Any similarity between the ideas expressed herein and your own perception of reality is not only coincidental, but worrying. Any similarity between the characters in this work and any persons, living or dead, is to be taken as an act of plagiarism on the part of the persons, rather than that of the characters, or their author.

No Hope Media
www.nohopemedia.com

Novels set in the NoHope universe:

No Hope for Gomez!
No Date for Gomez!
Sometimes I'm so Smart,
I Almost Feel Like a Real Person

And coming soon:

Welcome To Earth

Places to stalk Graham Parke on the internetwebthingy:
GrahamParke.blogspot.com, Facebook, GoodReads

On the off chance you don't hate this book, please consider leaving a review. It goes a long way towards ensuring future adventures of Gomez and his pals see the light of day ;)

I believe anyone can be forgotten. No matter how wonderful they are, no matter how unlikely they brim with kindness and inner beauty, you can get over any person.

The only trick is really wanting to…

A lot has happened since you left, Eric. For one thing, I had to deal with this really bad break up. Not one to waste time, I immediately turned to my oldest, dearest friend: Google. After all, more than 4000 years of civilization should've produced a cure, right? Countless generations suffered this fate before me, so the best way to deal with the rejection, the heartache, and that longing to spend the days with a special someone, it should be known by now. It should be Honed and Perfected. And, at a pinch, condensed down to a small pill or a fun little bullet list.

Not so.

Apparently humanity really dropped the ball on this one.

With over a million books and movies about love and relationships, I couldn't find a single serious effort on how best to *un-fall* in love. The only thing out there is corny advice on keeping your distance and giving it time. Which begs the question: what have we been up to? Why haven't we found a few moments to solve the most universal of all human problems?

Still, I was convinced exorcizing heartache could be reduced to a scientific exercise, and I set out to do just that. In fact, I captured my first efforts in a video blog series that I called: *How to get over someone in 600 easy steps.*

Okay, so I was still wallowing when I came up with that title. Deep down I didn't *want* to get over her, I just wanted a statement that explained how nonsensical my life had become.

Later I changed the title to: *27 simple steps to happiness…*

Still heavy on the sarcasm, true, but definitely a nudge in the right direction.

Anyway, my goals were simple: 1. identify the steps needed to return the love-sick mammalian brain to normal operating parameters; 2. condense these steps down to a single-sheet PowerPoint presentation. (After all, PowerPoint is how the modern hunter-gatherer deals with reality. Creating bullet lists and charts pass for survival skills in our society, and rightly so.)

So why bring this up? Well, due to my more than heroic efforts nobody'll ever have to suffer this fate again. They can simply follow my list and cure themselves. But before I tell you all about it, let me explain how I got into this mess in the first place. I'll call this bit of my story…

Part One

1

One of my strengths:

I'm like moss; you might not care for me at first, but when you're not looking, I'll secretly grow on you.

I finish the Waterton&Prince quarterly ahead of schedule and click around my desktop aimlessly. I move icons, open tabs, and re-check my empty mail box. There's enough to do, there always is, but I don't feel like starting anything new right now. I've earned a few *fuck-it* hours.

I peer over my cubicle wall to see if anyone else has hit a natural coffee break, but all heads are down. I realize why when I spot Gharity walking the floor.

Gharity's in his early fifties and sports a thick mane of pepper-and-salt. He has one of those wise and friendly faces, like a younger, slimmer Santa, and that can really throw you off because Gharity doesn't fraternize. Ever. He's one of those supervisors with a strict closed-door policy. In fact, many newcomers are tricked by his friendly appearance and dig themselves an early grave.

Of course, Gharity spots me immediately. A single head popping up above the cubicle garden stands out like a giant red flag. I decide not to show fear, though. Instead I give him a nod as if to say, *'Good to see you're checking up on our slower guys'*. Then I slide back behind my desk and click around some more. It really kills me that I've already checked all the blogs and gadget sites I follow. There is no new information for me out there.

Hushed whispers let me mentally track Gharity's route through the department. He's getting closer, so I'm still not safe. I call up the next account from my task queue to see what it is. No surprise there: another quarterly. I fiddle around with it, resizing the window and changing the font, then I peek over my cubicle wall again.

Gharity has disappeared. My penetrating gaze must have scared him off.

Supervisors are like that. They appear tough and intimidating but they have no idea how to react when a subordinate stares them down. They're not programmed for it. It's not part of the business school curriculum. Deep down, every supervisor knows you're only their subordinate by chance and contract, not by level of mental acuity. And this means that anarchy is always just around the corner. It's good to remind them of that. Keeps them on their toes.

With a little more breathing room now I start writing a script for a new YouTube video.

Although it's true that I kick fiscal ass on levels most humans couldn't possibly comprehend (supervisors included), my real passion is helping people in areas of the heart. I believe it's my duty to share my hard earned knowledge, my infinite stream of realizations and wise-isms, with other men. It's my duty to make the world a better place by teaching men how to better interact with women.

My upcoming vid will expand on the misunderstood differences between the sexes. I need to pass on some vital insight so men around the globe can successfully introduce themselves to their future wives.

Yes, I fully expect to save lives with my next post.

When I'm almost finished with my first draft, I notice a disturbance in the air. A small displacement of pressure accompanied by a hint of what some humans might consider an appropriate aftershave for the work place (they'd be wrong, however).

I don't turn around. Not just yet. Instead, I alt-tab between applications as if I'm looking for something. When I'm sure my screen is safe-for-work, I finally look up, pretending I've only just noticed Gharity standing behind me.

Here's why this works: getting caught is usually preceded by acting guilty, it's almost never preceded by acting cool.

When your supervisor looks over your shoulder he has no prior context. You might've been writing, say, a brilliant YouTube script, but all he sees is a screen full of text. If you leisurely browse through different applications your supervisor won't have time to read your screen, moreover he wouldn't have *reason* to.

Simply pretend you're not doing anything wrong. You'd be surprised how many times this trick has saved me.

"What're you doing?" Gharity demands.

He steps closer, torturing my finely tuned nostrils with his aftershave.

"I was just finishing up another quarterly," I lie.

"I thought I saw you typing a large piece of text."

"I might've been. Probably making notes about the quarterly."

"No." Gharity shakes his head. "You were typing something about women."

"Women? I highly doubt that, sir." I smile patiently.

"Yes, I definitely saw you typing the word 'women' as I walked past."

"Highly unlikely."

"And I saw the word 'kissing', too."

"I can almost definitely say you must've seen that wrong."

"I'm sure," Gharity says. "The word 'Kissing' came after the word 'women', and you were putting the word 'like' in between."

I shrug. "Can't say I remember."

"You did." Gharity gives me a hard look.

I decide to stay very, very still. Snake-charmer still.

Gharity huffs. "What kind of fiscal report could possibly necessitate the inclusion of the words, 'Women like kissing'?"

"It might have been some kind of elaborate typo," I tell him. "I'll fix it later."

"Didn't I warn you about flaking out during company time?"

I shrug. I really shouldn't allow Gharity to indulge in this 'artificial hierarchy' fantasy of his too long. It's not good for him. I subtly remind him who's actually doing the work that makes him look good, and I point out how far ahead of schedule I am. Then I direct his attention to the Waterton&Prince quarterly, which he has yet to approve.

He has no option but to change the subject.

"Don't let me catch you again," he says. "You're skating on thin ice as it is!"

Purely out of my own volition I decide to start working on a new quarterly. But Gharity doesn't move. In fact, he seems annoyingly reluctant to leave me alone.

Supervisors can be like that, too. I think this is either:

1. A natural defense mechanism (they need to leave on their own terms).
2. Their way of getting through the day (talk to enough people about nothing and, before you know it, it's time to go home).

So, for a few long moments, I consider developing the mental powers to make him evaporate. Not just leave, not just wander off, but make him lose actual molecular cohesion, move straight into a gaseous state, and waft away. But then I decide it's easier to put him in his place once and for all, so I mention that our personal evaluations are way overdue.

Gharity finally stalks off.

I allow a few minutes to pass as a buffer, then do a final touch-up of my new script.

YouTube Script:

Here's the big secret guys: *Girls aren't that different from us.*

This may come as a shock. After all, you've been trying to figure them out since kindergarten. (Why do they smell so different? Why do they refuse to throw sand at each other? ~~And why don't they ever pee in the snow? What's more satisfying than writing your name in yellow right into the earth?~~)

And for their part, girls haven't done much to dispel the mystery. They *want* us to think they're different, at some point probably even started believing they *are* different. But we all came from the same soup of primordial DNA. We're all built according to the same biological blue prints. The difference between the genders is merely one of perception.

[hold up chart #1]

The problem is, we've been befuddled by their mysterious handbags, inexplicable 'girl-problems', and whimsical tales of women's intuition – insisting they 'just know something is wrong' without ever feeling the need to produce a single shred of evidence.

But women want the same things we do. Women *like* being around us, women like kissing, they just show us in very strange ways.

[pause here for effect [and maybe raise one eyebrow? [could be too much]]]

So, why do they do this?
No one knows. ~~I'm not even sure they know themselves.~~
It's as if girls have this inner voice that works against us. It's their subconscious telling them lies and making life needlessly difficult. It tells them things like: 'If he likes me, then he'll figure this out.' And: 'He'll know that when I say the problem is A, that what I *really* mean is that the problem is B.'

Which is nonsense. You tell a guy the problem is a faulty A and he'll go out and fix it. Simple. What he won't do, is ask about A's feelings, or whether A is broken because of something he failed to say six months earlier. And he certainly will not, at any point in time, be aware of the existence of a B. Or the fact that B's sister bought the same dress just to piss someone off at a party.
No sir.

[sign off]

2

A test to see if she is The One:

When something interesting happens, do you think;
I wish She could see this.*
When you see a beautiful cloud, do you think;
I wish She could see this with me.**

*) This means she could be The One!
**) This means you're being a big sissy. Get over it. It's just a cloud!

I decide to leave work early.

And I do mean disgustingly, mind bogglingly, heroically early.

But Gharity deserves it, after all that 'artificial hierarchy' crap he tried to pull. And he doesn't try to stop me, either. He wouldn't dare. Then again, he doesn't appears to be in the office, so, lucky for him I guess.

On my way home I drop by the mall to pick up some art supplies and some peppered Brazil nuts. I always get my nuts from this cool little place called 'Ye Olde Peanut Shoppe,' which I'm pretty sure is the only place in town that stocks peppered Brazils. I have close to thirteen kilos of the stuff at home and I've never told a soul why I buy them.

On my way back from the Shoppe I detour past Sparky's for an Ultra burger. If you're familiar with this burger then you'll probably agree it is the best burger on the planet, not in the least because it comes with BBQ sauce so you don't have to bring your own.

I find a table in the food court and dig in.

As always, I analyze each bite, taking note of how some are heavy on one ingredient, like tomato, while others are an almost perfect blend of all ingredients.

Sadly, I'm interrupted by a guy who sits down at my table and attacks my delicate senses with an aftershave that's only slightly less intrusive than Gharity's. It is, however, more damaging, as it mixes in with my palette. Without warning the scent is translated into taste in that obscure way the olfactory organ has of overstepping its boundaries.

I hate when that happens.

"Are you him?" the intruder whispers. "Are you the guy?" His eyes flit about the food court, making sure we're not overheard. "You're him, right?"

I tell him I'm don't think I'm the guy he's looking for. I also ask him to seriously consider partaking in the underappreciated act of leaving me alone.

"I'm sure," he says. "I'm sure you're him." He finally meets my gaze and I notice one of his eyes is blue while the other is green. "Don't worry," he says, "your secret is safe with me!"

He rummages around in his jacket and produces a business card.

"This is me," he says. "Leopold. I'm in finance, bonds mostly."

I don't take his card. It'd mean putting my burger down and losing my finger placement. So far I've prevented all the burger's innards from spilling and this is no small feat. It is, in fact, a skill and the result of years of careful training.

Leopold decides to put the card on the table. "It's so great to meet you," he says. "I mean, you look different, I almost didn't recognize you, but, up close, it's unmistakable. You're him!"

"I'm sorry," I say. "I really don't think I am."

Leopold doesn't hear. "Do you like my teeth?"

"Your teeth?"

"Yeah. I had them done last Tuesday!"

He pauses as if that's somehow significant.

"*You know*," he prods. "After your post on Personal Appearance. You told us to take responsibility for our first impression."

It finally dawns on me that this must be one of my YouTube followers.

"And my eyes?" he asks.

Some part of me has been wondering about his eyes, yes, but it's been unwilling to ask.

"Contacts!"

"Ah."

"I got them yesterday, after your post on needing to stand out. You said there had to be something different about us. Something to make The One remember us, even if we didn't say much."

This is indeed one of my wise-isms, but one he has taken way out of context.

"I also have a red pair," he says. "For weekends."

I tell him he looks like a genetic aberration.

Leopold beams. "Thanks, Leverage!"

I cringe. That's my YouTube handle. My alter-ego. He's throwing my secret name around, out loud.

"Can I call you Leverage, by the way?"

"I'd rather you didn't."

He realizes he's stopped whispering and quickly lowers his voice. "Should I call you by your real name? Which is...?"

"You know what," I say. "Just call me Leverage."

It takes me a while to get rid of Leopold.

It's not that I don't like interacting with fans…

(Actually, this is an assumption on my part. As this has never happened before, I can't be sure.)

… it's just that I've had an idea for a new post. I have to get it down before I forget.

I let Leopold the green-eyed freak of nature know that brilliance is afoot. This appears to soften the blow.

"I can't wait to see your next video," he says, getting up. "Any chance you could, you know, mention me?"

I already feel my idea fading. I have to hurry and immortalize it. "In what capacity," I ask him, "would I mention you?"

"I don't know." He thinks it over. "As someone you've met?"

I'm not sure this would be the right thing to do. I cannot sacrifice the integrity of my art just to be *nice*. "Have you watched all my vids, Leopold?"

"Of course! Every single one. Several times."

"And do I ever waste time mentioning random people I've met?"

"Actually, no. You're exceedingly efficient with our time. It's one of the many things we appreciate about you."

"So, there's your answer."

Leopold gives me a salute. "Yes, sir," he says. "And may I say, it was an honor meeting you."

With that, he finally disappears.

I have to smile. So far my vids have been a one-way affair, but maybe interacting with other humans isn't always a bad thing.

I take out my tablet and start on a new script.

YouTube script:

Today I want to revisit a vital concept: The Intro.

The Intro represents the ten most important seconds of a man's life. It's the moment he first introduces himself to The One.

In future vids I'll talk about tools to survive the Intro, such as the all-important *Ear Catcher*, but today I want to focus on making sure the importance of the Intro is clear. Only when its monumental significance is understood can we begin to construct our own Intros.

I hope I don't have to explain that the Intro should be rehearsed ~~(if possible in front of a mirror with several recording devices running)~~. After all, we're not trying to pick up chicks here. We are after The One! There is no such thing as a second chance. Think of this as brain surgery, only slightly more important.

Let's analyze the Intro as implemented by the Average Hapless Joe (AHJ).

1. AHJ admires The One from across the room.
2. The One notices AHJ staring and is immediately creeped out.
3. AHJ notices her noticing and thinks they are *'having a moment'*.
4. Six weeks (and a lot of creepy staring) later, AHJ finally works up the courage to say hello.
5. The One runs away terrified. That *creepy guy* is after her!

If I have to say anything else to convince you that your default plan sucks on all levels, then you may be beyond hope, but if any of this is even slightly clear, then my work for today is done.

[sign off]

3

Ear Catcher:

"I read somewhere that all girls pee in the shower, is this true?"

I read my script back, counting the number of wise-isms to estimate its level of geniusness. It meets requirements, so I put my tablet away, finish my burger, and head home.

When I arrive, Mom's already complaining. Sometimes I think she starts before she even opens the door, perhaps warming up by telling the wall to stop slouching and stand up straight.

Today she's on my case about my room. Apparently there are charts and figurines gathering dust. The exact details remain sketchy as my subconscious immediately tunes her out.

Who does she think I am, anyway? Some kind of child to be chided? One so dependent on parental guidance he can't make it through the day without advice from his mom? No! I'm an adult and a fiscal genius with uncanny insight into the human condition. I'll damn well decide for myself when I clean my room!

However, the charts I left out so that the glue could dry are done, so I might as well put them away.

I give Mom a kiss and head upstairs.

(Never make the mistake of not kissing your mom just because she's being whiny. Being whiny is a natural state for some moms, they can't help it.)

The first thing I do when I get home is record a new YouTube post. My vids are basically five minute monologues that I shoot from two angles and then mix together, and I like to get them in one continuous take because that makes them feel more real, more genuine. But this can be a challenge, especially when Mom decides to call me for dinner. I have to yell down for her to give me five more minutes, then start my take over. However, Mom usually only manages to stay quiet for about four-and-a-half minutes, after which point she calls me again.

This annoying pattern will repeat itself until Mom finally allows me a full, uninterrupted five minutes to record.

Today she gets it in three tries. Some days, however, we keep this up for hours.

Mom can be very stubborn.

Okay, so maybe you think there's an easy solution to this problem, but there isn't. I can't record my vids after dinner because:

1. You only aggravate stubborn behavior by rewarding it.
2. You simply cannot schedule geniusness.

I have to record my vids when the muse takes me – usually around 6:42 p.m.

Think about it, what would've become of da Vinci if he had to plan his bouts of inspired genius around his mom's cooking schedule?

It would've been a disaster. We never would have heard of him.

Now I'm not comparing myself to Leonardo, of course, that would be ludicrous. After all, he hasn't done much too actually improve the human condition. But you know what I mean.

When I finally get my take, I head down to eat. As per usual, dinner is a difficult time for me.

Mom: How was work?

Me: Work was work.

Mom: Did you finally make some friends?

Me: Friends? I'm a highly-skilled fiscal genius. I set up quarterly reports for offshore multinationals. I don't go to work to *make friends.*

Mom: Still, it's nice to have a friend over some time. Remember that Tommy? Whatever happened to him?

Me: Tommy Moretti?

Mom: Yes, such a lovely boy. Why doesn't he come over anymore?

Me: His family moved away when he was twelve. He used to come over to play Legos and pick his nose!

Mom: But you had fun with Tommy, didn't you?

Me: Of course we had fun, we were twelve. Last I heard he was running some import-export business overseas.

Mom: Well, you should give him a call. Maybe he'll come over and play, you never know.

And dessert isn't much better:

Mom: When are you going to get a girlfriend?

Me: I can't tie myself down, Mom. I have too much to do. Anyway, so far no one has passed my tests.

Mom: You're not fooling anyone with your tests. If you don't find a date before the weekend, I'm calling Betsy. Her niece would love to go out with you.

Me: Of course she would. No one else will take her. She used to eat bugs. With ketchup. Who does that?

Mom: She's just a little shy, that's all. She has a nice personality.

Me: I'm not going on any blind dates and that's final!

Mom: Then you'd better call her and cancel.

Me: Cancel? You already made a date for me? How can you do that?

Mom: I have my knitting club coming over Saturday. We don't like your noise.

Me: I'll have you know I have a very busy schedule Saturday! I'm recording a master class for my YouTube channel!

Mom: That's fine, dear. Just pick up the phone and cancel.

Me: Mom!

Mom: What?

Me: You know I can't talk on the phone!

Mom: Of course you can.

Me: I can't! It makes me very… uncomfortable. And it's not my style. Phones are so last century.

Mom: It's up to you, dear. If you don't want to cancel, that's fine.

I give Mom a long, annoyed look. I remind her that Betsy is *her* friend and if she wants to avoid a disaster-of-unexpected-absence, then she'll have to make the call herself.

I go up to my room and start on the charts for my next vid.

These days it's pretty easy to splice a PowerPoint chart into a video or use all kinds of fancy effects, but I like to hand-draw my charts and hold them up to the camera. I believe handmade charts have a much higher impact.

People are so used to fancy presentations, they don't notice them anymore. You can talk about any subject while showing an animation of the lifecycle of a turd and no one would notice. Part of the brain is trained to assume PowerPoints and fancy graphics make sense, so we glance over them. That's why even a badly drawn chart is much more effective. It's an eye-catcher. The brain immediately goes: *'Hey! What's that badly drawn chart doing there?'* And then it's paying attention.

It's the same with women, when you think about it. You have to step out of their PowerPoint world and make their minds wake up and notice you.

Which reminds me, there's another script I should write.

YouTube Script:

Today I want to talk about: *The Ear Catcher*

The ear catcher (EC) lets The One know that you're different. That you're not like other guys. Being with you promises a whole different set of life experiences.

A good EC comes in the form of a sharp one-liner that her brain can't gloss over (so this means that *'What do you do?'* and *'Where are you from?'* are forever banned from the first twenty minutes of your conversations!) She can't respond to a good EC on auto pilot, so she'll have to 'wake up' and think about what she's going to say next.

[pause for effect]

ECs are not pick-up lines. They serve a very different purpose. They start out nicely familiar so they don't trigger her inner voice, which wants to block you. A good EC can fly under the radar of her subconscious mind and deliver its payload directly to her conscious mind. This payload, of course, is the second part of the EC, the part that she can't respond to on autopilot.

Deliver your EC with confidence. Remember, the best joke in the world still sounds creepy when told by a nervous, fidgety guy, while the worst joke will sound perfectly serviceable when told with unwavering confidence. ~~This is the reason (the only reason!) that confident people seem more fun.~~

And the more weird and offbeat your EC is, the more serious the delivery should be. Look deep into her eyes and wait patiently for her to answer the question/solve the riddle/explain the mystery.

Does she pee in the shower? If so, how disgusting! Why on earth does she do this? If not, then why not? The drain's right there, water all around, what's her problem? Discover if she'll play along, and scoop up any information she gives you in her response.

Warning: If she does *not* play along, she's unlikely to be The One. And you don't want to spend the rest of your life with someone who just doesn't 'get it,' do you?

[sign off]

4

A test to see if she's The One:

Do you like the person you are when you're with her better than the person you are without her?

I sleep well and my new charts are dry by morning. I put them away to avoid another after-work complaining session (even though Mom has received official notice she's barred from my room while I'm away), and I start the weekly backup of my vids.

My video archive has grown pretty large over the years, so every Wednesday I take a copy of my work to my storage locker at the bank – there's really no point keeping backups at home where they can burn down with the rest of your stuff.

And I remind myself I really should check the files I'm backing up sometime, make sure I'm not creating a vast archive of corrupt data. But, as brilliant as my vids probably are, I'm just not comfortable watching myself. Makes me feel weird, like I'm spying on some guy who looks eerily similar to me. It freaks me out. (Probably one of those quirky things that plagues all geniuses.) The small amount of editing I do while creating the vids is difficult enough, so, for now, I keep making copies of the same old files.

While the backup process purrs away for tomorrow's bank-run, I head down for breakfast, where I only have a small fight with Mom, and then I'm in my car, heading to the mall. Got's to get me some more of them peppered Brazils!

I enjoy a large range of nuts, as most human do, but the peppered Brazils have some very specific properties. Here they are in descending order of magnitude:

1. They contain selenium, which may or may not be good for testosterone production.
2. They are filling and stay fresh for a long time.
3. They are extremely unpopular, which is why they're stored in the back, and the clerk has to spend ages on your order.

On weekdays there's only one clerk on duty at Ye Olde Peanut

Shoppe and that's Emma. She seems pleased to see me.

I haven't actually asked her name, but to me she looks like an Emma. In my mind, Emmas are people with deep, dark eyes, the kind that radiate mysterious wisdom. And they often have straight hair that's cut in a bob. And they may well be short without being stocky, and when they smile their perfect smiles, with one little tooth slightly out of alignment, you just know something wonderful is going on in their minds. Something far beyond our mere mortal realm.

This particular Emma, I've noticed, is always in a good mood.

"250 grams of peppered Brazils, please," I ask her.

She smiles. "Roasted?"

"Sure, why not."

"Would you like to make that 500 grams? We have an offer." Emma points out a crudely designed flyer which I can only pretend to read because, for some strange reason, I can no longer concentrate. The flyer enumerates a number of restrictions which I have no hope of assimilating. Not in any kind of timely fashion. So, to minimize the risk of looking dopey, I just shrug and tell her that 250 grams will be fine. After all, my main goal here isn't saving money.

"No problem." She shoots me another quick smile, then disappears to the back.

While I wait, a line forms behind me, annoying me deeply. What are these people doing here so early? Shouldn't they be on their way to work or something? Or getting in line for their unemployment checks?

Emma returns and asks me if I'd like anything else. She captures me with her gaze and for a long moment my mind does nothing but ingest details: the way her hair falls over her forehead, the shape of the tiny birthmark on the side of her nose, the bit of crust caught in her eyelashes, her mouth opening as if in slow motion, showing me her brilliant white teeth, with that one little tooth slightly out of alignment, and her saying, "Hello? Sir? Is there anything else you'd like?"

I catch myself. "Let me see," I say. "I'm not sure…"

A groan from the line behind me. Not my problem. Serves them right for trying to procure nuts so early. What's wrong with people these days?

"I have my Brazil nuts," I continue. "So, I guess… I'm all set."

"Great." Emma smiles as she rings me up and I notice it's a particularly cute smile. I wonder if maybe this is not just a professional smile. What if this is a personal smile? One made just for me? That would be really interesting. I should find out if there's a way to tell the difference. Maybe Google knows. If not, I may have to invest some time in decoding this myself. Seems like an important skill to develop and share with humanity.

Emma hands me my change and I quickly search for something else to say, something fun and quirky. Something so cool she'll remember me, specifically as someone she'd like to hang out with sometime.

Sadly, by the time our transaction completes, my brain still hasn't come up with anything good and I can only thank Emma for her impeccable service and be on my way.

The line moves up with a sigh.

I leave, feeling a little sad for no reason.

Back at work I quickly start on a new script before it gets too busy around the office. My colleagues are already trickling in, throwing around boisterous hello's and peering over cubicle walls – not an environment conducive to time theft. I type fast. I only have minutes to spare before interruptions reach unbearable levels.

YouTube script:

You've heard the saying that you can't call a girl the next day. That you should wait at least 48 hours. But is this true? And if so, why?

Let's be clear: it *is* true.
You simply *cannot* call a girl the next day.

Even if she desperately wants you to call, you can't. If you do, her subconscious won't let her respect you. ~~It will signal her conscious mind that you're not worthy.~~ She won't even realize this is happening, she'll just experience a little loss of interest when the phone rings prematurely.

~~This is because her subconscious doesn't want to get a call from someone with time on his hands. It wants to NOT get a call from someone who is way too busy living his cool, exciting life.~~

So how do we get around this? How do we *help* her to stay interested? Simple: we create 'the illusion of scarcity'.
We do this by, you guessed it, waiting 48 hours. And this, of course, is the minimum amount, ~~to be used by guys who are going off to war or who have contracted a terrible wasting disease,~~ the rest of us are better off waiting a full week, or, if we can manage it, a calendar month. And, if it's relatively close, you might consider stretching it into the summer. Everyone knows summer dates are more fun.

When you do finally call, don't invite her on a date for that same evening, not unless you want her subconscious serenading her with songs about your utter unworthiness. You don't want her to think she's your last chance for a date. If you must see her that same night, then just ask her out on a tag along with your friends. Tell her it would be fun if she joins, but it's not expected. She's not actually needed.

[pause for effect]

So wait before you make that first call. It's a vital part of the dance. But don't overdo it. Leaving it more than, say, a full fiscal year, may well be overkill. ~~(Some actual field testing might be needed here).~~

[sign off]

The Leverage Credo

I am not a pickup artist.
I am not a Casanova or Don Juan.
I am a Dating Guru.

Pickup artists teach you how to get many women. Casanovas show you how to approach the most beautiful women. But these are not useful skills. They're parlor tricks.

A Dating Guru will show you how to get that One girl.

You know the one I'm talking about.
You've fantasized about her.
And not just about sleeping with her,
you've fantasized about just being near her and holding her hand.
A frightening number of times.
In fact, you're thinking about her right now.

You know where she works and you know her favorite color.
You know exactly what you'd do on your first date.
And maybe, just maybe, you've already talked to her.
But that was probably only in your mind.

I am here to give you a little Leverage.
I am here to
Change
Your
Life.

Your friend in this adventure,

Leverage.

Video #123 by *Leverage*. Views: 227

Comments:

WhipCrck: (5:01 pm) Who's watching this shit?? 227 views?? U gotta be kiddin me!! This guy's a moron!! He wears a Zorro mask for crying out loud! What's he hiding?

Agent12: (5:19 pm) Is this guy supposed to be some kind of wizard with women? Get ur ass to the Gym, dude!!

OnMyWay: (5:19 pm) Another killer vid, Lev. Saving my life here ;)

Leverage: (6:27 pm) Excuse me, Agent12, but we all know the camera adds ten pounds, webcams probably add double that! My weight falls well within the ranges set by most medical associations. WhipCrck; The mask is a style choice. You have way too much time on your hands if you can afford to worry about what I'm wearing!

GaryXXX: (8:35 pm) None of that explains the weird haircut, dude :*p

LeopoldGreenEye: (9:21 pm) Great advice, Lev. Will try it tomorrow on The One!

13Monkeys: (9:22 pm) <u>Get premium timeshares at discount prices here!!!!!!!!!</u>

GomezP: (9:23 pm) Lev *rocks* in serious doses! And he probably *rules* as well, but I have no way of measuring that ;)

Voodood: (9:26 pm) Leverage is exactly what's wrong with the net: too many idiots with webcams declaring themselves experts!

DissonantMelody: (9:27 pm) Another great vid, Leverage! Don't make us wait so long next time. You don't have to use the Illusion of Scarcity on us. We need our Leverage fix! :)

5

The trap:

*If you think about her too much, the girl in your head
becomes more interesting than the girl in real life.*

I sleep reasonably well – Mom's snoring only wakes me four times (my subconscious can't filter that sound out, perhaps due to its eerily intermittent nature) – and as I head to the bank to drop off my backups, my mind starts to wander. These videos represent such a large part of my life. It's not just the time invested in recording, uploading, and replying to comments, it's the hours spent pondering life and nursing ideas from embryonic impressions to full grown wise-isms.

In a way, my vlogs represent the passing of time. My life is a process that converts time into videos. And sometimes I wish I had someone to leave them to.

Eventually my YouTube channel will be lost in a maelstrom of meaningless data. The instant I stop updating, it'll drop back into obscurity. Nothing more than a needle in a stack of needles, inside a warehouse filled with stacks of needles.

YouTube is not an entity to entrust your legacy to.

If I want my wise-isms to survive so future generations can prosper from them, I'll have to pass them on, perhaps through these very backups.

I retrieve the previous backup from my locker and wrap it in my backup-protecting-towel before lowering it into my backup-transporting-backpack. Then I place the new backup in the locker, making sure not to nudge the sides of the metal container, and lock it back up.

At least my latest vids are safe… for now.

Back in my car, I think about all the people I'm helping. All the lives that'll continue along a slightly different path because of me.

A spotty-faced kid in Tijuana, who was sure his social life was over when all his friends started dating, he now finds the courage to crawl out of his shell. He'll grow up to be the CEO of a trading company.

A lonely widower in a tiny apartment in Rome finds just enough bravado to talk to the woman running the shop downstairs. This time he knows not to play it safe; he uses an edgy ear-catcher and two lonely lives are melded into a single, happy one.

An emo girl in Greece watches one of my vids and finally understands why the jock isn't right for her, and how deeply the shy kid with the brooding eyes really loves her.

But these stories won't reach me.

I'll never know any of this.

I crack a window. It's hot. I should've parked in the shade. I place the backup-transporting-backpack on the passenger seat and strap it in.

I might even have followers that I've met in real life, without even knowing. Perhaps the guys who bullied me in school. And the girls I had crushes on. They'll wonder why they didn't realize how special I was, and they'll assume it's too late to get to know me now.

It might be hard to believe, but I too was once hopeless with the opposite sex.

Maybe some of my colleagues are even watching.

And Mom's friends.

And maybe, just maybe, my dad.

I leave the parking lot and immediately slam on the brakes; a lady in an oversized SUV cuts me off. My right hand extends to catch my backup-transporting-backpack before the seatbelt brakes even kick in, while my left hand gives the lady the finger. (And I make a face that clearly communicates that she doesn't need *that* much metal and plastic to transport her tiny frame to step-class, but now that she's decided that she does, she should at least be responsible enough to keep her eyes on the road while maneuvering her tank across town.)

And get off the damn phone! I mouth at her.

She shows me one of her fingers and drives off, without ever lowering her cell from her ear.

I file into traffic behind her and switch on the radio.

Every once in a while that image pops into my head: my dad secretly following my vids, tracking my progress through life from the other side of an anonymous internet connection.

It could happen, I suppose, but do I even want it to? I push the thought away, check the time; another forty minutes before Gharity arrives at work. There's still time for my second stop.

Emma's on duty in Ye Olde Peanut Shoppe and she smiles politely, but I'm not entirely sure she recognizes me.

"Can I help you?"

"Sure," I say. "Why not?" I make it sound as if it's an unexpected offer. How nice of her to help me out.

Her smile warms up. "I meant, what'll it be?"

"I'd like some nuts, please." I look around as if unsure of my location. "Do you have any of those?"

Emma grins. She cocks her head to the side in a way I find almost unbearably endearing and says, "You're in luck, we still have a few. Are you looking for any particular kind of nut, or I do I get you one of each? Because that could take a while."

There are many levels of recognizing someone. There's the level where you know you've seen a face before but you can't quite place it, and you rack your brain trying to recall where you met and whether you're still on speaking terms. There's the level where you remember everything about a person except their name, and you spend the entire conversation trying to avoid having to use it.

There could be an infinite number of levels of recognizing somebody...

"I'd like 250 grams of peppered Brazil nuts, please."

"Of course. We might have some in the back. Let me check."

...So I'm sure Emma remembers my face. It's unlikely to appear entirely new to her. She may even recognize me as one of her regulars, but that doesn't mean she remembers our last conversation, or the fact that it took place yesterday...

"Would you like to make that 500 grams?" She returns with a scoop of Brazils, ready to weigh them. "We have a special offer." She points out the flyer on the counter.

...Or maybe she can't quite place my face.

"No," I tell her. "250 grams will be more than enough."

Emma finishes up my order and hands me my change.

I realize that if I want her to really recognize me next time, I'll have to make her laugh. And how cool would that be? To see her laugh at something I've said, to have my thoughts running around up there, tickling her brain. Luckily, I know exactly what to say to make that happen. I've practiced it. Honed the delivery of my EC to perfection.

Sadly, when Emma looks at me with that deep, penetrating gaze, I suddenly forget everything. My mind goes blank and I hear myself say; "Crazy weather we've been having, don't you think?"

I can't believe I just said that!

What's wrong with me?

Emma stares at me a moment, then nods and says, "You're a bit weird, aren't you?"

"I sure am," I say, relieved. "Thanks for noticing."

Her gaze lingers on me, as if she might say something more, but then another customer enters and the moment passes. She smiles and wishes me a nice day.

I panic. I could make another attempt, I suppose, there's still a little time, but I realize the light isn't coming through the windows the right way, and it doesn't make sense to attempt another EC under these harsh conditions. No, I have no option but to bail out.

I leave the store and head to work, and I do *not* spend the entire trip analyzing whether Emma meant I was 'weird' in a good way, or whether she was expressing genuine concern for my mental health.

YouTube script:

Let's talk about the Trap. It's perhaps our second most fearful enemy.
While women have a little voice telling them to dislike us, we have an equally annoying voice telling us to like them *more*.
~~That's right; evolution is secretly stacking the odds against species survival!~~

[show chart #1]

Our inner voice starts out reminding us of something She's said. Something cool or funny. Then it'll romanticize it, finding hidden meaning, inventing new subtexts just to keep us thinking about Her. Pretty soon, we're imagining events that never even took place, like her giving us special looks, making in-jokes, performing acts of advanced body language...

~~Don't deny it; you've imagined her liking your favorite music and mentioning that obscure movie you didn't think anybody else liked.~~

Slowly the girl in your head grows more and more perfect. So perfect, in fact, that when you finally speak to her, you come off sounding like an idiot.

You know what I'm talking about. It's the reason you subconsciously start speaking louder whenever a cute girl stands near you at the bar (never mind the fact that what you're saying isn't all that interesting). ~~It's that time you were convinced you were naturally deep and funny, but still couldn't think of a single thing to say past 'this weather is crazy, isn't it?'~~

So you have to cut that inner voice off. In fact, don't even let your mind wander. Think of it as an addiction: if you let the voice speak, you'll get used to it, start *needing* it. Similarly, once you've successfully muted the voice three days in a row, it'll fade. The addiction will break and you'll be in the clear.
All it takes is three days of not making stuff up about Her in your head.

By all means, remember the little things She did. Analyze them for future reference. But, as soon as you find yourself thinking about things that haven't actually happened, CUT THE VOICE OFF!

[sign off]

6

The complaints start as soon as I open the door. There's talk of rooms needing tidying, trash that should be taken out, lightbulbs that may or may not need replacing, mysterious drops found on toilet seats, pieces of underwear that have narrowly missed hampers post-flight, cartons of milk that suffered a diminishment of content without any accompanying cups having been used and, perhaps most importantly, there are suspicions of cookie theft, most notably from a jar that was labelled 'Mom' for previously misunderstood reasons.

It seems my complaints filter is working sub-optimally today.

I quickly sidestep Mom and run up to my room. Alas, before I can record a new vid she bursts into my inner sanctum uninvited.

"I made you some tea," she says. She holds up a cup as proof, then looks for a place to set it down. Unable to locate an empty surface, she places it on one of my charts, causing an immediate ring.

"You need a nice cup," she says. "You're far too stressed lately."

There's no point getting angry about the ring, or even the intrusion, it'd just take that much longer to get her out of my room. So I just say, "Thanks, Mom."

I try to look on the bright side. Perhaps this means dinner isn't ready. It doesn't look like she's even started. Maybe I'll get to squeeze out an entire take uninterrupted after she leaves. That would be a cool, positive experience for once.

"So," Mom says, lingering at the door, "trash pick-up is early tomorrow morning…"

"Is it?" I put the cup on the floor and assess the damage. I could cover the ring with a patch, but the edges might show. I'll have to do a few test shots.

"They'll be here before pretty early …"

"That's great, Mom, but I don't understand why you keep informing me of these non-events. It's not like I'm planning to get up at the crack of dawn to take pictures."

"You'll just have to take the trash out tonight," Mom continues, a little louder. "And it wouldn't kill you to pick up your underwear from time to time. You don't get points for *almost* throwing them in the hamper. I still have to bend down to pick them up."

"That never happened," I say, appalled. "Whoever did that, it wasn't me."

"I don't see who else it could be."

28

"Your ability to intuit the real culprit is not the issue here," I tell her.

"And I still don't have a working light in the basement!"

I let out a sigh. "If it is your intention to force me to listen to all your complaints on life, then you should consider waiving my rent. I mean, seriously Mom, this is no way to treat a paying lodger!"

Mom's jaw drops. "This is no way to treat your mother!"

I was afraid this might happen. I should've cleared this confusion up much earlier. "Either I'm a lodger," I tell her, "or I'm a confidant. But a lodger doesn't get verbally assaulted and a confidant doesn't pay rent. Which am I?"

Mom's dumbfounded. I decide to charge on. "And, while you're at it, you may consider the fact that you're not paying me for my fiscal services. Work of my level doesn't come cheap. Some people might think a thank-you would be in order."

Mom declines to give this the consideration it deserves. Instead she says, "I just don't see why I have to be confronted with a wet toilet seat every single day. Can you tell me that?"

I shrug. "That has nothing to do with me, so what can I say on the matter other than that life is mysterious and unfair? And, at your advanced age, you should know that already."

Mom doesn't seem to hear. She charges on, reiterating every single problem she notified me of at the door earlier.

"You know what?" I tell her. "You've given me a million dollar idea."

Mom stares at me, unsure where I'm going with this.

"I've decided to set up a hotline."

"What are you talking about?"

"I'm talking about my new business, Mom, paid for entirely by bored moms. I already have a name and a number: 0800-complain-my-ear-off."

"Don't talk nonsense."

"No, it'll work. Just imagine, for only fifty cents per minute you can call an operator and talk about your problems. It's much better than talking to a therapist because my people will just listen. Nothing more. They won't annoy you with actual solutions or point out the myriad of flaws in your logic. But these operators will need to be trained, of course. Hardened to take the abuse, like commandos. And they'll have to work in shifts, have access to counselling. In fact, that can be a spin-off business: desensitizing courses for men. I'll give men the armor to withstand attacks of up to thirty minutes of unfounded complaints and up to an hour of useless hearsay."

"You can *hearsay* yourself," Mom retorts. "Because you won't be getting a second dessert tonight!"

And with that totally unfair decision, she finally vacates my room.

Mom keeps her promise and the evening is a strained affair.

It's followed by another strained day at work, and by the time I leave the office, I'm in dire need of some peppered Brazils.

Emma is on duty at Ye Olde Peanut Shoppe and I know exactly what to say. My inner voice won't make me forget this time. Emma and I will finally have a long, meaningful conversation!

The queue moves up and a smile of recognition crosses Emma's face (I quickly tell my inner voice to look up the words 'polite professional smile,' so it won't put advanced misconceptions in my head).

"What'll it be?" she asks.

I request some peppered Brazils, about 250 grams worth.

When Emma returns from the back, I feel a little prickle at the back of my neck as I'm about to launch into my pre-fab opener. I must've picked up an insect somewhere because it can't be nerves. The great Leverage doesn't get nervous around female humans! But when Emma looks up, something inexplicably switches off in my brain and the words that come out of my mouth sound eerily similar to, "Crazy weather we've been having, don't you agree?"

I'm absolutely mortified!

My subconscious betrayed me!

Again!

Emma regards me quizzically. "Well," she says after a long pause, "there is this high pressure front moving in from the east, which should bring more stable weather. But recent storms have saturated the air causing some unexpected side-effects such as, but not limited to, showers and freak storms." She hands me my nuts on a platter. "So I suppose you could call that crazy weather. Yes."

"Eh, right." I take my nuts and pocket them. "You seem… very well informed."

Emma smiles brightly. "Of course. You never know when one of your customers will be overcome by the sudden urge to discuss the weather."

"Sure," I say. "That makes perfect sense."

"Or perhaps…" She smiles more mischievously now. "I just made it all up on the spot."

"Ah." I think this over. "Did you?"

"As a matter of fact," she says. "I did."

I smile back. "Very good, very clever."

I wish my brain would start working already.

"Don't look so surprised," she says. "They don't just let anyone serve nuts, you know. It's very responsible work. You need degrees in physics and meteorology, obviously, and ornithology if at all possible."

"Of course," I say. "Otherwise there'd be chaos."

"Exactly."

"So," I ask her, "you have all of those?"

"Nah," Emma says. "I only have two degrees. All birds look alike to me. Just bags of feathers with beaks."

"Too bad," I say. "So ornithology is out, then."

I realize I say this not just to keep the conversation going, but also to show her I actually know what ornithology is.

"Yup." Emma takes my cash and counts out my change. As she hands over there's this weird little moment.

Her eyes seem to say; *anything else?*

And; *are you satisfied with your order?*

And then they seem to add; *don't you think we'd make a perfect couple?*

I smile back, but already her gaze drifts away from mine and what she actually ends up saying is, "Who's next?"

I can still make a move, of course. I can still throw out something funny and insightful, but I decide not to. It just wouldn't be fair. By now my skills are so honed, so developed, it'd be like shooting deer in the headlights. Fish in a barrel. She wouldn't stand a chance. In fact, she'd fall for me so hard I wouldn't even be able to convince myself she really loved me for me. So, instead, I leave.

But I drive home with an odd little spark glowing inside of me.

Video #126 by *Leverage*. Views: 113

Comments:

Hopeless72: (8:23 pm) Great vid leverage! Will def. try this out!!!

LeopoldGreenEye: (9:15 pm) Love your ECs, Lev! Tried to make up my own but, no luck. Can't seem to make em either funny or clever :(But I used your Pee-in-Shower EC with great success on The One yesterday! Here's what happened:
I was making small talk and she was going on automatic (she's in retail), so I decided I had nothing to lose and asked her if it was true that all girls pee in the shower.
The effect was amazing! At first she gave me this blank stare, and I started to panic, but then she started laughing! Amazing! It was like her eyes opened and she saw me for the first time! And then we started bantering (not just talking, bantering!) I can't even remember what we talked about, just that it made me very, very happy :)

Leverage: (9:27 pm) Leopold, great to hear my ECs are working for you. Yes, you should make up your own, and you'll get the hang of it soon enough. Until then, feel free to use mine (there will be a few more coming this week!) So did you ask her on a date or get her number? Don't forget to keep the momentum going. If you didn't, be sure to intro her with another great EC as soon as you see her again. Don't just wait until the conversation stalls!

WhipCrck: (9:28 pm) Nerds!! Bantering? Who talks like that?? That's your whole problem with women right there!!

LeopoldGreenEye: (9:28 pm) I will. In fact, I'll make sure not to run into her until I have another killer EC lined up (either yours or mine :)

GomezP: (10:09 pm) Hey Lev. I've been following ur advice and now I'm dating this girl (actually, I think we're dating, I'm not really sure. One night I got drunk at a party and she took me home so I could sleep it off on her couch. Since then I've returned to her place after work because I thought maybe she expected me to. So far she hasn't complained, so I guess it's okay. In fact, we may be living together, although we haven't specifically discussed it). Anyway, my question is, how do I make sure she doesn't get bored with me? How can I keep the relationship interesting for her? (She's really smart and special!)

Leverage: (10:27 pm) Good question, GomezP, and one I have answered in many vids already (go back and check, you'll find gold!) Be sure to remember this: while guys appreciate clarity (are we living together or not? is that other guy who's using your shower your BF or just a lost neighbor?), girls care far more about drama. The way to keep her interested is to make sure there's always enough drama in your relationship. This means communicating with her on an emotional level. Don't give her facts ('had some problems at work'), but give her feelings ('I hated it when this guy at work tried to look at my screen.' and so on). Hope this helps.

Agent12: (10:32 pm) Unbelievable!! People are actually taking advice from this moron? I thought this was one of those ironic channels! Seriously, these posts are jokes, right? This guy is an actor?

Leverage: (10:42 pm) Getting The One is no joke, sir! I suggest you stop watching my vids if you feel they are not for you.

7

A test to see if she's The One:

Do you find yourself inexplicably mesmerized by little things she does?
The way her tongue touches that tooth that's slightly out of alignment, the face she
makes when trying to decide whether something is either funny or inappropriate?

Saturday.

No work. No shopping. No vids.

It's not that I don't have inspiration, it's just that I don't want to saturate my market. My followers need time to digest, recoup. To practice.

I still rise at 7 a.m. though, I don't have much choice. Mom gets annoyed when people sleep in past 6:30. She feels the day is wasting away. Try as I might, it's impossible to sleep with her standing at the bottom of the stairs wondering loudly what has happened to the younger generation and whether they even realize it's time to take out the garbage.

Passive aggression is a bitch.

I brush my teeth and take a shower, return to my room and discard the clothes Mom's hurriedly laid out for me. I call down to warn her again about sneaking into my room while I'm showering.

(She balks at filling the bedroom-entry request forms I created, objecting on the grounds that it's *her* house and she shouldn't have to apply for a temporary visa to go through my closets. (And she flat out refuses to fill out the forms in triplicate, even though that's clearly the only number that makes sense from an administrative standpoint.))

Yelling down at her, I remind her that as long as I pay rent she has no legal grounds to enter my inner sanctum. It is per ipso facto a piece of sublet property subject to the strict rules and regulations of civil law – I cite the corresponding jurisprudence for good measure.

To which her defense is an annoyed, "Jurisprudence, smurisprudence!"

And with that the weekend has officially begun.

I watch cartoons while eating breakfast.

Astonishingly, there are still adults who fail to realize how insightful cartoons can be. They carry a plethora of sub-layers, embedded secretly by the writers and animators. As I scoop up my cereal, I carefully dissect the hidden wise-isms imparted by our generation's hieroglyphographers, and marvel at references I failed to notice on previous viewings.

"I knew you were going to watch cartoons all day!"

Mom blocks the TV, hands on hips like some 1930s poster of an indignant housewife. "What did I tell you?" she asks.

"I *just* sat down," I say. "Look, my bowl is still half full." I show her that my cereal still floats in a generous measure of milk. "And differences of perception and definition notwithstanding, I don't believe anyone on the planet would classify this fragment of time as 'all day.'"

"I warned you, didn't I?"

I grumble at her. I just missed a great bit of insight imparted on the second sublevel of *Adventure Time with Jake and Finn,* which is a real shame. Now I'll have to watch this episode again, from the beginning.

"I told you I wouldn't stand for it!" Mom says. "My knitting club is coming over and we don't like your noise!"

"Your knitting club will be here in" – I check my watch – "five hours? I'd say there's more than a fair chance I'll be finished with my breakfast by then."

Mom isn't in the mood for logic. "I thought you had such a busy day," she huffs. "I thought you had all these important things to do."

"I do. It's just that not all of them can be done at eight in the morning on a Saturday."

"Well, I warned you, didn't I?"

Mom seems really upset.

She's whiny most of the time, annoying and irrational intermittently, but she rarely gets upset. Being whiny is her natural state, but being upset is where things get dangerous.

"Why do you keep saying you warned me?"

"Because I warned you," she says. "Now you'll have to suffer the consequences."

Any other time that would sound laughable, right now, though, a chill runs down my spine.

"What did you do, Mom?"

Nightmare scenarios flit through my mind. I'm reminded of the times she tried to destroy my charts, soak my comics, tidy my room. She can go from zero-to-psycho in seconds, and what's more, she has no working sense of value. She'd just as easily destroy seven years of vids as she would delay my dinner by an hour. It's all the same to her. Just a friendly little warning.

"What. Did. You. Do?" I can hardly keep my voice level.

"It's more what I *didn't* do." She smiles now. *She actually smiles!* I feel the blood drain from my face. I feel light headed. I want to run up to my room to make sure my little kingdom is still there, hasn't been burned to the ground, re-arranged into oblivion, but she couldn't have done anything like that, could she? There wasn't time.

I switch the TV off and get out of the reclining chair, balancing the cereal precariously. "I'm up, I'm up," I tell her. "Now tell me what you did!"

"Remember Betsy?"

"Oh no."

"Oh, yes."

"You didn't. Tell me you didn't."

"No, I didn't," Mom says. "I didn't cancel your date with her niece."

"But you promised!"

Mom bristles. "You promised not to watch cartoons."

"I never did. And I wasn't going to anyway. Not all day. You have to call Betsy and cancel!"

"Too late. Betsy already took her niece to the hair salon, and after they're going jeans shopping."

Mom's expression suddenly softens. "Don't worry," she says. "It'll be good for you." She reaches out to ruffle my hair. "You'll have a wonderful time. You'll see."

It seems she's been pushing the cartoon issue just to dish out this punishment. It was planned from the get-go.

"You'll finally have someone your own age to play with," she says. "And, who knows, maybe she has a you-pipe-trench as well…"

My brain does a double take. "A *you-pipe* what?"

"A *you-pipe-trench*." Mom looks at me as if I'm slow.

I sigh. "Do you mean a YouTube channel? I doubt she has one. There's probably not a webcam on the planet that can color-correct her weird-ass makeup jobs."

Mom twists my ear. "Be nice!"

I head to the mall, wondering if Dad ever had these problems with Mom. Maybe that's why he left. I'm sure she never forced him to date weird looking near-relatives, but she could've found other ways to get under his skin. Or maybe Mom was telling the truth when she said he died in a freak accident – an accident that somehow caused his body, as well as his wardrobe and belongings, to go missing forever.

If not, there's really no excuse for him not being in contact with his only son for over two decades.

I turn onto the highway and give a warning-beep to another yoga-mom before she can cut me off.

My day merely continues going downhill.

I'm not sure why this surprises me.

Two clerks man Ye Olde Peanut Shoppe on Saturdays and when I enter, Emma's helping someone else. I get stuck with the new girl, a mousy type with a long nose and earrings in weird places. I stall for time, browsing the display cases hoping Emma will free up, but she's involved in a lengthy discussion with a guy who's ordering three different kinds of nuts (the show off!)

Dejected, I order my peppered Brazils from Mousy Clerk. When she disappears to the back, I turn to Emma and give her a special smile, one inundated with deep, secret meaning.

My smile says, *Too bad we missed each other today.*

It says, *I would've loved to talk to you.*

And it adds, *You look great, by the way. Just… wonderful.*

But Emma doesn't notice. She's engrossed in her work and misses my brilliantly layered facial communication completely. In fact, the whole time I'm in the Shoppe, she doesn't once glance in my direction.

My day is ruined!

I take my nuts and head to the food court. I'm supposed to meet Betsy's niece in a few minutes and I already feel weird and panicky. There's nothing in the Leverage arsenal about blind dates. Of course there isn't. Blind dates go against all that Leverage stands for. A blind date is just dating for the sake of dating. It's… it's… evil!

I remind myself that at least it's not a nighttime date. At least I'm not expected to take her to some club and then drive her home.

(At least she can't try for a good-night kiss.)

(At least there's no such thing as a good-afternoon kiss… is there?)

I make my way through the food court and it dawns on me that if I wasn't such a humanitarian, I could've found a way out of this. I wouldn't have to suffer on my very first date. I'd have been able to save it for someone special.

It's not difficult to spot her. Betsy's niece is by far the strangest looking person in the food court. You'd spot her even if you weren't trying to. In fact, I notice several people doing their best *not* to spot her – trying to keep her out of their peripheral vision so they can enjoy their meals.

Not only does each item of her clothing clash with every other item of her clothing (which is quite a feat), her make-up could only be described as highly experimental and likely chemically unstable. Then there's the way her generous number of chins wobble when she moves, and none of it is in any way compensated by her unsettling complexion or her mean, beady eyes.

My knees suddenly buckle and I drop gracelessly into the nearest chair. I don't think I'm getting even close to the right amount of air.

To calm myself, I take out my tablet and boot it up. Strangely enough, even at this darkest of times, brilliance is afoot. I've just had a sizzler of an idea. I should get it down before facing enemy fire. After all, who knows how long it'll take my sensitive brain to recover from what's about to transpire?

YouTube script:

The bulk of our work takes place in the 'venue.'

The venue is a place where you can repeatedly run into Her without it looking forced or unnatural. She can be found there with clockwork regularity and you have legitimate reasons for showing up there yourself. Reasons that don't involve her in any obvious way.

[show a chart with places crossed out]

The venue is unlikely to be a club/supermarket/bar/party. More likely it's a place of business/social hangout/office.

We need the venue because our work is done in small, incremental steps over a long period of time. You cannot get The One by simply walking up to her in a one-off situation and asking for her number. This would be considered a pick-up, and The One won't go for a common pick-up. Most she will do is give out a fake number to get rid of guys who haven't proven to be *her* One yet.
And this is actually a good thing. You don't want her to disappear into the arms of someone else just because he happened to stand in line with her at the supermarket and offered to call her sometime, right?

[pause for dramatic effect]

As an added bonus: the third time you 'happen' to bump into her at the venue, you can comment on the serendipity of the situation. "We keep meeting like this, are you stalking me?" ~~Don't forget to smile!~~ This will create an instant little bond.

Note: don't use this EC if it's clear she doesn't remember you. Her inner voice would put up a giant red flag, *he likes me more than I like him!* And that's a big problem. If that thought ever crosses her mind, you've lost the battle. Her subconscious will do everything it can to make sure she ends up in the right place, and, sadly, it believes the right place is in the arms of a man who likes her slightly less than she likes him!
~~Perhaps this is because there's far more drama to be had in that type of situation. Always keep the drama going!~~

[sign off]

8

Of course I think about it. Of course that nasty little thought crosses my mind: *Just keep walking! She hasn't spotted you yet, just go home and have Mom call and tell her you were overcome by a sudden case of the plague.*

But I can't.

I'm not that kind of guy.

Sadly.

There's something about social situations that curbs my free will. It turns me into an embarrassed robot programmed to do whatever is socially expected. Even if it's something highly uncomfortable.

So I put my tablet away, take one last, deep breath, and wobble over to my date's table.

"You must be… my date," I say, realizing I never actually bothered to ask after her name. I really hope that doesn't turn into a thing.

"Yup!" she says, nodding enthusiastically. "Are you getting anything?" She points at her food. "The Ultra Burger at Sparky's is really good!"

"I'm familiar with the Ultra Burger," I tell her. I look away so I don't have to see what she's doing to hers. She's clearly spent little time developing her finger placement; bits of vegetable and escaped sauce paint her plate. Her whole burger is falling apart at the seams.

"I'll just go and order," I say. "Be right back."

"Okidoki," she says. "Don't get lost!"

As expected, the 'date' starts off really, really rough. But, surprisingly, it actually becomes slightly less painful after a while. Bearable, even.

For all her weirdness, at least the girl can talk. Whenever I need a moment to compose myself, whenever I need to look away from her bright, colorful face to give my eyes a rest, she keeps the conversation going. There are no awkward pauses, no silences. She just talks and talks and talks. And, although nothing she says is interesting enough to lodge itself in my memory, I'm grateful for not having to worry about what to say.

Her name even comes up;

"So then," she says, "that bitch tells me, 'Sorry, Ms. Fox, but we only have those jeans in normal colors.' So I tell myself, 'Calm down, Samantha, she knows not what she's saying. It's not her fault.' But then, get this, I found these really amazing jeans in–"

My brain does a backflip.

Did I hear that right? Her name is Samantha Fox?

Seriously?

Samantha Fox?

How did that happen? Didn't her parents realize that with the subpar genes floating inside them such a name was out of the question? Way too exotic and sexy? I mean, you wouldn't call a fifteen pound albino baby Angelina Jolie, would you? Of course not. That wouldn't make sense. It wouldn't be fair to the baby, who'd grow up to constant looks of disappointment, nor to other Angelina's, who'd surely possess and maintain the correct levels of exoticness to support the name.

Samantha Fox, really?

There should be a law against that.

Or at least some kind of regulatory body. It could perform checks on, say, a yearly basis, making sure the Samanthas and Angelinas and Roxannas of this world don't stray too far off course and start confusing us all.

'*Sorry, ma'am. Your baby just doesn't have the dark, brooding eyes required for the name Keira, and we can't let you have Ashley either, because, well, her legs just aren't straight enough. See how they bend outwards here and here? No, it wouldn't be right. Those aren't what we call Ashley-legs. Tell you what, you work on those legs and come back in five years' time, then we'll see. For now, just call her Sue. Next!*'

I realize Samantha's staring at me.

I might have missed a question. I have no idea what it was, though, and I don't want her to repeat her story, so I try; "Yes?"

"Fine," she says. "You know what? If you don't want to be here, just go."

"Excuse me?"

Samantha crosses her arms. "You heard me."

"Well, not really–"

"It's obvious you're bored, don't think I can't tell. You keep looking around and giving me that weird, forced smile."

"Come now," I say, panicking. "That's not true."

I have no idea why I lie. It's the embarrassed robot, it has to be. I just can't be openly mean. I don't possess that skill. But, for a fleeting moment, I do wonder what it would be like to have the courage to just get up and run.

"I know the signs," Samantha says. "Don't you get that this happens to me all the time? Right now, you're thinking: what if I just get up and run?"

I'm appalled. "How can you even think such a thing?"

"Just go," she says. "I'd love to have a burger and chat with you, but if it's so hard, if it takes so much effort to be around me, then just go. I'm used to eating alone."

I suddenly feel sick. Did I really make her feel this way? Am I the bad guy here? How did that happen? I was being such a brave boy!

"I told you," I stammer, completely lost. "I don't *want* to go."

I just want someone to drag me off so it won't be my fault. So people can see that I wasn't being mean.

Samantha shakes her head. "I just don't understand why you have to be so cruel."

"Cruel? How am I cruel?" I'm taking a bullet for humanity here. I should be getting a medal. How is this date cruel to anyone but me?

"It's easier for me to be alone than to be with someone who was forced to spent time with me by his mom," Samantha says. "Do you really not get that?"

"No, no," I say, "that's not how it is. You've got it all wrong."

With all this drama, I've yet to touch my burger. I can sense it growing cold and slightly less tasty.

"How is it, then?" Samantha demands.

"Well..." I wonder why I continue to lie. Why can't I just be normal and tell her that I have to go because I left my cat on the stove or something? "I remembered you from that party a few months back, and I thought..." Where am I going with this? "And I thought, now that's someone who, eh, seems like a nice person. I'd like to have a burger with her sometime."

Samantha snorts. "Nonsense."

"It's not."

"Your mom forced you to come, admit it."

I'd love to. I really would. But, I can't.

"Listen," I say. "I don't know how things are at your house, but my mom doesn't plan my social life. Furthermore, if you have trouble believing anyone would want to have a burger with you, then that's both sad and very much your problem."

Samantha's jaw drops, but she recovers quickly. "Okay, then," she says, staring me down. "Prove it!"

"Prove what?"

"If you think I'm such a nice person..." She puts air quotes around the word nice, "Then why don't you kiss me?"

"Kiss you?"

"Yeah," she offers me her cheek. "Go on, stud, give my cheek a good smooch."

For a moment the world turns upside down.

I have trouble breathing.

"Come on, big boy," Samantha chides. "If you like me so much, kiss me!"

"I'm sorry," I say, mercifully feeling my brain start up again. "I just don't believe we're at that stage in our relationship. I don't go around kissing every girl I get a chance to, you know. I'm saving myself."

Samantha glares at me. "So now we're in a *relationship*?" She throws up her hands. "And when exactly did that happen?"

"Of course we're in a relationship," I say, feeling a wave of relief wash over me. I'm finally back on familiar ground. I sit back and rattle off one of Leverage's monologues: "We're in a relationship in the sense that every two people on the planet are in fact in some kind of a relationship. A relationship, after all, is merely an indication of the way people relate to each other. For instance, the relationship between myself and my mailman is that he brings me my mail. And the relationship between me and that woman over there," I point out a random mom who appears to be force feeding French fries to her overweight baby, "is that we've never met."

I feel a little better now. I pick up my burger, mindful of my finger placement, and search for my first bite site. "Those are all relationships," I tell Samantha. "All ways of relating to people."

Samantha squints at me. "Really," she says. "And what exactly is the nature of *our* relationship?"

She thinks she has me cornered.

Poor girl.

"Well," I say, after I take a bite which, surprisingly, isn't too cold. "We're two people who've just met up for, as you stated so eloquently before, a friendly chat and a burger."

Samantha deflates. "Whatever," she says. "You talk a lot but I think you're just too scared to kiss me."

My mind falters a moment. Was that an attempt at reverse psychology? Does she really think I'm going to kiss a strange cheek on a dare?

I really feel for her, but not to the point where I'm willing to subject my lips to her greasy, chemically-colored skin. No sir!

"Think whatever you want," I tell her. "But we're not kissing. Our encounter today will remain entirely kiss-less. Just so you know."

I'm relieved to find the social robot allows this kind of honesty. It's thrown me under the bus a couple of times, but at least it's picked me up before the truck came along.

Samantha shrugs. "Whatever," she says. "You're just like the rest."

I ignore the passive aggression and finish my burger quickly.

As far as I can tell, this is a lunch date. I've finished my lunch, so that signals the end of the date. Especially as Ms. Fox has already shown she doesn't stand on formalities. After all, she did start on her meal before I'd even arrived. I'm sure she won't mind me leaving before she finishes hers.

"It was nice to see you again," I say, to indicate that I'm leaving. "I wish you and yours well."

Samantha looks up. With a full mouth, she says, "Yeah, sure. You run home to mommy."

I turn and feel a weight drop from my shoulders. But, as I finally escape to sweet, sweet freedom, I hear Samantha's voice one last time.

"So," she calls after me, "I'll friend you on Facebook, yeah?"

9

A test to see if she's The One:

Whenever you meet another woman, do you subconsciously think; that's <u>not</u> Her?

I delete my Facebook page.
   It's the right thing to do.
   After all, I'm not a sixteen-year-old girl, so I don't really need one.
   I'm just a little surprised at how difficult it is to delete a profile.
   They could make that a bit more user friendly.

"And?"
   Mom stands in my doorway.
   I'm quite sure I'd closed my door.
   And locked it, from the inside.
   "How was your date with Samantha?"

I don't sleep well that night.
   So many thoughts going through my head.
   None of them very important.
   But they come anyway.
   Begging for attention.

Sunday rolls around, starting off eerily similar to Saturday, with me minding my business, watching cartoons and eating cereal, and then all hell breaking loose.
   A terrifying sound travels through the house. A deep reverberation that cascades down the stairs and makes my blood turn cold. I rocket out of my chair and shoot up the stairs. I have to hurry. Mom's vacuuming my inner sanctum!
   I enter my humble domain and immediately dive to the floor, rescuing a vintage Jayce and the Wheeled Warriors action figure from the clutches of the vacuum.
   "Stop!" I yell. "For the love of all that's holy, please stop!"
   Mom ignores me. She guides the nuzzle around my crestfallen body.
   "Mom, all my stuff's still on the floor!"
   She pauses a moment, hands on hips. "And when exactly should I vacuum?" She leaves the monster running, it's hard to hear over the

noise. "Tell me," she says, "when would be convenient for his lordship?"

"*Any* other time," I tell her. I get up off the floor. "I'm at work over fifty hours a week, just fill out an application for a temporary visa, in triplicate, and pick any of those hours. That's close to two-hundred hours each month to choose from!"

"I shouldn't even be doing this," Mom bristles, my logic gliding off her like water off a duck's back. "You should be cleaning your own room. How will you ever learn to fend for yourself? I'm not going to be around forever you know!"

"So let me do it," I beg, straining to be heard over the noise. "I didn't ask you to vacuum, did I?"

"No," Mom says. "You just want to turn my house into a pigsty. If I don't vacuum, your room won't ever get vacuumed!"

"Not true. Just leave the vacuum here and I'll do it myself. I promise."

Mom harrumphs. "You won't vacuum," she says. "You'll just bury my vacuum under dust and toys and comics."

"Dust and collectables and graphic novels!"

Mom shakes her head and goes back to vacuuming.

The noise drives me crazy.

I scurry around like a madman, picking up my precious things.

"You never do anything when I ask you to," Mom says. "I always have to give you warnings."

She hits the legs of my table roughly as if she's doing her best to knock it over and spill my charts. I can't watch this. It's more than one delicate soul can bear.

I drive angry for a while, end up at the park.

Which is an odd place for me to be.

I think the last time I was here I came with my dad. Which tells you how long it's been.

It's my personal philosophy that nothing good comes in green (the only exception being the Jedi master). Nature is the home of bugs and worms and creepy things. Ever looked at a tree? Really looked at one up close? There's like a million things crawling and growing all over it. Tree bark is a moving tapestry of infestation.

Hug a tree? I don't think so!

I switch off the engine and let out a sigh. I managed to pick up all my collectables so no damage was done. And I might still be able to salvage part of my day. I could have another stab at having breakfast – I won't be able to watch my usual cartoons, and I'll feel a little full from the first breakfast, but I could still start the day over right.

Mom will be vacuuming for a while, though, so I'll have to kill some time. I get out and start walking.

The park is much smaller than I remember. All the spots I loved as a kid are still there, but they're crammed together as if space itself has contracted. The pond where dad and I tried to fish once now sits directly next to the playground. And the field where we had some failed attempts at playing baseball is directly adjacent to the midget golf course, even though it used to take hours to walk from one to the other.

Walking here is like walking through a miniature model of my past.

But at least the park is peaceful. There are only a few people about. There's a couple on a blanket near the pond – being all lovey-dovey – and a lone woman on a bike.

I walk on, keeping an eye on the woman. There's something familiar about her. It takes me a moment to recognize her – perhaps because I don't expect to see her in this context. But, even before conscious recognition sets in, there's this sudden breathlessness. This attack of nerves. This flood of happy feelings. Then Emma makes eye-contact and slows. "Hey!" she says, "aren't you the guy who always buys Brazil nuts?"

She remembers me!

"Yes," I say, quickly closing the gap between us. "Yes, I am."

"Isn't that weird," she says. "Running into each other like this?"

For a moment I cannot answer because I'm lost in her deep, brown eyes. I've always known her eyes were amazing, but I've never seen them in sunlight before. "Yes," I say, "it's truly amazing."

I do my best to recall some of my own advice. Luckily, a recent ear catcher does surface.

"Hey, I read somewhere that all girls pee in the shower. Is this true?"

For a moment it looks like Emma might laugh, but then she says, "Do all guys say that? Are you all reading the same blog or something?"

"What?"

"A guy asked me that exact same question yesterday."

"Really?"

Damn! One of my fans is using my advice on my Emma!

"Could be," I mumble. "Could be."

She shakes her head, "You guys are so weird!"

What? No!

I want to yell out that not all guys are weird, it's just me. I'm the weird one. I'm the weirdest of 'em all. That was my line, not this other guy's. He's a fake. A poser. He gets his dating advice from the internet, how sad can you be? But I can't tell her any of this. Not without sounding desperate and divulging things about myself that are worse (like how I'm handing out perfectly good ECs before ever using them on her. She deserves better than second hand ECs. She's special!)

Emma smiles and says, "I'm Emma, by the way."

46

I shake her hand and tell her my name, shocked to find hers really *is* Emma. Just like I imagined.

Maybe this is serendipity. Fate. The heavens giving me a sign that this was meant to be.

Or maybe, just maybe, I overheard her name in the Shoppe.

"Would you like to get a coffee with me, Emma?" I ask, surprising myself with my sudden boldness.

"Why not," she says. "Sounds like fun."

"Okay, great," I say. "That's really cool."

Emma looks at me a moment, then says, "You know that I have a boyfriend, right?"

I gasp for air. I must've been kicked in the stomach by an invisible assailant – perhaps a midget from the nearby golf course. Luckily, I manage to keep my expression unchanged. I cannot show Emma how hard that hit me. I'm not sure why, but it seems like the right thing to do. "Don't worry," I tell her, "it's just coffee, not a marriage proposal."

I smile magnanimously.

At least I think I do.

I can't feel my face.

"There's a cool little café down the road. How about we go there?" My voice sounds weird, but I'm hearing it from inside my head, maybe it's not so bad on the outside. Emma gives no sign she's heard anything strange. "Great," she says. "Lead the way."

I lead the way, even though my legs are wobbly, as if they suddenly need detailed instructions on how this walking thing is actually accomplished. I also realize there's a very important vid I need to put up as soon as possible.

YouTube script:

Most men assume there are two categories of women:

1. Single women.
2. Women in a relationship.

And this may well have been true in the nostalgic-past of yester-year – I'm talking castles, sea monsters, and dowries here. But these days the 'Single Woman' is a mere myth. A fantasy.
Let me make this very clear: There are *no* single women!

There are indeed two categories of women, but the categories are as follows:

Category 1: Women in a committed relationship.
Category 2: Women with a placeholder boyfriend who want to trade up.

Where there's a woman, there's a guy who thinks he's her man. He may know he's just a placeholder, a backup to keep her from getting lonely while she waits for someone better, but most likely he's oblivious.

Here's the good news, though. Whenever a woman tells you she has a boyfriend (or husband/sex slave/shopping assistant) it means one of two things:

1. She's indeed in a committed relationship (cat1: get the hell out!)
2. She's not convinced you are special enough yet. (cat2: there is some hope!)

You have to understand that a woman in category two isn't lying, not exactly. She does sort of/kind of have a boyfriend. So she's passing along real information in that mysterious, non-direct way her subconscious prefers. But, deep down, she may believe a worthy suitor will see through these vagaries and know what to do.
Bless her little heart.
Also, she might not even realize she's in category two. Her inner voice may have her convinced she's in category one. ~~It is simply waiting for the opportunity to replace the placeholder with a genius or an internet philosopher.~~

So don't get scared when a girl tells you she has a boyfriend. Just get good at spotting category two and you'll be fine.

[sign off]

48

Video #131 by *Leverage*. Views: 75

Comments:

GomezP: (6:06 pm) Lev. I liked what you said about guys wanting clarity and girls needing drama. I actually sat down and prepared some drama for my girl on paper, then acted it out for her last night. It seemed to be going well (she got very emotional!) but we slept in separate rooms and she hasn't talked to me since. I was hoping you could tell me if this is normal or if I made a mistake somewhere.

Leverage: (6:27 pm) Tell me exactly what you did!

GomezP: (6:29 pm) You rock! Okay, she was talking about making me some tea and I pretended to mishear and told her that she could damn well make her own tea. She gave me a surprised look and said, "I *am* making my own damn tea, I just offered to make you some damn tea too!" So I told her to stop whining about the tea and leave me alone.
Her: Why are you doing this?
Me: No reason, do what you want. Just ignore me like you always do.
So she went to the kitchen and came back with two cups of tea.
Her: Just in case you changed your mind, I made you some damn tea.
(I decided to turn up the drama further.)
Me: Oh, what's the use, I can't hide it any longer; I'm in love with your sister!
Her: What?
Me: It just happened. We didn't plan for it. We didn't want it to happen. It just did.
Her: What sister?
Me: Both your sisters, actually. You see, they're so much taller than you, and they have great penmanship. You just don't see that anymore.
(I admit, I was struggling a bit here...)
Her: I don't know what's gotten into you. Please stop it!
Me: I couldn't help it. It just happened.
(At this point I noticed the drama was really working, she was getting very emotional!)
Her: I don't understand any of this. I don't *have* any sisters!
Me: I'm sorry, honey, I didn't want this to come between us. They mean nothing to me, I promise. Let's forget this ever happened and get back together.
Her: Get back together? When were we apart?
Me: Honey, it feels like we were never apart, and it feels like we were apart forever.

LoathingAndFear: (6:33 pm) Are you too small? Make your member HUGE here!!!!

GomezP: (6:33 pm) So it all seemed to work perfectly, but for some reason, after she stormed out of the room, she didn't return to make-up and she didn't want

49

to talk to me anymore.

Leverage: (6:35 pm) I have no words for this...

WhipCrck: (6:37 pm) First smart thing leve-rag has ever said. Guess it was bound to happen sometime.

GomezP: (6:37 pm) Lev? Are u still there? What does all this mean? Is it good or bad? Did I overdose her on drama or should I give her more? What do you think?

GomezP: (6:49 pm) Lev?

LoathingAndFear2: (6:50 pm) Are you too big? Make your member SMALLER here!!!!

10

A test to see if she's The One:

Do you already miss her five minutes after she leaves?

It's always over.

Ever noticed this? How the fun stuff is always behind you? How it's never actually happening *right now*?

At this moment, I should be on a date with Emma. I should be sitting across from her, watching her fingers touch her cup, her hair fall across her face. I should be telling her something stupid and making her smile.

I really should be looking at her smile right now.

But I'm not. For some annoying reason all those moments are already over. They're behind me. I'm sitting on my bed, in my room, and it's getting dark. I'm sitting alone in the dark thinking too much.

I guess wonderful moments are always over because when they're happening, we're never fully *in* them. We never interrupt a wonderful moment to spend time appreciating it. By the time we realize we should appreciate a moment, it's already gone.

With Emma, I was probably overthinking things. Worrying about what to say, about my body language, my shirt, my teeth, my smile. I didn't get a chance to relax and enjoy myself.

Plus, she drank her coffee really fast and then had to go.

That didn't help.

But it *was* nice. The whole thing was kind of wonderful and cool and fun. In fact, I've been running our conversation back and forth through my mind ever since we parted.

It also occurs to me that we should, by now, have invented some kind of technology to record moments.

Not just the video and audio of it, but the entire moment, with all its intricate emotions and feelings and physical interactions. We should be able to relive any part of our lives. After all, it's *ours*. We made it happen and we should be able to do whatever we want with each moment. Live it again. Live it back to front. Upside down. Over and over in a loop. Whatever we feel like. Our moments should be our property forever.

Why should a moment happen only once and then be lost in time forever? That's as silly as buying a movie you can only watch a single time. Where every scene becomes instantly inaccessible for eternity after you've watched it.

I really should be able to press a meta-physical rewind button and relive my almost-date with Emma.

For instance, I'd really liked this bit:

Emma stared out across the street at an office building as she stirred her coffee. She said, "Wouldn't it be cool to own that building?" It was a towering, modern affair, with cool reflective windows. "What if the whole thing was yours and you had the money to change it anyway you liked?"

I felt a glow spread inside me. "You do that too?"

She nodded. "Of course," she said. "And I know exactly what I'd do with that building. I'd put a tennis court on the roof. A spa on the ground floor. And in the middle, I'd put one of those giant movie theatres."

I nodded. "I can't even get on a plane without sectioning it off in my head. First four rows: replace with a nice living room set – a couch, big screen TV, media center. Next five rows: a luxury bedroom so I can sleep on long flights. Next five rows: a game room."

Emma laughed.

"So," she said, "you want to land your plane on my building?"

I did. In fact, there was no way I'd ever be able to aptly express just how badly I wanted to land my plane on her building.

"That would be great," I told her.

And another bit I want to relive for ever is:

I put my coffee down and Emma reached over to touch my hand. "Look," she said. "There's Steve Buscemi!" She nodded in the direction of a middle-aged couple drinking tea – looking jaded and dehydrated, the way older people tend to do.

I had no idea who Steve Buscemi was, but I didn't care. All I cared about was that Emma had touched my hand and was *still* touching my hand.

"Doesn't that guy look exactly like Steve?"

"Sure," I said. "The spitting image of Steve. It's amazing, really."

I could only hope this Steve wasn't an ex-boyfriend.

Our hands were still touching.

Emma smiled mischievously. "Should we take a picture?"

"Maybe, but I didn't bring my cell. I left the house in kind of a hurry."

"Wouldn't it be fun to ask him for his autograph? Just to see what he'd do?"

"It'd be crazy," I said.

Still touching.

"So, should I? Should I go over there?"

"No," I said, perhaps a little too quickly. I just didn't want to risk her moving even the slightest. It would result in our hands no longer touching, and that was unthinkable. "Let's watch him a little longer. Who knows what he'll do next?"

And, more importantly, who knew when our hands would (accidentally?) touch again?

"You're right," she said. "He's probably discussing contracts or something. Who do you think that lady is? His agent? Or a secret mistress who wants to star in one of his films?"

Perhaps Steve Buscemi was some kind of movie star, or an infomercial guy. It didn't really matter, all that mattered was that the *'Hey, look over there'* window had expired. She only had to touch my hand for a second to get my attention, anything beyond that was, well, purely recreational.

"Could she be his mom?" Emma wondered. "Beyond a certain age, it's so difficult to tell, don't you think?"

Still touching.

What did that mean?

Did she like me?

Did she *like*-like me?

Did she… love me?

"I once met this guy who was the spitting image of George Clooney," she said, her eyes glazing over.

Or did she just forget where she'd put her hand?

"He's so sexy," she said. "In a rich, rugged, pepper-and-salt kind of way, don't you think?"

I shrugged. "I suppose. If that's the kind of thing you like."

"Ooh," she said. "Steve's getting up!"

The couple left some money on the table and disappeared into the street. Emma pulled back her hand to snap a quick picture with her cell.

And here's a moment I didn't like so much:

Emma took her last sip of coffee and smiled over her cup. We had one of those long eye-contact moments. You know the kind. It really looked as if she was about to say something meaningful. Something like, *'You know, after talking to you, I realize you're a really cool guy. We should hang out again sometime.'* Or maybe even, *'You know what? We should hang out every day from now on.'*

To which my reply would be, *'Hey, that's a really great idea. We should totally meet up every day from now on.'*

And then we'd smile because we'd made a pact.

A pact for life.

But, instead, Emma broke eye contact to check her watch, then said, "Got to run. Promised my boyfriend I'd iron his underpants." She looked up with a crooked smile. "He just loves to have them all nice and warm."

"Oh," I said. "Sure. Great."

"Does your girlfriend iron your underpants?"

I shrugged.

"You should get her to do that." She said, with a conspiratorial smile. "You'll love it."

I really didn't appreciate how she kept bringing up this fake boyfriend. Hadn't we passed that station? Hadn't she just made love to my hand?

Emma stood to go. I was too shaken to react. By the time I got up she'd already put some money on the table, thereby crushing any hope that this had been a date.

We said our goodbyes outside and went in opposite directions.

There were more moments, of course. Good ones and bad. And even the bad ones were good in a way. The kind of way where I'd give my right arm to relive them again. But nobody's bothered to invent a metaphysical rewind button so I guess I'll keep myself busy writing another script. Something to help those less fortunate than myself. Those who haven't attracted the attention of their Emmas yet.

YouTube script:

Today I want to discuss an important concept: Male Invisibility.
You probably don't realize that, even though you've made eye contact with The One, and you've talked to her, it's still likely you're completely invisible to Her.

She has no idea that you've been pining over her. She doesn't know you've already worked out, in explicit detail, why you two would be perfect together. So, unless you've made her specifically aware of the fact that you exist, through your Intro or your Ear Catchers, she probably doesn't remember you.
That wonderful little moment of eye contact, for her that was just eyes crossing paths. It happens to her all the time. And that delightful conversation you had, if she even remembers it, she won't be able to recall the specific details, such as whether she was having this conversation with a girl or a guy.

[show hand drawn chart #1]

It's a difference in the way men and women perceive the world. Subconsciously, men divide everything in their field of vision into two

54

categories:

1. Women
2. All other objects

We're very aware of the women around us. We know how cute they are, where we've seen them before, and if and why we're interested in them. All the other objects around us we're only aware of to the point of making sure we don't crash into them. But we'd never accidentally *not* notice a woman we're interested in.

We could be on our way to hospital, with a broken leg, a punctured lung, and one eye poked out, and we'd still notice The One if she were sitting somewhere in the distance. We'd still find the time to admire the way she read her book and ignored us.

[hold up badly hand drawn char #2]

Women, on the other hand, divide their field of vision into a multitude of categories:

1. Shoes
2. Other women
3. <Assorted elements of clothing>
4. Shoes, again
5. All other objects

And this is the problem men face: women group us in the *all-other-objects* category. This means that if we don't do anything to stand out, we'll register as brightly on their mental radars as old ladies, lamp posts, and dogs. They won't exactly crash into us, but they won't remember us, either! If we want to be noticed, we have to drop our cloaks of invisibility.

So remember this next time you convince yourself that a chat or eye-contact is probably good enough, that there's no need for an amazing EC:
She. Won't. Remember. You!

[sign off]

11

Possible EC:

Do you think people can sneeze in their sleep?

The annoying woman tells me to take my bag off her conveyor-belt-scale-thingy and put it back on the floor. "Please, sir," she sighs. "One bag at a time."

I lift my bag back onto the floor and wait while she taps away on her keyboard, pretending to do something vitally important even though we both know I'm already in her system and her work is essentially meaningless. I've already checked in online, our bags just need to be tagged to the right ticket numbers, that's all. A computer could basically do this. In fact, there are computers behind me doing this and more right now. Alas, I still have to interact with this woman because my travel companion doesn't trust the computers. She's convinced they'll send our bags to the wrong side of the world.

Soon, though. Soon these manual systems will be deprecated and this annoying woman will sit at home watching the shopping channel while eating her already impressive body weight in corn chips.

I can't wait.

In the meantime, I comply with her every whim. Of course I do. Unlike her, my actions aren't motivated by a hunger for dominance over other humans through meaningless acts. No, right now I'm motivated by the knowledge that compliance is the path of least resistance. The quickest way to get to our flight.

So, off the conveyor-belt-scale-thingy my bag goes.

"Passports, please," the woman snaps.

I wait patiently but she gives me an exasperated look. "I need *both* your passports, sir" she says. "Yours and hers."

Of course she does. It's only logical that during this part of the process she does need everything together. I should've guessed. Consistency is not something airlines are known for. I sigh and dig my passport out of my fanny pack, then hide the fanny pack back under my shirt.

The woman taps away on her keyboard.

"Your bag, sir."

The other bag rolls away into darkness and I lift mine back onto the conveyor-belt-scale-thingy.

"You'll be boarding at gate 68D," she says. She hands us back our passports – together with some comically large boarding passes which we won't be able to store anywhere comfortably without folding them – and dons a fake smile. "Please make sure to be at the gate at 11:45. Thank you."

We take our wad of papers and go.

Before we reach the gate, Mom gets severely sidetracked. "Duty free!" she exclaims.

I groan inwardly. From experience I know this expletive is short-hand for: 'I'm going to buy five kilos of overpriced chocolate which you'll have to carry half way round the world without accidentally melting it with your beefy hands after which I'll completely forget about it and you'll end up eating it all, even though you're trying to cut back.'

I'm not a big fan of duty free.

I'd buy some alcohol to numbify my senses but my finely honed intestinal tract won't allow it. So, instead, I head over to the newsstand to check out the graphic novels.

It takes forever for the plane to take off.

Some people can't find their seats.

Some people can't find enough overhead storage.

Some people can't find where they put their baby.

It's always something.

The aircraft finally rumbles down the runway and then makes the precarious jump into thin air. This is the moment I switch off all logic so I can ignore the fact that the numbers just don't add up. This much metal, people, and luggage can't possibly leap into the air unpunished. Not at these speeds. This doesn't look nearly fast enough. So out the window my logic goes and I start taking the universe at face value (which is the only way humans can make use of air travel).

Mom nestles into her window seat. She's like a little girl on her first flight. She must've flown over a thousand hours but she never stops being amazed. It's really annoying.

"Look at all the small houses!"

"Yes, they're very small."

"And the trees, see how small they are?"

"Yes, they're small too."

"And the cars, look at the cars. They look like toys! Don't you just want to pick them up and play with them?"

"Mom, I'm a grown man. Even if they were toy cars I wouldn't play with them."

"Don't be grumpy!" Mom attempts to pinch my cheek, I try to stop her, it turns into a whole thing.

"You're always so grumpy," she complains. She takes the in-flight magazine to check the airline's latest scams. "You shouldn't be so grumpy. After all, we're on holiday." She smiles cheekily. "Why don't you take a holiday from being so damn grumpy?"

But she doesn't know.

She can't know.

No one can comprehend the dark forces I'm battling. I can actually *feel* the distance. It's a force as real as gravity or electromagnetism. It pulls on me harder and harder as the distance between Emma and myself increases. We're linked by this invisible cord.

For me there's no such thing as 'out of sight, out of mind.' With every second that passes, I miss her more. And the most annoying thing is that I know she doesn't miss me. If she did, this wouldn't be so bad. The shared experience would give us both solace. But Emma doesn't even know I'm speeding away from her. She'll have no idea why I won't turn up at Ye Olde Peanut Shoppe the next few days. I didn't get a chance to tell her. Things just didn't come together right.

What's worse, I have no control over how she'll interpret my absence. For all I know she'll go through a miniature Kübler-Ross grief cycle culminating in her acceptance of my absence and her moving on. I may well lose this fresh new thing that only just started to almost grow between us.

Maybe she'll even think I'm cheating on her, getting my nuts from another vendor.

I fidget in my chair. It appears I've opened my own in-flight magazine. There's an ad for tobacco-free cigarettes. It shows a mostly nude female. And there's an ad for jewelry, because the one thing you really need to procure through a magazine when you're traveling is fragile, expensive neck garnish.

I put the magazine away. It kills me that I can't drop Emma a note. There must be a thousand ways to contact her and I don't know any of them. I don't have her number, her email address, her chat handle, her Facebook link. I don't even know her last name!

It's too insane to even contemplate. I could tell her everything she needs to know and more if only I knew the right fifteen or so characters. That's all it would take. It seems so trivial it almost makes sense to guess them.

emma@miss-u.net?

ClerkEmma@ye-olde-peanut-shoppe.com?

emmagrl@shes-an-angel.com?

Why isn't there an app that takes everything you know about a person and then composes a thousand likely email addresses to which it broadcasts your message? There must be a market for something like that. I'd certainly buy a copy. Maybe even two.

It makes you wonder how people survived in Victorian times.

I try to imagine writing out a letter, long hand, with a quill, perhaps running out of ink half way and having to wait till Monday to buy more. Then I ride to the post office in the next town on some type of tall animal. Waiting in line and trying not to scream when I find out the last coach has just left and my letter will sit in a sack at the back of the store for at least another week. After which it will finally start its eight day journey to my beloved, who won't be able to get word back to me before the end of the month. And that's assuming neither coach gets robbed.

No wonder people died so young!

"Would you like something to drink, sir?"

An air-waitress has appeared at my side to give me a precisely crafted smile. Her cart is parked halfway into my arm rest and my elbow throbs. Mom's already drinking water with a bit of lemon. I ask the air-waitress for a Coke and orange juice and, when she takes out two plastic cups, I stop her.

"Please mix them together," I tell her.

The air-waitress hesitates. She cannot process this information. She struggles for a moment, then gives me two cups anyway, filling one with Coke and the other with orange juice. She quickly moves to the next row.

"Oooh," Mom croons. "They have duty free chocolate!"

I take the in-flight magazine away from her and start sectioning off the plane.

First four rows: a little studio to make vids while travelling (a nice backdrop, some quality lights, three different cameras for interesting angles, and some software to fix the audio track).

Next five rows: skylight room (replace the entire top section of the fuselage with clear material, like the opposite of a glass-bottom-boat, and place a hot tub underneath).

Next five rows, no, make that six: a luxurious bedroom (king-size bed, some ultra-modern version of magic fingers, two nightstands, reading lights, mirrors on the ceiling with embedded 3D TV and a big closet for Emma's clothes).

Next three rows...

"Doesn't that cloud look like an apartment building?" Mom points out the window excitedly.

Next three rows: a cinema, so Emma and I can watch our favorite–

"It does! It looks exactly like uncle Harry's building. And that cloud over there is the spitting image of Harry himself! Imagine that! Take a picture with your phone, quick!"

I sip my drink and wonder if Emma ever orders Coke mixed with orange juice. If not, would she think it's weird or endearing?

I decide she'd probably find it endearing. I picture Emma in her building (with my plane parked on her roof), holding a pitcher of Coke-and-orange, inviting me to join her in her Cineplex.

Coke-and-orange juice, that could be our thing.

Like our song, but with liquids.

It's hot.

Searingly so.

Instead of hiding inside an air-conditioned building like sane people, Mom insisted we lay out by the pool so we could burn our skin off.

Because we're on holiday. Any moment not spent burning our skin off is a moment wasted. Mom's actually like an accountant in that respect; divide the cost of the holiday over the number of sun soaking hours to arrive at the cost per hour. The more hours to divide over, the lower the cost. In fact, burn off enough skin and your holiday is practically free.

"We should get up earlier tomorrow," Mom says. "All the best spots are taken. Tomorrow we should sit closer to the pool."

It's 10 a.m. but it already feels like we're baking in the midday sun. All the plastic recliners round the pool are occupied, lethargic tourists lying around like beached whales wrapped in oversized towels and colorful shirts – the kind of shirts they wouldn't be caught dead in back home.

"Do my back, will you?" Mom hands me the lotion and turns over.

Factor 40. It's like rubber cement. It'll take me a good twenty-five minutes to grind this stuff into her skin. I shudder at the thought. Skin should never get old, there's no point to it. Or perhaps it's just an evolutionary deterrent.

You've served your biological purpose. You're not supposed to reproduce anymore, so now you get to look like dried fruit until you die.

Mom gets impatient. "What are you waiting for? I'm can feel my back burning!"

What am I waiting for?

I'm thinking of a way to get out of this without starting a huge, embarrassing fight.

I'm thinking of the precedent this will set. If I do this now, I'll be rubber-cementing her the rest of the holiday.

I'm thinking that this isn't very efficient. With this stuff it takes forty times longer to get a tan. Better leave it off and we can get back to the room that much sooner.

I'm thinking, where does Emma go on holiday? Does she tan or

60

burn? Does she bring stacks of books and guides? Does she get drunk and sleep around or does she maybe, just maybe, go on holiday with her mom and think about me?

The thing about this holiday is that it was booked and paid for before Emma and I went for that coffee. Before I'd even given her that first EC.

Mom books our holidays very early. She gets early-bird specials in January. She gets two-for-one discounts in January. She even starts packing in January.

For both of us:

'Do you think you'll want to wear this t-shirt between now and June?'

'I don't know, Mom. Get out of my room!'

'What about your swimming trunks?'

'Mom!'

'I'm going, I'm going. Just tell me if you think you'll go swimming between now and the holidays.'

'Out!'

'Who am I kidding, you're not going swimming. When do you ever go swimming? I'll just pack them.'

'Leave them! I'm going swimming next week!'

'You are? With who?'

'With *whom*. And it's none of your business. I don't have to justify my swimming exploits to you.'

'Nonsense. I'm packing your trunks. If you do go swimming you can just take them out again.'

But this time I really didn't want to go. I wanted to stay home and work on my ECs. I wanted to ask Emma out on another sort-of-date. I wanted to start on my winter stock pile of peppered Brazils. But Mom threatened to kick me out if I cancelled, and said she'd go into my room every day while I was away at work.

So, again, I chose the path of least resistance. It was pure survival instinct.

Yes, these are the survival skills of the modern man. Forget about hunting and gathering, killing alphas who covet our females, warring with tribes who worship the wrong deities, our survival skills are reduced to finding the path of least resistance when communicating with other humans.

And, believe me, that's important stuff.

"I want one with all those little umbrellas."

"You mean a Piña Colada?"

"Is that the one with chocolate? I don't like chocolate."

"What do you mean you don't like chocolate? You just made me carry five kilos of the stuff all the way here!"

"You know what I mean, I don't like chocolate in my cocktails."

The hotel entertainment has just started, some kind of singing/dancing/magic show. Right now, there are two couples on stage dancing to loud samba-like music while urging the guests to join in.

Mom and I found a table at the front so Mom won't miss a thing. The other tables are slowly filling up as people return from their after dinner strolls. It's starting to get dark and one of the hotel staff members is lighting the candles on the tables.

"Piña Colada is coconut," I tell Mom, "not chocolate."

"Okay, then. Get me one of those. I *love* coconut."

"No you don't. You always complain when I want to do Indonesian takeout because they use coconut."

"I mean, I love coconut when I'm on holiday."

I sigh and make my way to the pool bar. I get a Piña Colada for Mom and select a suitably colorful drink for myself, some virgin version of the local brew.

On some level I realize that going out for cocktails with your mom could seem embarrassing. It's all very well going on holiday with your mom to share costs, just as long as you go out with cool people to crazy beach parties at night. But when you actually skip the nighttime insanity then, well, then it could all seem a bit sad.

But I don't see it that way.

For one thing, Mom always books just out of season so the hotels are cheaper and filled with pensioners and childless couples. These are not people to feel embarrassed around. Most of them look at us admiringly, probably thinking what an awesome son I am for taking my dear old mom on a holiday.

For another thing, I have neither the desire nor the need to go to crazy beach parties. I'd rather sit here and think about Emma. And with how much fun I had with Emma on our almost-date, it's unlikely anything any other girl could say or do could possibly interest me.

I pay up and take the drinks back to our table.

"Oh," Mom says, clearly disappointed. "Thanks. That looks… good."

"What's wrong?"

"Nothing, dear. I'm sure this will be fine."

"Something's obviously wrong, just tell me."

"It doesn't matter."

"You asked for a Piña Colada, this is a Piña Colada."

"No, *you* said I wanted a pina-lada, all I asked for was a drink with little umbrellas. This drink has exactly no little umbrellas. Not a single one. But that's fine, I'm sure it won't be too horrible."

"I can get you some little umbrellas."

"No, dear, don't worry about it. Sit, relax. This drink is clearly not supposed to have any little umbrellas, adding little umbrellas now is not going to make it taste any better. Just forget it. Enjoy your own drink. Enjoy the show."

I sigh. There's nothing about this show that a truly sentient human could enjoy. But, with nothing better to do, I sit and sip my virgin.

Something Emma said on our almost-date suddenly gnaws at my brain.

She'd already heard my EC. The one about peeing in the shower.

Did she overhear it somewhere or was it used directly on her? And if it was, did she realize what was happening? Did this guy stop being invisible to her? Did she realize he was coming on to her? Did she maybe even *like* him?

I might, in fact, have a rival.

An adversary, who's basically cheating.

And I wonder whether this adversary even knows he's my adversary.

But I shouldn't worry. Obviously I can beat any mystery admirer with one half of my brain tied behind my back. Then again, with my ECs and advice going directly to him though my YouTube channel, half of my brain *is* tied behind my back.

Shadows play over the ceiling.

I'm lying in bed listening to the noise of the old people by the pool who should know better. They shouldn't be trying to have fun like this, dancing and drinking after midnight. Who are they kidding?

But they don't bother me, not too much. I'm pretty busy. I'm designing the perfect holiday for Emma and myself. I'm picking destinations, clothes, books, movies. I'm deciding on food, conversational topics, drinks.

It's going to be amazing!

I'm already playing out fun moments in my head.

There's the time she'll smile at me as we run down the beach on an early morning. There's the time her expression will turn to excited surprise when I unexpectedly push her into the pool (and she pulls me in after her!) There's the time her eyes will light up as we sit in a quaint little restaurant, eating by candle light.

Suddenly the noise-level increases. It jars me from my musings. I stare at the patterns on the ceiling and try to regain my calm. Disco light plays a quick dance in my peripheral vision and gets me more irritated.

They really don't need to turn up the music right now. It confuses the old people. They forget they don't like loud music, they forget that what they really, truly like, is being in bed by 9 p.m.

I wonder what Emma's thinking right now.

I wonder if she misses me, if she's even noticed that I'm gone.

And I try *not* to wonder if anyone is using my new ECs on her.

Snag Yerself A Cool Guy!

A dating blog by Emma

There are still a few cool guys out there. Let's snag them up before the army of blonde bimbos gets its hooks into them, breaks their spirits, and turns them into wusses!!

Post #123: Practice, Practice, Practice!!

Listen up grls, today's post is going to be different!! I'm having a lot of fun with this blog, and judging by the comments, so are you, but today I'm going to give you an assignment. Yup! You're gonna get off your asses and actually do something. But, I promise, you're going to have fun.

If you're anything like me then you get a little insecure at times. It can be intimidating walking up to a **cool guy** and just starting a conversation. So here's what we're going to do. Today we're going to go out and practice, practice, practice. Dad always told us practice makes perfect, right?

Okay, so here are the ground rules:

1. This isn't the Dark Ages. Don't waste time feeling weird about making the first move. Guys like it, even when they don't immediately assume, from looking at us, that we've escaped from a supermodel mansion.

2. But play it cool. Don't scare off the wildlife. If he's a 9 and you're a 7, don't be too flirty!! (You *know* your number!! If not, rate yourself **here**.) Instead of being flirty, just ask an innocent question – what's the time, where did you get that cool watch, whatever. After he answers, pretend to walk away, but then turn back for one more question. And then another, and so on. Pretty soon you're in a **conversation**.
The clue is not to make him feel cornered if he's 2 or more points higher than you.

3. Start out small. Practice on easy targets. Strike up a conversation with a 5 or a 6. When you get more confident, move up to a 7. It's easier that way. (But never set your sights on a 10!! There's no way to get out of a relationship, or even a conversation, with a 10, without some kind of emotional damage!! Just leave it.)

4. Have your exit strategy ready. If he gets too close or goes too fast,

casually mention your BF. But make sure to really be casual about it. Don't just blurt out: 'Hey, I have a boyfriend!' Guys see right through that. Instead, drop the BF bomb as if by accident: *'You know, my BF said the exact same thing yesterday.'*

You can also use the BF bomb to feel out the guy's level of interest. Is he shocked? Sad? Relieved?

Don't worry, you can always take it back later if needed. Just say something like, *'Actually, he's not a real BF, more like a good friend, you know?'*

So stop reading right now!! Turn off your cell or laptop or tablet or smoke-signal interpreter and head to the mall!! I expect your reports in the comments section below with a minimum of five guys per reader!!

Go!!Go!!!Go!!!!

~Emma

12

Observation:

Humans aren't that different from the quantum particles they're made up of.
They don't feel they truly exist until someone observes them.

The office is buzzing. Gharity's making his rounds again so I quickly close my script and check out my current task; apparently I'll be spending the next two weeks on Questionable Deductions (QD).

A QD is a task so shitty no one can do it for long without suffering an unacceptable drop in work quality. That's why they made it a floating task.

The way a QD works is, whenever we come across a seriously questionable deduction from one of our clients, we tag it to this task, and whoever is on QD duty gets to solve it.

It's a pain because it's not about figuring out whether a deduction is actually legal or not. That'd be too easy. The person on QD duty has to find a loophole. A reasonable explanation for why a particular deduction is not only legal, but completely logical given the circumstances. And, to make sure we don't slack off, a score is kept. A whiteboard on Gharity's door shows the percentages of QD's rendered *un*questionable by each employee.

It's not entirely clear what the penalty for having a low score is, but it's safe to assume it's nothing particularly good.

I stare at my screen and note how fast that holiday feeling disappears when you're back at work. The surface of a desk must be an ultralow-resistance conductor for holiday feelings. As soon as you touch it, holiday feelings are sucked right out of you. Even wearing rubber gloves probably wouldn't help. Once you come into contact with that surface, you're back in the real world. In fact, the conductivity is so high, you instantly feel as if you never left, as if you've never been on a single holiday in your entire life.

In short, I already feel like I'm in desperate need of another holiday.

I really wanted to drop by the Shoppe to seen Emma this morning but the jetlag messed me up so badly that I overslept – even Mom wasn't up until 7:13! Dropping by the Shoppe would've meant missing the morning stand-up meeting which in turn would've meant taking a half-day. I wasn't willing to do this. I'm saving my days, I won't touch them until Emma and I are a couple and we can spend them together.

Still, it kills me that I haven't seen her in such a long time (only slightly shorter than forever, it seems).

"What's going on?"

Gharity steps into my cubicle.

"I'm sorry?"

He taps my desk. "You're halfway through your stint on QD duty and you haven't cleared a single deduction."

I'm not sure I follow his defective reasoning. "This is my first day on QD. I was on holiday last week."

Gharity frowns. "On holiday?"

"Yes."

He mulls this over. "You sure?"

"Yes, pretty sure."

Gharity's not convinced. "Didn't we talk about the RedChip account last week?"

"Not really, no."

"Then who did I talk to about that?"

I shrug. "I wouldn't know, I wasn't here, I was on holiday."

"I'm pretty sure I saw you getting a coffee."

"You didn't. I wasn't even in the country."

Gharity gives me a look as if he still expects me to come to my senses and realize that I'm the one who's mistaken.

I stare back at him.

"Either way," he says, "you can't just disappear for a week. That's not how we do things around here. Nobody knew you were gone. You have to tell Amy so she can put it into the system."

"I did. And I sent you an email months ago with the dates. And I repeated the email the Friday before I left."

"You sure?"

"Yes!"

Gharity shakes his head. "Well," he says, "you'd better get cracking, you only have a week left on QD. Got to get your score up."

He turns to leave, then steps back. "Are you sure you didn't come into my office to complain about the quality of the bottled water in the soda machines?"

I ignore him. I'm no longer here. In my mind, I'm on a trip with Emma.

Sometimes I fantasize about the most mundane things. For instance, right now I'm picturing Emma and myself at an airport, waiting for our bags at the carousel.

She's checking her cell, finding us a place to stay. I'm watching the carousel like a hawk, ready to secure our belongings.

That's it. That's the entire fantasy. But, for some reason, it's very powerful.

There's a commotion. I peer over my cubicle wall and see my colleagues huddled around Gharity's office. He's stalked off to update the QD chart.

This sucks.

There are sniggers.

I really should work all through lunch to catch up, but I don't. Instead, I take my coat and head to the mall. Which turns out to be frightfully busy. It takes me a quarter of an hour just to find a parking spot.

Who are all these people slacking off during the work day?

I have a good reason to be here, I'm on a onetime mission. But what about these other people? They can't all be on onetime missions. Why aren't they working? Or domestic engineering? I hazard to think what will become of the world if we're all at the mall in the middle of the day!

I hurry to Ye Olde Peanut Shoppe and, as I approach, I suddenly don't feel well. Out of the blue I get sweaty and panicky. I don't understand this, I didn't have anything weird for breakfast.

I enter the Shoppe clutching my stomach and get in line behind some slackers. When it's my turn, Emma smiles at me and asks, "What'll it be?"

Even though I'm crazy happy to see her, my upset stomach curbs my enthusiasm. I barely managing to blurt out, "Oh, you know, just the usual."

Emma's smile wavers. "The usual?"

This isn't good.

My voice cracks, "Yeah," I say. "Just give me 150 grams of the nuts I always get."

Please remember me!

"Hold on." Emma looks over at Mousy Clerk. "Maybe you ordered with Tamarin last time?"

At the mention of her name, Mousy Clerk looks me over. She shrugs and returns her attention to her customer.

"Sorry," Emma says – and she really does look apologetic. "Tam doesn't remember you. Did you order ahead?" Emma moves over to her ancient computer to check the orders.

"I'll just have some peppered Brazils," I mumble, wishing I hadn't come. Wishing I wasn't even on this stupid planet. And I feel even more ill now. I definitely have food poisoning. I should find a doctor before I collapse.

Emma returns with my nuts and rings me up. "You probably want something to go along with that," she says.

I'm not sure what she's talking about. I may have missed something subtle in our communication. It's no surprise, after all, I appear to be dying.

"Don't you usually take your peppered Brazils with a nice, detailed weather report?" Emma grins mischievously.

It takes me a moment to process what's just happened, then another to recover from the shock.

She does remember me!

"Because there's a lot going on with high and low pressure fronts at the moment," Emma continues. "It's like an epic battle, right over our heads. Marvel could do a whole series of movies about it."

"No, thanks," I say, playing along. "I don't need any more weather reports. I have quite a collection already. I'm actually thinking of auctioning them off."

"Really?" Emma seems very interested to see where I'll go with this.

I am too.

If only I knew.

"Yeah," I venture. "I was thinking I could get a good price for them on one of those reality TV shows where they pawn stuff. Some of the reports are really old, they'll fetch a good price. I may have to learn to haggle first, though. It's not part of my natural skillset."

"Hold on!" Emma says. "Some of those reports are copyrighted, you know. I'll expect a nice cut of the profits."

"Of course." I make a magnanimous gesture. "And you could put it towards buying that building you liked so much when we had coffee."

Emma laughs.

There's a long moment of eye contact.

"We should probably talk about your cut over another coffee, don't you think?"

She nods. "We should."

I'm not sure if she thinks we're still joking.

"How about today, after work? I'll pick you up."

Something is violently tearing away at the lining of my stomach, I can only hope I'll be out of hospital by then.

"Oh," Emma says, her smile waning. "I can't, I'm sorry." She makes an apologetic gesture. "I have some stuff to do today."

"Sure. No problem."

That was pretty clear. And I really don't feel well. I should leave. I turn to go, but Emma calls me back.

"Wait," she says. "How about tomorrow?"

Back in my car I notice my stomach is suddenly much better. Whatever was attacking me must have given up.

13

Observation:

*You are both going to end up miserable if all you can show
her is how tongue-tied you get around her.*

The rest of the afternoon passes in a haze. I manage to close some
Questionable Deductions, but the full force of my brilliance isn't behind
them. Instead it's huddled at the back of my mind, together with my
subconscious, planning tomorrow's almost-date.

At least, that's what I think they're doing. From time to time little
ideas surface; snippets of conversation, questions to ask, ways to stand,
looks to give Emma.

I'm fully confident that by tomorrow lunchtime it'll all be worked out.
Fully confident.

I return my faltering attention to my screen. The next QD is for the
construction of an indoor pool (heated and self-cleaning), deducted by a
Sole Proprietorship and constructed at the owner's home rather than his
business address.

Straight away my sense of honor feels bruised. I want to delegate the
request to the bin – much like any government auditor would. However,
my professional pride, urged on by the memory of the sniggers at the
QD score chart, causes me to spin an elaborate tale about the
therapeutic properties of warm water coupled with the scientifically
proven regenerative stimulus of underwater exercise. I also send a quick
email to the client telling him to see his doctor straight away about the
work-related back pains he must be suffering. And I remind him to
make copies of any and all prescriptions and store them in a safe place.

Another QD vanquished!

My subconscious sends up an image of a black tuxedo. The monkey-
suit I wore to my cousin's wedding two years ago.

Yes, I'd look pretty smart in a tux, but I'm not fully convinced it'd be
appropriate attire for an almost-date with Emma. I park the idea and
suggest my subconscious keep working.

The next QD concerns a collection of fine Scottish whiskeys. Twelve
bottles of thirty-five year old single malt, purchased at an estate auction
using a company account.

The tuxedo image resurfaces, this time with some context. My subconscious explains it'd really make me stand out. Like an EC, but expressed in clothing. Not only would I be the only guy in the venue wearing a tux, I might even be Emma's first tuxedo date. She'd definitely remember that.

I park the idea again. I'm not sure the thing even fits. At the very least it's unlikely to overly flatter my new, more manly proportions.

I start typing; thirty-five year old single malt is too valuable to drink. It's not a consumable, rather, it's a display item, exuding a dense air of wealth and prosperity, which is difficult to accomplish these days. So, in a very real sense, the whiskeys serve the same purpose as, say, premium ad space. I email the client to bill them to the marketing budget rather than general expenses, and remind him to procure some display cases for his business (I also mention that he may want to display some cheaper spirits in said cases for now, just in case he doesn't remember to ship the fine Scottish whiskey from his home to his business).

The day rambles on.

The tuxedo image surfaces a few more times, and I have to admit, it's starting to grow on me.

Mom's on the phone when I get home. I hang up my coat, take off my shoes, give her a kiss. She quickly thrusts the receiver into my hand. "Someone wants to talk to you," she says.

I stare at her. "I have no desire to talk to Betsy!"

"It's not Betsy," she says. "It's Sam."

"Sam? Sam who?" I push the receiver back towards her but Mom jumps out of reach. She can be surprisingly agile when she wants to be. Moreover, she knows about my social robot flaw, and is not above exploiting it.

"Sam wants to thank you, that's all."

Which makes no sense. I know of neither a Sam nor anybody who'd want to thank me.

The robot makes me put the receiver to my ear. "Yes?"

"Hi!" a female voice says. "It's Sam! I just wanted to thank you."

Which does exactly nothing to help me determine what's going on.

"I had a really great time last Saturday," the female continues. "Did you?"

I think back. Last Saturday wasn't all bad. I made a cool vid, wrote an even better script, and vanquished an entire cheese cake. "Yes," I mumble. "Last Saturday was pretty neat."

"Great!" The voice is young and energetic and not, I have to admit, entirely unsexy. It continues in breathy tones, "How about repeating it?"

Another day like Saturday would be amazing. If we could put days in jars... Alas, I don't suspect this is what Sam is alluding to.

"Let's hang out again," she says. "Anytime you want. How about

72

tonight?"

I shoot a look-of-many-daggers at Mom. She's set me up. This is not some hot, sexy, mysterious Sam. This is just Samantha Fox, Betsy's unaptly named niece. And she's trying to trick me with her sexy voice and name. But I already did my bit for humanity. It's someone else's turn to take her out. This should be like jury duty.

"Do you want to get another burger with me?"

A good response here is: *'No!'*

An even better response is: *'Hell NO!'*

And the perfect response is: *'Hell NO, never again!'*

Alas, the social robot won't let me be that honest. It won't let me be hurtful in any way. This is why I should not be allowed to talk on the phone. Ever. To anybody. But I won't let the robot force me into giving a definite 'Yes,' or even a definite 'Maybe.' I still have one last card to play. I can still be evasive. Oh yes.

"I'm really sorry," I tell her. "I'll have to get back to you. My schedule is frightfully fluid at the moment. I'm shifting gears, chasing opportunities. I cannot possibly make any plans right now."

"Oh." Samantha sounds disappointed. She sounds as if she hadn't even entertained the possibility of an evasive answer. I almost feel guilty about *not* being the kind of bastard who'd lead her on by taking her on another fake date. But, I won't do that. I'm too much of a gentleman.

"You have to understand," I explain. "I'm no ordinary man. I have great responsibilities towards my fans. I've started a journey with them. I've taken their trust and their time. I cannot bail on them. I'll leave no fan behind!"

Sam sighs. "Sure," she says. "I see what you're saying. And it's very noble and everything, but, during all that not bailing and not leaving any fan behind, you still have to eat, right? I mean, you're not on a hunger strike, are you?"

"I may eat," I concede, "if and when I have to. I may travel to the mall or have food delivered to my headquarters. The point is, due to my specific and special circumstances, there's no way for me to plan ahead. It'll all be spur of the moment eating."

"I see," she says. "No problem. Tell you what, just give me a buzz when you leave and I'll meet you there. I just love last-minute plans. And I can always eat."

"Fine," I say, heading toward the only way to wrap up the conversation; "I'll try to remember to call you, if I happen to eat out sometime in the near future, how's that?"

I'm skirting the very outer edges of what the social robot will let me do here, but I really hope it summarizes the significant level of vagueness to our non-plans.

"Great!" Sam says, sounding chipper again. "Looking forward to it!"

Apparently not.

"See you soon!" She hangs up.

Mom beams at me. "See? That wasn't so bad."

"Of course it was bad! It was terrible! Don't ever do that again!"

I throw down the receiver.

Mom tries to pinch my cheek. "I told you," she says, "once you get over your shyness you have no trouble talking to girls."

I want to explain the difference between being shy and being mortally terrified of wasting valuable lunch time, but I don't. "Just don't do that again," I repeat. "If I want to talk to people, I can call them myself."

"Nonsense," Mom says. "You always procrastinate. Be honest, it was scary at first, but you actually had fun, and now you even have a second date."

I shudder. "It's not a date, Mom. It's just a plan to almost certainly not meet in the future."

Mom smiles. "Sounds like a date to me."

I roll my eyes and go up to my room. It's time to reap the fruits of my subconscious labor. I'll make a list of all the things I want to say and do on my almost-date with Emma, then I'll study it. I'll go over it so many times I'll remember all of it even if my conscious mind decides to go offline again.

YouTube Script:

Here's the biggest secret anyone will ever tell you:

You cannot make a girl fall in love with you.

It simply can't be done. No man can make any woman anywhere fall in love with him. Period. In the entire history of humanity, this has never been done. ~~Not even by yours truly.~~

So what are we doing here? Why are you even enlisting my help? Well, I can lift the curtain for you, let you see the mechanism behind the magic. The cogs and wheels that turn behind the clock face. And that's important, because when you know about the mechanism, you're better equipped to interact with it.

What actually happens is; a girl *allows herself* to fall in love.

That's the secret. That's the whole deal. At some point, a girl simply lets herself fall in love. All we men can do is try and help her along and not get in the way too much.

Remember this and half your battle is over. Understand this and maybe three-quarters to four-fifths of your battle is over. ~~Maybe a little less, though,~~

~~because four-fifths is a lot, it's 80%, and you'll still need to do many things right, and be at many places at exactly the right time, so maybe it's more like three-fifths. Let's just call it three quarters to be on the safe side.~~

So how can we stay out of the way while still maintaining enough of a presence so she'll remember us?
Well, not much.
But here's what we can do:

First of all, we can make sure we've made contact using a killer EC. One that really made her wake up and take notice. ~~Even if some other guy has already EC-ed her with one of our best lines!~~ Secondly, we make sure to run into her from time to time, at the venue, causing a subconscious refresh signal. And, lastly, we make lists. Yes sir, we do. ~~The last thing we want is to get tongue-tied (or brain-tied) when we run into Her.~~ We have to have some go-to material on hand. Things to say, interesting questions to ask, places to take her. ~~After all, it makes absolutely no sense to rely on your brain to come up with decent ideas when you're making eye-contact with The One!~~

So is this kind of preparation dishonest in any way? Is working out conversations ahead of time a bit like cheating?
Of course not! Remember, this is not a pick-up! You're not trying to con random girls into liking you. You're simply giving the woman of your dreams a better chance of falling in love with the right guy. So making lists is actually your sworn duty! How on earth is She going to end up with the perfect mate if she never gets to find out who you really are? ~~You're both going to end up miserable if all you can show her is how tongue-tied you get around her.~~

[sign off]

14

Observation:

Women are like horses in that you cannot seem nervous around them, it scares them off. They need to feel you know what you're doing. Always exude confidence!

I get up extra early because I noticed a few saplings of neck hair last night and so I'm in for a complicated shave. I would've done it right away but a freshly shaven neck itches and interferes with sleep. Now I'm standing in front of the mirror, realizing I need at least a second mirror to pull this off. And, as I look around, there's nothing on hand.

"You're up early!"

Mom enters the bathroom without knocking. Before I can voice my utter shock, she takes up position on the toilet.

"Mom!"

"What?" She looks at me innocently.

"Can't you wait til I'm done?"

"What? This?" She shakes her head at me. "Don't tell me this embarrasses you!"

"It's not just embarrassment," I gasp. "It's also hygiene, politeness, and, to be frank, I'm a little busy here. Please await your turn."

"At my age," she says, "when it's time to go, it's time to go. You can wait outside if it upsets you."

I think of a devastating rebuttal. One which would have her respecting my bathroom privacy from now until the day the sun expires. Alas, I already hear Mom doing her business and no amount of sparklingly clear logic will stop her flow. I have no option but to flee.

On the other side of the bathroom door I mentally go over my rights as a lodger. I may need to retain legal counsel.

"Don't worry," Mom calls through the door. "I'm almost done."

I shudder.

When she finally emerges, I ask her for a hand mirror – the least she can do is help me make up for lost time.

"A hand mirror?" She gives me a look. "What do you need a hand mirror for?"

"I just need to shave my neck."

"Your neck? What's wrong with it?" She runs her fingers over my neck. "It's not so bad."

I feel time draining away.

Lost and wasted forever.

"I'm not asking for a debate, I just want a hand mirror."

Mom steps back into the bathroom. "Come on," she says. "I'll do it."

I hesitate. Flashbacks of forced holiday intimacy re-surface.

"What are you waiting for?" Mom waves the razor at me. "I don't have all day."

I check my watch and relent.

"I can't remember the last time I did this," Mom says. She lathers up my neck and wets the razor with warm water. "What's the special occasion?"

"No special occasion. It just noticed it and then it started bothering me."

"Sure it did," Mom says, "but *why* did you notice it? That's the most interesting question…"

I try to subdue a sigh, but fail. Had I known the favor would come with an unhealthy dose of third degree, I would've passed. "I'm sure," I say, "that on this vastly complex planet, in this ever expanding and mysterious universe, that cannot possibly be the most interesting question."

"Maybe," she says, "but I bet it has something to do with a girl." She sounds excited. "I know! You *are* planning a date with Sam, aren't you?" She sounds pleased with herself. "Didn't I tell you the two of you would hit it off?"

"I'm just doing this for work, Mom."

"Of course you are." She shaves away the first strip of neck hair and I wonder if she'd still help if she knew I have no intention of ever seeing Samantha again. That I'm planning a completely Samantha-less life from here on in.

"You're doing this for the same work you've never shaved your neck for before," Mom says. "I believe you."

She nicks my skin.

"Careful!"

"Stop fidgeting!"

I put as much finality in my voice as I can. "They shave my neck when I get a haircut, so I usually don't have to bother."

"And yet," Mom continues, not missing a beat, "and yet, you're bothering now. So it must be a special occasion."

I cannot believe I'm still having this conversation. Isn't a conversation supposed to be a two-way deal? Surely with only one willing participant there can be no conversation? "Fine," I say. "If you're hell-bent on making me say this, then I will, but you won't like it... I do have a date."

"I knew it!"

"But it's not with Samantha. It's with an infinitely more interesting female. Someone much more my intellectual equal."

"Ooh," Mom croons. "A new girl!" She takes off a few more strips, shaving more carefully now. "Where did you meet her?"

"She's in the nut business."

"The nut business?" Mom shaves on silently, undoubtedly forming a very strong opinion on the recently stated business. After a long moment she says, "Well, that's a good business. People will always need nuts."

I replay the comment in my head, looking for the passive aggressiveness, hidden jibes, catty edges. Surprisingly, I can't locate any. Mom seems genuinely happy for me. Somehow I expected her to be loyal to team Samantha. Apparently, as long as there's a potential grandchild bearing female involved, Mom's onboard.

That's a bit of a relief.

"So," Mom says, "tell me more about nut-girl."

When my neck is clean Mom follows me to my room. She looks over my chosen outfit and sucks air in through her teeth.

"Are you sure you want to wear *that*?" she asks.

"What's wrong with it?"

"It's jeans with a tuxedo jacket…"

"Yes, it is."

"Well, that's what's wrong with it."

She rummages around in my closet and she's made me just insecure enough about my choices that I let her.

She takes out a few shirts, looks them over, throws them back. "I really wish you'd let me take you shopping," she sighs.

I think about rebutting but I'm on a tight schedule. I shouldn't slow her down by getting her defensive.

She takes out a few more shirts, holds them up, throws them back.

"You dress like a homeless person–"

"Mom!"

"… on crack."

She picks out some stuff and stands me in front of the mirror.

"How about this?"

I know what this looks like, but it's not so much that my mom is dressing me. It's more like I have a private wardrobe consultant. One who also happens to be related to me.

That's all this is.

I barely make it to work in time. Gharity's already doing his rounds. I hear him telling one of the new guys about his strict closed door policy. I keep my head down and handle a couple of QDs, then leave the building at precisely twelve, reaching 'Ye Olde Peanuts Shoppe' just as Emma steps out.

This upsets me a little. I'd expected to have a few moments to check myself and go over my opening statements. Instead, I'm staring at Emma with kept breath.

This happens every time I run into her unexpectedly. I get a little star-struck, as if I'm meeting a minor celebrity. It's very annoying.

Emma spots me and comes over. "Hi!" she says. "You're right on time!"

I nod. There's a funny response I could make, but I'd have to go home and sit at my desk for a couple of hours to find it. So I just say, "Yeah!"

"Where should we go?"

I'm back on solid ground. I have it all worked out. I know she doesn't have much time. I know it's too early in our almost-relationship to take her away in my car. I know that sometimes more is better but often it's not. So, taking all this and more, into account, I've come up with the perfect venue for our almost-date.

"How about we get some Ultra burgers?"

Emma beams. "I love the Ultra burger!"

Of course she does. Logic dictates all highly sentient humans do.

I lead the way to the food court.

Emma sounds a bit nasal today. I think she has the sniffles. I watch her touch her nose and realize being ill actually suits her. It's kind of cute. And I spot a hint of makeup, also. She's applied a light dusting of eye shadow. I wonder briefly, very briefly, if she did this for me.

As we make our way to the escalators, I'm acutely aware of walking next to Her. Of Her walking next to me. Of Us walking together, next to each other. And it occurs to me that people watching might assume we're together. Which we are, I suppose. At least on some level.

I take a few seconds to imagine what that would be like, Emma and myself as a couple. It would mean we'd meet up again after work today. We'd make dinner together, fight a bit over the remote, then snuggle up to watch a movie.

I push the thought away, it feels too damn good.

Emma suddenly touches my arm, "Hey, is that a tux jacket?"

'This old thing? It's just something I threw on on my way out the door.'

"I believe it could be," I say. "Yes, I guess it is."

"It's nice," she says. "It really suits you." She looks me over appreciatively and I feel all warm and fuzzy. I should probably find more ways of having her look at me like this.

"It brings out your eyes," she says.

"Thank you." I'm not entirely sure how to act (cool and aloof seems a

79

good way to go). "You look great too."

She snorts as if I'm joking. Which makes her even more adorable. I look away before I get too nervous to actually talk to her.

"So, are you going to a funeral later?"

"What?"

She shrugs, "I just thought you had a funeral or something."

I have no idea why she'd think that.

Maybe I should smile more. Maybe I look sad.

She changes the subject. "Do you get Ultra burgers often?"

"Not really," I say. "At least, not as often as I'd like."

Once a day and twice on weekends. That's just barely the minimal human requirement. In a more optimal reality I'd step it up to a respectable number, alas timing, finances, and cholesterol prevent reality from being more optimal.

"Me neither," she says. "In fact, I can't remember the last time I had one."

"You know in some cultures that's considered a mortal sin," I tell her. I remember to smile. "The Ultra burger gods are looking down at you right now, trying to decide what do to with you."

"Oh no," she says. "You think they might smite me?"

"Smite you? That's the least of your worries."

"But you'll protect me, right?"

"I'm not sure," I say. "This actually puts you on my black list too."

Emma grins. "I promise I'll eat Ultra burgers for breakfast for the rest of the week. Does that make up for it?"

"It's a start."

I consider her ultra-cool breakfast idea, then our hands accidentally touch and my mind goes blank. I don't pull away and she makes no effort to pull away either. I hold my breath and enjoy the sensation. We travel down the escalator with our hands casually connected – skin touching skin – and she still doesn't pull away.

Is this just an accident? Is she aware this Is happening?

I want this to last as long as possible (forever?) so I remind myself to breathe again, just in case it does.

"It's so nice that you kept lunch simple," Emma says. We round a corner and head into the food court. I feel a pang of loss when we sit and our hands finally disconnect. The loss doesn't last, though, because now I get to look into her eyes. And it occurs to me it should be illegal for women to have such amazing eyes. After all, thousands of guys will see them and end up dreaming about them, but only one guy gets to take them home. For the rest of us, it's just torture knowing that they exist.

This should definitely be illegal, for anyone but Emma.

"Some guys take me to these elaborate champagne lunches," Emma says. "Or to fancy candle-lit restaurants. It makes no sense. What's that all about? Don't they get that I only have an hour?" She smiles. "I'm so happy you didn't do anything dopey and romantic."

"Well," I say, somewhat hurt, "the Ultra burger is somewhat romantic."

Emma laughs as if I'm joking. She leans over to squeeze my hand. I like her laugh and I love her hand-squeeze, so I decide I probably was joking.

Emma and I have a lot in common.

We're like the same person.

Only in two separate bodies.

With two separate minds.

I might be losing the thread a bit here.

"You're right, I forgot," Emma says. "Burger Aficionado magazine did vote the Ultra burger the most romantic burger of the year, three years running."

She sounds so cute making jokes in between sniffles, it just makes me want to hug her and kiss her and blow her nose for her.

I have no idea what that means.

Lunch is over far too soon.

Of course it is.

And when we return to the Shoppe there's an awkward moment where I feel as if I'm dropping her off at home. I almost consider going in for a kiss.

Do people even kiss goodbye at the mall? Is that accepted behavior? Is it expected, perhaps? I really don't know.

Then my train of thought derails because Emma slips her hand into my pocket. I have no idea how to react and Emma's expression doesn't reveal a thing. She just smiles this casual, friendly smile. Then she pulls out my cell and says, "I'll give you my number. In case we have to message each other sometime."

When she's done she puts my cell back and gives me a quick kiss on the cheek, then disappears into the Shoppe.

It takes a while for my head to clear and to realize I'm supposed to go away. Back to work or something. Back to the real world.

YouTube script:

Guys enjoy an introduction at any time, day or night. It doesn't matter what we're doing, who just died, we're always in the mood for a conversation with The One.

In fact, if an interesting woman were to break into our home and wake us up just to say, 'Hi, my name is Emma, what's your favorite color?' we wouldn't really mind. We'd appreciate the interest. ~~In fact, on some level, we're actually *waiting* for this to happen.~~

But women are different. They're more like the sea; they have high and low tides. They have moods. There's a cadence to what they enjoy.
Even the most amazingly perfect introduction will fail during low tide, when she's stressed, upset, or just focusing on something else. While a moderately bad introduction will still work well during a high tide. It's all about timing. Her reactions aren't based solely on your approach or you as a person.

To grasp this really strange concept, think of it as being offered a nice, juicy Ultra burger. Ultra burgers are great, ~~and they come with BBQ sauce, so you don't have to bring your own,~~ but imagine being offered that burger after you've already had three, and you're carsick. Someone offers you this fourth burger and now you want to vomit in their face. Same introduction, same burger, different timing.

So what causes these tides in females?
The obvious one is hormones. It's a scientific fact that there are times of the month where she feels more flirty, and others where she'll be more stubborn or introspective.
Less obvious factors are: having had a fight with her best friend, not having slept well, having had a fight with a family member, having found out someone died, having had a fight with an impolite store employee, having realized she doesn't own enough shoes, having had a fight with her computer ~~(or any other electronic device (except for cell phones, which they can always figure out for some reason)).~~

The list goes on, perhaps indefinitely. The point is that you need to look for signs of a high tide situation.

[sign off]

Video #136 by *Leverage*. **Views: 69**

Comments:

LeopoldGreenEye: (6:12 pm) U were so right about men being invisible to women! I was on a date with The One and I asked her about the times we met before we started dating, and, just as you predicted, she didn't recall any of them! The times we made eye-contact (prolonged eye-contact!), the times we talked (5 times!), the time we shared an elevator (very special!), she didn't remember any of it! It's as if it never happened. The only person on the planet who knows this ever took place is me :(

Leverage: (7:27 pm) It's important to put this into perspective. Don't attach any special meaning to it. Just because she doesn't remember some moment that's meaningful to you, that doesn't mean you guys aren't right for each other. But let this be a good lesson about ear catchers. Unless you make her brain do a back-flip, you will probably remain part of the background noise of her life.

TheLizard: (7:37 pm) When you explain it, Lev, it makes so much sense. I can't believe I didn't realize any of this before!

Agent12: (7:37 pm) My balls hurt when I read this shit! Over-think much?? Prolonged eye contact – what the hell is that? Just talk to the bitch and see if she'll put out. I should start my own channel, teach you guys how to spot the bitches who won't so you can move on!

DissonantMelody: (8:27 pm) So why don't you, Agent12? Set up your own stupid channel and stay clear of this one. No one here is interested in what you have to say!

OldMan1951: (8:27 pm) I need to talk to you son.

Leverage: (8:38 pm) The truth is, Agent12, for all the fun you think you're having, you live in a sad, sad world. You don't even realize what you're missing. It's like you've been watching movies without sound all your life and you're boasting about how many movies you've seen. On this channel we inherently understand you haven't truly seen a movie until you've seen one with sound!

TheLizard: (8:38 pm) Yeah! Tell him Leverage!

Agent12: (8:39 pm) Movies without sound? What the hell is wrong with you? Who talks like that? I don't understand a thing ur saying!!

Leverage: (8:40 pm) Which is exactly my point.

OldMan1951: (8:44 pm) How can I reach you?

15

Observation:

We should feel bad for all the beautiful people;
they don't get much of a chance to struggle.

My charts are starting to slide off my desk. It's a pretty hefty stack after almost a year of vlogging, I look around for somewhere safe to put them.

Cool and aloof as I am, I should throw them out. I never reuse materials, even if I explain similar concepts. I always present my followers with fresh new charts to help them concentrate. Still, throwing them out feels so final.

What if my vids suddenly go viral? What if they go global? At any moment, humanity might collectively realize how much wisdom can be found in my vids, then fans might battle over an original, hand-drawn Leverage chart.

I'm not bragging, I just don't want to make a silly mistake and throw out something that'll be valuable someday. I mean, imagine how stupid Van Gogh's neighbor felt after losing the little sketch he received as payment for some bread?

That won't happen to me.

For all I know, future generations will display my charts in museums.

'These charts, dear children, are the earliest records of the Enlightened Age. Before Leverage, men simply didn't have a clue. They took dating advice from TV and cinema. Our species was headed for extinction!'

Okay, that isn't a likely scenario, at least not during my life time, but I don't want to be so foolish as to rule it out completely.

However, the charts are gathering dust and beginning to tear, so where to put them?

I'd keep them under my bed but with Mom's penchant for rough hovering it'd be akin to storing them in the opening of a particularly aggressive shredder. And I don't want to fold or roll them, so my bookcases are out.

I scan my room. I suppose the top of the cupboard is the only option. If I stack them neatly, cover them with some plastic, they should be okay for a couple of years.

I get up on a chair and clear away the debris that invariably accumulates on top of cupboards: old consoles, limited-edition Coke cans, movie posters, Kenner figures that refused to appreciate as excessively as predicted, pieces of lava rock 'borrowed' from Pompeii during a short holiday, tiny sombreros, pens that are also lights, lights that are also key-chains, and a dusty old shoe box. I compress everything into the cupboard, everything except the shoe box, which goes onto the bed for further inspection. I have no idea what's in it. I don't even recognize the box, it looks like it might have housed a pair of Clarks, child size.

I take a moment to sit on the bed and go through it. On top I find medals, the kind they give out to kids for attendance of recreational events. Nothing special, although I must have believed they were at the time. Underneath are some cut-outs: cars and houses I was going to buy, places I would visit. I vaguely remember these. The next layer is an assortment of cereal box prizes – plastic insects, magnifying glasses, rings with special powers.

I'm on a miniature excavation here, brushing away layer after layer of debris, descending deep down into my past.

I find old school photos, each with a little red circle on it. A magic marker halo around a little girl's face. These, I recall, are my childhood crushes, the girls who first set my heart aglow. I smile. How clueless I was back then. How little I understood of the female mind. I never even talked to any of these girls, I just admired them from afar, waiting for them to suddenly and inexplicably realize how amazing I was. Hoping to capture their little angel hearts with meaningful looks that somehow displayed my hidden depths as a kid-philosopher.

I check these faces now with the magnifying glass from layer three, seeing if I can still recognize the traces of angelic magic I spotted as a child.

There's Katherine, with the cute overbite, who always wore homemade dresses. Mandy, with the ponytails and freckles, who punched me in the stomach. And Lenora, with the baggy pants and pigtails, who invited me to her birthday party.

I realize now she probably invited everyone, but that didn't occur to me at the time. I spent the entire afternoon following her around, waiting for that special moment when she'd take me aside to tell me what she so obviously felt for me.

Of course, we never spoke.

They look so very different now, these girls. Alien, almost. They've become children when before they were equals. I'm looking at faces frozen in time.

How different my life would've been if any of these girls had spoken to me. Or if they'd just treated me like any normal human being, just another kid in their class, no worse, no better. But, well, I suppose there was just something about me that made people uncomfortable.

For a moment my mind travels the path not taken. What kind of person would I've become? Would I have been able to develop my trademark insight and my carefully crafted wise-isms, or would complacency have arrested my emotional development? Would early success with the fairer gender have removed my drive to become more insightful?

A scary thought.

Perhaps a psyche molded under the influence of beautiful memories might believe, deep down, that the world is a nice place. I'm not sure that kind of delusion helps. Perhaps it only hinders.

I go through the pictures one more time and it occurs to me how much stronger childhood feelings were, how everything was intense and all-consuming. Every single emotion was either life or death, there were no in-betweens.

It's probably because the mind needs time to get a handle on emotions, just like it needs time to learn how to ride bikes and climb ropes. Once you reach adulthood, you've got it more or less under control. The lows aren't so low anymore, the highs not that high. A tuning process has taken place allowing you to put things in perspective. The most extreme outliers are reserved for things that really are life or death, everything else just gets muted, turned down.

I haven't felt anything as intense as my childhood crushes. Nowhere near. Not until a year ago, when I first met Emma.

I put the pictures to the side and check the next layer: TV Guide cut-outs of the shows I wanted to live in. Here are the star ships and green body builders and talking cars and lots and lots of actresses in spandex. Here are renegade teams of ex-military, child-sleuths uncovering mysteries no adult could ever solve and all manner of talking pets and aliens and alien talking pets.

The next layer has some collectable cards. Then bubble gum wrappers. Then lists of graphic novels.

I dig deeper. Getting younger. Travelling back in time.

More old pictures. These are scratched and yellow, the paper starting to fray. They've been handled often and I recognize them instantly.

Picture 1: Dad at the hospital, holding a one-year old and a round, purple baby. Dad's hair is too big, his moustache too wide.

Picture 2: Dad handing me an ice-cream cone at the beach. I'm about nine, still missing some teeth. I'm wearing a t-shirt over burnt shoulders and Dad's moustache is gone, his hair has started to thin. Neither of us notices the camera.

These pictures aren't in any particular order. They were simply dumped at the bottom of the box.

Picture 3: Dad letting go of my bike. I'm six and my face is a study of terror. I remember the house in the background, but only from pictures like these, and I only remember the rooms that were photographed. I have no idea what the kitchen looked like, but I clearly remember the living room at Christmas.

Picture 4: Mom holding a large present, smiling at the camera. She looks so much happier and un-whiny.

There are no pictures of the four of us.

Picture 5: A yard full of people. I'm ten, blowing out the candles on a birthday cake. When I squint I can make Dad out in the background, staring off into space.

There are more pictures, but Dad isn't in them. There isn't even an empty space for him to be.

I'd go through the rest of the pictures but for some reason they are all out of focus. In fact, the whole room is now out of focus. I hate when that happens.

I blink a few times and put everything back into the box. I wonder, very very briefly, if Dad, wherever he is, knows what still goes through my mind whenever I see an unknown face in the crowd: *Are you him? Are you my dad? Are you secretly checking up on me?*

And I'm curious about what he'd say about my vids and my wise-isms. Would he be proud of what I've done, of who I've become?

Would he want to know someone like me?

I put the box away. It doesn't matter. Dad's long gone and there's no time to think about stuff like this, I have important scripts to write.

YouTube Script:

Here's why I feel sorry for the beautiful people.

Life is like a game of Russian roulette. A game of chance that can leave you dead or mangled at every turn. First, millions of sperm (millions of possible you's) travel down the fallopian tubes, but only one makes it to the egg. The rest dies. If you make it, you're literally one out of a million. But that only means that your struggle has begun.

Another spin of the wheel, another roll of the dice. Good parents or bad? Nice part of the world or no? Hereditary deceases or not so much?
Let's say you luck out again: nice part of the world, okay parents, no diseases. Woohoo!

Alright, so at some point you'll pick up a mirror. Are you ugly or beautiful? Chances are you already know. If you're beautiful your aunts and uncles have told you thousands of times (can't trust your parents, they have a blind spot). And if you're ugly, or different in any way, your pals at school have found very efficient ways of notifying you of this, also.

You're still not sure? Well, that just means you're one of the beautiful people. You don't know any better. You may even have silly questions like:

Doesn't everybody hear; "My, what pretty eyes you have!", throughout their childhood? Doesn't everybody have boyfriends and girlfriends all through high school? Doesn't everybody have people fall all over themselves trying to help them out?
Actually, no. They don't.

Doesn't everybody get their dream job handed to them when they smile during an interview? Isn't that how the world works?
It most certainly is not.
It's just how things work temporarily, inside the Beautibubble.

But who are the lucky ones here? Who drew the longest straw?
Is it those who never learn to work for anything, who breeze through life on the kindness of others? Those who grow up thinking that the world is filled with smiling, friendly people waiting to offer help?
Or is it those who have to fight every step of the way, for every friendship, every job, every single break in life. Those who actually have to work to earn each smile they'll ever see?

In my humble but well researched opinion, the beautiful people got the raw deal. All growth comes from adversity. All knowledge is born out of frustration. Every invention is preceded by a problem. As a race, we are problem solvers. We *need* to find things to fix and improve. The easier life is on us, the fewer tools we develop. Emotional tools, physical tools, mental tools.

Who needs to develop a personality when things seem to come along just fine without one? How often do we hear: She has a pretty face, but when she opens her mouth, she ruins it? But it's not her fault. She was taught she was perfect from the beginning. Why change when you're already perfect?

But when beauty inevitably fades, when the Beautibubble bursts, she's thrust into the real world, unprepared for actual existence. And that can't be easy. ~~But every rule has its exceptions. There are creatures with beauty inside and out. They have it oozing from every pore. But she's hard to find.~~

[sign off]

16

My promise:

Pretty soon she'll realize she likes you. From then on it's an uphill battle, you and her against her subconscious.

Another Saturday morning with cartoons and cereal. But halfway through Adventure Time disaster strikes: the phone rings! I panic. My adrenal glands shoot into overdrive. I call up to Mom, but she's in the shower, and, try as I might, I can't get her to budge.

Why does the really bad stuff always happen to me?

My mind racing, I go over possible could-have-beens and might-have-happeneds. If only I'd left the house a minute ago, before the phone rang. Can I still leave? After all, what's a minute in the lifespan of the universe? It's so insignificantly small, it practically doesn't even exist. Leaving now or having left a minute ago, it's basically the exact same moment.

But I already called up to Mom. She knows the phone rang and that I heard it.

I stare at the receiver, I just know it's bad news. It always is. It's someone trying to sell me something. Or one of Mom's friends, whom I haven't spoken to in years and who'll feel obligated to catch up.

It's a municipal worker.

A slow cousin.

It's... Dad.

My hand hovers over to the receiver. I take a deep breath, then lift it. "Yes?"

"Hi! It's me!"

I do a double cringe. First, because I hate it when people assume I can infer who they are from just three words. Second, because I actually infer who this sexy, breathy, size-zero voice belongs to. It's Samantha Fox, my soon-to-be stalker.

"I guess you've been eating in your room," she says.

"My room?"

I notice I sound a bit nasal.

"Yes," she says. "Remember we were going to get a burger as soon as you had some time?"

"Ah. Well, I told you that was very, very unlikely... I have all these

89

scripts and ideas and–"

"Relax, I'm teasing," Samantha says.

But she doesn't sound like she's teasing.

She sounds needy.

I cradle the phone on my shoulder and take out a handkerchief. My nose is itchy, like it's about to run.

"That's not what I'm calling for," Samantha says.

I relax. I don't know why that hadn't occurred to me. Samantha is Mom's best friend's niece. Of course they have thousands of inane messages to pass along their ranks. I shouldn't have worried.

"Mom's in the shower," I say. "I'll tell her you called."

"No, silly," Samantha says. "I have other business *with you*."

I tense up again.

"You probably need a break from all that hard work, don't you?"

"Not really," I say. "I love hard work. I thrive on it."

Samantha snickers. "You're so funny," she says. "Well, I won't let you work yourself to death. I'm going to save you. I'm giving you permission to take a night off. How's that sound?"

It sounds like a trap. A trap she's carefully laid out. She's prepared this conversation in advance, worked out crafty responses to whatever I'm likely to say, and here I am, completely unprepared. It's not fair!

"I'm taking you out on the town," she says.

"Oh, you don't have to," I tell her. "In fact, I won't let you. Your time is far too valuable to waste on me."

Thinking on my feet is not my strong suit, but I'll be surprised if she expected that response.

"Come on," she says. "You'll have to watch a movie sometime, won't you?"

She's got me there. Movies are essential to mental survival. Her logic is flawless.

"Who's that?" Mom asks. She's appeared beside me in her bathrobe, brandishing a curling iron. There's a towel wrapped around her head. My stress levels double. I put my hand over the receiver. "It's Samantha," I tell her. "Betsy's niece."

Mom takes the receiver.

"Wait!"

I was almost out!

I was just about to hang up!

"Hello, Samantha," Mom says sweetly. "How are you, dear?"

I try to get the receiver back but Mom deftly turns away from me. I'm having trouble breathing. Mom's not only likely to make an appointment in my name for tonight, she's perfectly capable of making a standing appointment for every Saturday night until the day of my demise – which could turn out to be very soon.

"I'm sorry, dear," Mom says to Samantha. "I've just grounded my son. He's been very naughty. He's not to leave the house. It's straight home after work for him from now on."

There's a pause as Samantha speaks, then Mom continues. "No, dear, I'm sorry. I'd love to make an exception for you, I really would, but what kind of signal would that send?" Mom's tone turns conspiratorial. "You have to be so careful raising children these days. They need structure. They need to learn that no means no."

My jaw drops.

"Yes, dear, I understand." Mom gives me a wink. "But he was far too naughty. I'm not sure he'll ever be allowed out again."

I'm flabbergasted.

Mom tells Samantha to remind Betsy to bring the crackers for the knitting club, then hangs up. She gives me a stern look. "Call me next time Sam tries to trick you into going out," she says. "You know you can't say no over the phone!"

I'm still not sure what just happened. "I thought you wanted me to go out with her?"

Mom waves it away, heading to the kitchen. "Let's just see how things pan out with that nut-girl, shall we? I was never overly fond of Samantha."

I'm about to respond when my pants start to vibrate.

It appears I'm receiving a message. I quickly dig out my cell.

em: Hi! what r u doing?

A message from Emma!

Holy smoke!

She's completely ignoring the 48 hour rule, how cool can one girl be? But my excitement turns to dread as I realize I'll have to answer. I'll have to think on my feet, again.

For a moment my thumbs tremble over the virtual keyboard, then I remember how effortlessly we talked on our almost-date, how much fun we had, and I try to bring that feeling back. I imagine Emma sitting across from me, smiling and laughing and not at all thinking what a weirdo I am.

me: Oh, just teaching underprivileged rhesus monkeys to read, how bout u?
em: HA! ;) taught all my rhesus monkeys to read yesterday, now moving on to gnus, much more of a challenge!! ;p

I really would've liked to start our chat relationship on a more brilliant note, but it appears Emma enjoyed my lame joke. Enough, at least, to respond right away, and that has to be a good sign. Maybe I'm not doing so badly here.

Mom returns from the kitchen. "What's wrong?" she says. She stares at me.

I put my cell away. "Nothing's wrong."

"You look ill." She touches my forehead. "You're all red and sweaty."

"*You're* all red and sweaty!" I retort, realizing too late how juvenile that sounds.

Mom frowns at me.

I brush past her and run up to my room.

I read Emma's messages again. I can't believe how wonderfully wonderful she is. I want to reply to her latest message but I'm not sure I should. What we have now is such a nicely contained thread, I might destroy it if I try to add something funny.

So I wait for something else to happen, but nothing does.

And now I've left it too long. I sit on my bed and stare at the wall. Samantha's call and Emma's messages have thrown me off, derailed my Saturday. I have trouble finding my tracks. What would I be doing right now if none of that had happened?

I look around the room. Should I prepare yesterday's script for recording? Try to write a new script? I don't really feel like doing either. I'm far too unfocussed, too excited.

My pants vibrate again.

My heart jumps.

em: bored out of my skull!!!
em: where are the magic time-pixies when u need em?

I forget all about my day and type my reply.

me: I heard they're on strike. Something about needing more time off. Ironic, when you think about it
em: true, but sucks 4 me.
me: yup. just close up and head home, no one will notice :)

After that, Emma doesn't respond anymore. Probably busy with customers.

I'm dying to go to the Shoppe but there's no way that wouldn't seem awkward and desperate. And even if it didn't, I'd find a way to make it so. So, instead, I spend an hour or so re-reading Emma's messages, trying to interpret them in different ways. And all the while my nose runs. I must've caught Emma's sniffles when she kissed me. Now I have millions of tiny bugs multiplying inside me, ravaging my immune system.

And that's kind of cool. At some point these creatures were living inside Emma and now they're inside me. It's like we're raising this life-form together.

The day disappears somehow and I head down for dinner when Mom calls. As per usual, dinner turns out to be a difficult time for me.

Mom: You're not eating!
Me: Yes I am.
Mom: Look at your plate!
Me: My plate is almost empty.
Mom: That's because you didn't put anything on it. How can you keep up your strength if you don't eat?
Me: I'm large enough to survive on a few less calories.
Mom: Where did that come from? You never talk like that!

17

Observation:

When you're not in love, this entire planet doesn't make sense.

The next few days I spend more time on my cell than I do on my computer. I get a little work done, but only in between messaging Emma. It seems she has a lot of downtime between customers. Either that or she likes me so much she's blowing off her customers to message me.

(Unlikely.)

(But fun to consider.)

Even after what seems like a hundred or so messages, I still feel that tingle of excitement whenever a new Emmanism arrives.

> **em:** why do so many of my customers look like Barney?
> **me:** them's the breaks, my dear.
> **em:** seriously, every one of them seems to be short and round!
> **me:** guess it's a popular model, and easy to maintain.
> **em:** sure, but just once I'd like to serve a Clooney or a Pitt!!

I've noticed Emma mentions celebrities a lot. I wonder if this should worry me.

> **me:** The Clooneys and Pitts of this world aren't half as interesting as the guys who look like Barney. think about it; who needs to develop an interesting inner life if they look like Da Vinci carved them out of marble on one of his extra good days?
> **em:** that's a long sentence ~~
> **me:** but probably true
> **em:** i dont' care, i just want to serve someone sexy for a change!
> **me:** won't your bf get jealous?
> **em:** ???
> **me:** didn't u say u have a boyfriend?
> **em:** did i?
> **me:** yeah. u had a whole story about ironing his socks
> **em:** oh :) could be, i do that sometimes. no bf :(
> **me:** no bf?
> **em:** nope
> **me:** poor em :P

em: yeah, but who knows coon?
me: coon? Why coon??
em: sorry, that should be: 'soon' : |
me: ah...

I wait a few minutes, but there's no response. I notice my hands are trembling. I prop my cell up against a stack of manuals and re-read our conversation. Why is Emma dropping the boyfriend pretense now? I think back to my previous analysis on the pitfally subject of fake BF's, but I draw blanks. Somehow I can't think clearly. I guess it's a good sign she's coming clean, though.

"Hey!" Quiton-James passes my cubicle on his way from the coffee machine and peers over my wall. "Didn't I see you playing with your phone twenty minutes ago?" He gives me a meaningful look. "Is that thing glued to your hand or what?"

I shrug and smile. His remarks don't bother me in the least.

"Are you planning to do *any* work today?"

"Planning? Yes. But we all know how fast plans can change."

I smile some more.

Quiton-James shakes his head. He was passed over for promotion twice, each occasion coinciding with me finding a glaring error in one of his reports. I don't think he likes me very much. Instead of thanking me for preventing his ineptitude from being made public, he's been, well, bitchy. And I think he's made it his mission to annoy me. Today, however, he has no hope of succeeding, which will probably upset his declining mental balance even more.

"Anything else?" I ask pleasantly.

Quiton-James frowns, then walks away.

I congratulate myself on being so cool and collected. I suppose it's because I feel sorry for him. Sorry that he doesn't have an Emma in his life. Sorry he won't receive a tingle-inducing message any time soon – and, really, that's no way to live. No wonder he's always in a bad mood. Everybody should always be at most five minutes away from their next tingle-inducing message. You're just pretending to be alive without it.

I read Em's last message again. I'm still baffled, but my memory slowly uncoils. I remember writing that all girls have boyfriends. Either real ones, placeholders, or made up ones. The made up ones are used to ward off unwanted advances. You can't expect a girl to simply confess she doesn't have a boyfriend, not straight away. If she does, she's either lying or needy. I'm not sure how the rest of my vid went, if I ever figured out when the fake BF ruse is supposed to be dropped.

I reread Emma's messages five more times.

Then another forty.

Is she asking me to be her boyfriend?

Could that actually be what's happening here?
My cell buzzes.

em: so, u coming to the store tomorrow?
me: why? i'm not sure you deserve to see me
em: of course i do! i'm, like, totally cool, remember? :P
me: not when you talk like that ;)
em: hey, no fair. i was doing a silly voice in my head, that totally counts!
me: sure it does...

I want to find out more about her fake boyfriend, but I don't know how to bring it up. I can't just type *'Won't your BF mind?,'* every other sentence. Too obvious. And I certainly have no idea how to write, *'Are you asking me to be your boyfriend?'* because that's probably spelled very differently in the real world (more subtly, and with lots of different words). The same holds for, *'We'd be perfect together,'* and *'There isn't much point in ever being apart again.'* You can't just throw stuff like that out unprocessed. You have to set it up right.

em: hey, aren't u supposed to be working?
me: u should talk!
em: don't have customers right now, but u get paid by the hour, r?
me: tru, in fact, u don't want to know how much our conversations have cost so far.
em: ouch! should I feel guilty?
me: just enough to agree to another lunch with me :P
em: nonono, I owe that debt to your clients, sir, not to u
me: ah, of course..
em: sly guy ~~
me: yup that's me
em: seriously, tho (or somewhat seriously) I think without u I would've gone insane already
me: are u sure u haven't?
em: is that a compliment or an insult?
me: probably a compliment, but don't let it go to ur head.
em: don't worry, like most things, it went straight to my hips ~
me: ??
em: that's prob a girl-joke, don't worry aobu tit :P
me: great, I love things I don't have to worry about.
em: anyway, u r a bad influence on me!!!!
me: of course I am (but why do U think so?)
em: I don't think i've ever written this much in one day :) :)
me: u c, u simply cannot live without me ;)
em: sure, sly guy 8^) (I'm rolling my eyes at you right now, can u tell?)

I stay at the office an hour longer than usual. Not to make up for lost time, but because I can't tear myself from my cell long enough to get my coat, never mind drive all the way home. When I'm sure Emma's gone home herself, I finally leave to start on a new script.

YouTube Script:

Let me explain why women are so attracted to celebrities. Why they get giggly over actors, rock-stars, artists, and infomercial presenters.

I won't waste valuable YouTube real-estate expanding on the obvious; it's not just their status, confidence, money, and unfailing good looks. Those count, but they only make up a small fraction of the equation. They're like side dishes: nice to have, but not absolutely necessary. And that is exactly why so few men have figured out what I'm about to tell you.

Collectively we've assumed it was just the fame and the money. And our next move was to try and acquire said fame and money. However, we should've stopped for a moment to analyze the situation.

First, you have to understand it's much more attractive for women to have something that *other* women want than it is to have something that only they want.
This holds true for many things; clothes, houses, shoes, you name it. ~~You only have to take a look at a Fendi bag to know what I'm talking about – google a picture, you'll see. These bags are so ugly that even men notice them. However, because women were cunningly led to believe that *other* women coveted this type of bag, they've become a huge success.~~

The reason I'm telling you this, is that the same principle applies to boyfriends and husbands.
Women don't want that fun exciting guy who will make them happy. What they want is that fun exciting guy that *their girlfriends* want to make *them* happy. And what's more attractive than a celebrity? A guy that every single woman in the world has heard of? A guy that every girl she'll ever meet has spent time thinking about?

But that's not all.

In dating a celebrity, there's always the immediate danger of being dumped for a better model. In fact, every second a celebrity's girlfriend spends *not* being dumped, is like a personal victory. It's an implicit validation of her entire existence.
Think about that.
There's no way a normal guy can supply that much validation, certainly not by doing absolutely nothing. And this is a key point. Going out of your way to give her validation won't even work. Constantly giving her presents and compliments will just make you seem weak and needy. Her subconscious will despise you. The key to validation is that it needs to be given more or less

effortlessly. Basically by the guy doing absolutely nothing. ~~Coincidentally, doing absolutely nothing is also the preferred amount of effort men like to put into relationships – but more on this later.~~

On to the next point: the drama.

Ever read a romance novel? Ever seen a romantic comedy? Of course you have. You don't have to admit it out loud, just agree with me in your head. So what do all these stories have in common? Where do they all begin and where do they all end?

They begin with the girl wanting a guy (and not just any guy, it has to be a guy that *other* girls want, badly!) And where do all these stories end? At the exact moment the girl gets this guy.
There might be a wedding ceremony, some kind of ritual of moving in together, but that's it. To the female mind, there's nothing interesting left to say. The guy is in the bag and thus the fretting is over. There's no more thrill, no more romance. Case closed.

In fact, there's only one way to keep the story going, and that is to throw some ~~artificial~~ drama into the equation. (Most women subconsciously try to accomplish this in real life by looking for arguments and disagreements, ~~this is why the big fights start the day people get married.~~)
And what better way to get constant, effortless drama than to be the girl who constantly has to look over her shoulder, scanning for females with designs on her celebrity boyfriend? The constant cycle of drama/validation, drama/validation, this is what attracts women to celebrities.

~~Luckily, there are some girls who transcend this odd biological design flaw. They may mention celebrities in passing, but it's only for joke value. They are secretly wise to the lunacy of it all.~~

[sign off]

18

Sometimes I'm so smart, I almost feel like a real person.

It's a weird morning. I'm out of bed before the alarm sounds. I'm dressed by the time I usually hit the snooze button. And I'm brushing my teeth before I normally poke a toe out of bed to estimate ambient temperature.

This is not like me.

And after I'm dressed, I bound down the stairs full of energy and I even contemplate, for a very fleeting moment, doing some exercise.

Which is really not like me.

Later I notice my toast is still partly frozen, cold and hard at the center, and I don't for a moment consider throwing it at Mom's head. Instead, I just eat around the permafrost and get on with my day.

Nothing can faze me. I'm on fire!

While Mom chatters away about something wildly unimportant I take out my cell to check my messages. There is a new message and I feel an immediate tingle. How wonderful to wake up to a new message!

em: hey you!

I check the time, it was sent at 1:54 a.m. That doesn't tell me much, or at least, not enough. Did Emma stay up late or did she wake in the night longing to talk to me? And what does 'hey you!' actually mean? Is it one of those hey you's as in: *'Hey, I've decided that it's you. You're the one for me!'* Or is it more like a, *'Hey I'm bored, are you there?'*

Mom glares at me.

She's asked me a question.

I shrug and start typing.

me: hi, wasgoingon?

Mom rattles some plates to get my attention. "Do you want the last pancake or not?"

I almost say yes – in that Pavlovian way I've developed – but I decide no. I don't really need the calories. I'm not even hungry. I shake my head and get my coat.

"See you later, Mom."

Mom sticks out her cheek for a kiss but she's not tricking me with that one. When I'm finally on the road my cell buzzes again. Another message! I end up driving more by feel than by traditional visual cues as I take out my cell.

em: oh, nothing. just wanted to know if u were still up so we culd tlk.

I suddenly have the overwhelming urge to park on the shoulder of the highway and reply. And, for a long moment, that seems entirely reasonable. Logical even. Then it passes. Not only would it be illegal, if we started chatting now I probably wouldn't make it into work until 4 p.m. at the earliest.

Some idiot cuts me off and I place a curse on him and his offspring, five generations down. Then my cell buzzes again.

Today's shaping up great!

But traffic lurches and I slam the brakes to avoid bumper-kissing the idiot. Meanwhile, my brain is overthinking things. Where is Emma now? Is she up or is she messaging from her bed? Is she wearing cute pajamas? Does she always check her messages this early or is it because of me?

I let the distance between myself and the idiot increase, then take my eyes off the road just long enough to read the latest message.

em: hey! u never answered my question. r u coming to the store today?

Of course I'm coming to the store. It's the highlight of my day.

Traffic keeps hiccupping but never comes to a complete stop so I can actually reply. On top of that, something strange is happening. For no apparent reason, and without my consent, my brain has started a mental conversation with Emma.

It began when I turned on the radio:

'Oh, I love this song!' the Emma in my head says.

'It's Land Down Under *by* Men at Work,*'* I tell her. *'Apparently it was Australia's unofficial anthem when they won the America's Cup in 1983.'*

'You're so smart,' she says. *'I didn't know that.'*

'Not many people do.'

I kinda feel this should worry me, but for now I enjoy talking to this Emma in my head. Let's see where it goes.

As expected, I have no hope of concentrating at work. Luckily, this doesn't bother me. I'm just biding my time. As soon as lunch rolls around, I get up, grab my coat, and race over to the mall.

As I step off the escalator bringing me up from the parking level, I notice someone vaguely familiar coming toward me. He's dressed in a grey, pinstriped suit and his height and build are fairly average. I can't quite place him, but I instinctively know I don't want to lose time talking to him. So, while I'm racking my brain to identify him, I make sure not to make eye contact.

'*Who* is *this guy?*' I ask the Emma in my head.

'*A friend or a colleague maybe?*'

'*No, I'm pretty sure I don't know him from the office.*'

'*Someone from a convention?*'

'*I don't think so.*'

I move all the way over to the left, as if I'm browsing shop windows. I'm only a few doors from Ye Olde Peanut Shoppe so maybe I can make it without being spotted. But, from the corner of my eye, I notice the guy doing the same thing. He's moved to the right and now we're back on a collision course.

'*What a weirdo!*' Emma blurts out.

'*Yeah, what's wrong with him?*'

I pick up my pace. I suddenly feel it's imperative I reach the Shoppe before the collision point. And, much closer now, I finally recognize the guy.

It's his green eyes that give him away.

This is my fan.

Leopold.

I do my best to slip into the Shoppe unseen but Leopold cuts me off, stepping into the Shoppe himself. I have this horrible *a-ha!* Moment: I'm now absolutely certain that Leopold is the guy who's been using my ear catchers on Emma!

I can't believe he's been so bold: using *my* ECs in *my* mall on *my* girl!

I quickly remind myself it probably doesn't matter. It won't do him any good. He's going head to head with his master, his creator. He doesn't stand a chance. That green eyed freak of misconstrued advice is doomed to fail.

Leopold picks up his pace and we end up rushing inside, neck and neck. A measure of not-so-accidental shoving follows. We end up at Emma's counter simultaneously but I still feel victory is mine: Emma makes eye contact with me first.

"There you are!" she says. "Took you long enough. So, what'll it be?"

I feel a surge of pride, happiness, elation. It electrifies my body and soul.

I smirk at Leopold. He has no idea how deeply Emma and I are connected. We're over two-hundred quirky messages into... well... into some kind of relationship.

And that's a big deal. That's a real thing.

"How about some peppered Brazils and one of your famous weather reports?"

Emma doesn't have time to react, Leopold cuts in rudely. "Hey, Emma," he says, "that's a really nice dress."

Emma blushes. "Thanks, Leo."

Leo?

"That floral pattern is so safe and generic," he continues. "You could probably still wear that when you're eighty."

For a moment Emma seems dumbstruck, insulted. I grin. Taken down by his own treachery, what an amateur. Clearly Leopold didn't gauge the mood correctly. Serves him right for stealing yet another of my ECs!

But then Emma starts to laugh. She leans over and punches Leopold in the shoulder. "Hey!" she says. "Play nice!" She gives him a wink. "You're so bad!"

And I really don't care for the way she says the word bad. She makes it sound way too good.

For a second I consider explaining exactly how bad Leopold is. That he's feeding her scripted lines which he didn't even script himself. This guy doesn't deserve her attention, doesn't deserve her laugh. He deserves nothing. He doesn't even deserve to have his name start with a capital letter!

But I can't tell Emma this. Not without revealing way too much about myself. So instead I say, "Don't mind him, Em. He was born without a sense of style. It's a terrible affliction. I'm thinking of starting a charity, raising some money. We can beat this thing."

Emma doesn't hear. She's showing leopold her pinky ring. He's asked her something about it and now he's touching her hand.

He's Touching Her Hand!

I don't feel well.

"Oh, I almost forgot," Emma says. "I was going to get peppered Brazils, wasn't I?" She finally pulls her hand away, gives me a curt nod, and disappears to the back.

leopold grins at me. At least I think he does. I cannot be sure, I'm studying the lettering on the windows. It's really intricate work. Very well done. I wonder if it was a manual job.

Emma returns with my nuts. I take them and pay up.

"Thanks, Em," I say. "Perfectly done, as always."

"Of course," she says. "By the way, looks like clear skies the rest of the week."

"Great."

'Thanks for that really short weather report.'

And with that, the well runs dry. I want to throw out some freshly minted ear catchers, but I can't think of any. There's nothing interesting going on in my head. Meanwhile, leopold has cut back in, asking Emma about her ring again, and throwing out all these lame ring jokes that Emma eats up.

"You're so weird," she tells leopold.

"And proud of it," he says. "My brain doesn't operate according to expected parameters."

Which is a mangled version of something I've said in a vid.

I guess I'm expected to leave now, but I can't. I want to stay and reanimate our deflated conversation. I want to be the last guy to leave the Shoppe. But I have no obvious reason for still being here. On top of that, leopold has stepped in front of me and now I look really out of place, standing slightly to the side, listening in on their conversation.

I'm out of options. It appears leopold has won this round somehow and, with a heavy heart, I leave the Shoppe.

On my way back to the car the Emma in my head tries to console me.

'Come on,' she says. *'You're not sulking, are you?'*

'Of course not,' I tell her. *'But I really wanted to talk to you and you hardly noticed me.'*

'I was probably just being professional. I didn't want *to talk to him, I* had *to.'*

'But you called him leo…'

Emma sighs. *'Well, maybe I couldn't remember his full name.'*

That could be, I suppose. That could very well be.

I head back to the office and start on a new script.

YouTube script:

I've been thinking about instinct lately. Sometimes I wonder whether all the advanced thinking that humans do, all the forward planning and strategizing, if it isn't missing the point entirely.

Birds fly south for winter, beavers build dams, lions hunt antelope. They don't discuss their strategies with friends beforehand and they don't look for tips on the net. It's all pure instinct. They're born with the all the knowledge they need to thrive in their respective environments already built in.

But what do humans do? We use our much larger, more sophisticated brains to introduce new concepts to precede all of our actions, such as worry, over-thinking, and fear. And not just the kind of fear that could help us, like the fear of tigers and long winters. No, we busy ourselves with made up fears that need far reaching concepts such as insurances, pensions, and aggressive bumper stickers.

It's the fear of having less than others, of people taking some of the stuff we don't need but which we feel is ours. The fear of things that may or may not happen in distant, extrapolated futures. And it's this fear that creates the real social diseases like hatred and crime, which in turn foster the need for artificial protection structures such as police, government, and a penal system.

Yay for the human brain.

[hold up chart #1]

So perhaps we're on the wrong track here. Maybe we made a big mistake the first time we came up with a complicated, cerebral solution to a fairly straightforward problem. A solution that, through its complexity, actually caused more spin-off problems than it solved. Which in turn called for more solutions, which each created yet more problems. On and on until we'd created this vast social structure that by its very nature needs to grow continuously to keep from collapsing in on itself.

Maybe we need to take a step back and evaluate. Look at what instinct tells us to do. After all, our instinct has evolved over countless generations, adjusting only when needed. And instinct doesn't try to anticipate problems that don't exist yet. It doesn't try to head them off with solutions that cause immediate problems in the present.

Take girls for instance.
Before guys started overthinking things, reading articles and taking advice from romantic comedies and valentine card commercials, what was our first instinct? What did we do about it, the first time a girl made us feel funny inside?
We decided to tease them and pull their hair. We made fun of their clothes and hid their lunch boxes. Maybe that was in our species' best interest. Maybe that kind of behavior activates something buried deep within the female brain that allows her to appreciate us.

~~It certainly didn't send out that one devastating signal that most of us are sending out right now: *I like you more than you like me.*~~

Perhaps little dudes inherently know the best way to approach women. If it's part of our genetic code, hardwired into our survival instinct, then instead of overthinking things, we should just observe little dudes in the playground to understand how to treat females.

~~Actually, I'm not really sure.~~

[sign off]

Video #142 by *Leverage*. Views: 57

Comments:

LoveLost: (7:54 pm) Lev. I've been taking your advice but I'm not having much of luck. Here in my country maybe girls is different. Please help. I can type about my date and you can analyze and give wise-isms? Like you did for the guy with the drama?

Leverage: (8:27 pm) Sure, LoveLost, fire away.

LoveLost: (8:28 pm) Ok, so I meet girl in club and she's very pretty so I know lot of guys will try to get close to her. So I do everything different from other guys, but her reactions are not so as expected.

Leverage: (8:28 pm) Tell me exactly what you did. Give me ur whole conv. word for word.

LoveLost: (8:29 pm) Ok. So I stand next to her at bar with hands behind back.
Me: Hi.
She: Hi.
Me: I have something for you.
She: Let me guess, you bought me drink.
Me: No, I bought you puppy.
(I give her puppy)
She: ....
Me: I thought, you have lots of drinks, but you don't have puppy.
She: ...
Me: Is everything okay? Do you like puppy?
She: ...
Me: Is it wrong color? They have other colors...
She: Are you giving me dog?
Me: Yes. Most puppies is dogs. In fact, all puppies is dogs, I think.
But now girl leaves. Which is what usually happens when I talk to pretty girl, so I know what that means. I'm not stupid. But last night I don't know what it means, because this girl took my puppy. So I guess my question is, Lev, what does it mean when girl doesn't want to talk to you but she does want your puppy?

Leverage: (8:30 pm) Which country are you from? When you say puppy, do you mean an actual puppy? Like a small animal?

LoveLost: (8:30 pm) Yes, puppy is very small.

Leverage: (8:31 pm) Okay, so you did in fact bring a small dog into a bar?

LoveLost: (8:31 pm) Of course! Not good to bring big dog into bar. Hard to hide and girls don't like them.

LoveLost: (8:46 pm) Lev? You still there?

LoveLost: (8:59 pm) Lev?

WhipCrck: (9:06 pm) See, that's the kind of idiots your breading, man!

DissonantMelody: (9:27 pm) Don't you mean "breeding"? I don't think Lev has been going around putting his followers between slices of bread, Moron!

OldMan1951: (9:42 pm) Hello lev, this is your old man.

TheLizard: (9:43 pm) Hehe :) Nice one, Melody!

OldMan1951: (9:43 pm) Strange meeting like this on the world wide web, isn't it?

LoveLost: (10:43 pm) Should I try some other animal? Maybe bird or rabbit? I have magician friend, he can teach me to hide in top-hat. Should I wear top-hat, Lev?

OldMan1951: (11:23 pm) Lev, I know it's been a long time, and how can you even be sure this is me, right? But I'm really trying here. Look, I'm even using your world wide web name, Lev, see?

OldMan1951: (11:58 pm) Okay, so ask me any question. I'll prove it's me.

19

'I'm sorry we haven't talked much lately,' the Emma in my head says.

'That's okay,' I tell her.

'No, it's not. I always have so much fun with you. I really miss you.'

'Can I tell you something? Something yucky and emotional?'

'Sure! I love yucky and emotional!'

'Don't laugh, but if I'd known we'd meet some day, life wouldn't have been so bad.'

'How do you mean?'

'I mean, if someone had told me when I was twelve, "Look, kid, life's going to suck from time to time, more often than seems fair, and it's going to be really rough for a couple of years there, but in the end it'll be okay, you'll meet Emma, she's waiting for you." If that had happened, I could've handled just about anything.'

'That's so sweet!'

'Told you it'd be yucky…'

Some really weird followers have turned up in my comment's section. I do my best to ignore them – turns out you get idiots everywhere, even on the internet – but when I check my private messages, I find even more weird stuff. Tucked away between the usual thank-you's and hate mail, I find this:

OldMan1951 wrote:

Hey son, how's life?
I've been trying to get a hold of you. I found your TV channel, the one on the world wide web. It looks like you're getting really popular. I always knew you'd land on your feet. Anyway, let me know if you want to get together for a talk sometime.

Your Dad

I stare at the message in disbelief.

It appears the entire time I thought Dad was dead but secretly hoped he was alive somewhere and following my vids, he was actually alive somewhere and secretly following my vids.

If this really *is* him, of course. It'd be easy enough to set up an account and impersonate him. But who even knows he's missing? I don't share any personal information in my vids, and what would be the point of impersonating him anyway?

The sad thing is, I have no idea if this even sounds like him. I have nothing to compare the writing to. Not so much as a Christmas card or a goodbye note. I don't even know if it's physically possible for him to be writing me.

And Mom isn't much help.

"Maybe it's one of those computer errors," she suggests.

"What computer errors?"

"You know, you're searching for lawn furniture and suddenly the screen goes white and there's a message saying you need to pay to unlock your computer."

"A virus? You think a virus wrote me a message pretending to be my dad?"

"Could be."

"A virus wrote to tell me that it's following my YouTube channel and wants to meet up..."

"I think so." Mom hands me back my tablet. She's hardly looked at the message. "You should get a virus-murderer," she says. "They have those now. Maybe even for your weird flat-computer."

"And what would be the point," I ask her. "What would this semi-sentient virus stand to gain? It's not like it's asking me for my credit card."

"Not *yet*," Mom says. She taps the side of her nose.

"So it wants to meet up so it can hit me up for money."

"They're cunning little bastards," Mom says. "Betsy had a virus that knew her email address *and* her phone number. It stalked her for a year!"

I sigh and shut down my tablet. "Look, Mom, I asked you a simple question. I didn't request a technical analysis, I merely wanted to know... is Dad dead or not?"

Mom shrugs.

"Come on, did he die or didn't he?"

"It's hard to say," she mumbles. "But whatever happened, I'm sure he's dead by now, so don't worry about it. I have to start dinner."

She heads into the kitchen.

"Mom!"

"What?"

"Come back here."

Mom whirls round, eyes wide. "What do you want me to say? He disappeared, alright? He just left. He never called, he never wrote, he never visited. Not once. You are not to contact him!"

I'm stunned by her sudden fierceness, but I recover. "That's not your call, Mom! You can't tell me what to do!"

"Maybe not," she says, her voice smaller now, shaky even. "Maybe you're too old for that. But I'm still your mother and I won't let him hurt you any more than he already has."

She turns, but not before I notice some odd moisture in the corners of her eyes.

I don't know what to say.

There's a long, tense silence, then Mom sighs and goes up the stairs. I hear her bedroom door open and close.

When I look out the window I realize it's dark already. I've lost a large chunk of time. My tablet lies on my desk, battery light flashing.

There are a few remnants of thoughts lingering in my mind, hinting at where the time has gone. Not surprisingly, they're of Dad. In them he's in prison. Not for a crime, though, but for doing something heroic, and pissing off the wrong people. He couldn't contact us for our own protection. He was doing it all to keep us safe.

I chastise myself. That's just like me. I'm way too positive, always seeing the good in people. I have to stop doing that.

I look down. My tablet shows my YouTube inbox; it appears I've been re-reading Dad's message.

Has he really been following me online? I started vlogging about a year ago, before that I had almost no online presence, so he can't have been following me long. And it's unlikely he's been following me from the beginning, so it's not like he's been trying to find me for years, turning over every stone, hiring detectives, working with police and FBI.

Sure, Mom and I moved a few times, we had to, there was just so little money, but we were never hard to find. We stayed in the city. In the same area. And we kept his last name. So what stopped him from sending me a single birthday card?

I stare at his message, tempted to press reply. Not because I want to re-initiate contact, not because I want to start up a conversation, but because I have so much I need to get off my chest.

How could you forget about me?

Do you know I thought about you every day?

Do you know I look for you in crowds? Examining every face, every set of eyes, hoping to find you checking up on me?

But, no. I close my tablet. He can't possibly have any answers that would satisfy me. Besides, I had to wait decades for my first message, it would be insane to send him a reply on the very same day.

Why couldn't you just love me?

It doesn't matter. I have my job, my fans, and above all, I have my Emma. I don't need anything else.

In fact, it's about time I sent her a message. I've punished her enough for being so callously friendly to leopold.

me: Hey Em, there are some very important developments in the weather we should discuss.

I get a reply within minutes. An intense tingle shoots through my body, letting me know Emma really is The One.

em: Cool! Shoot!
me: nono, way too complicated for a chat, we need to discuss in person!
em: ok, when?

So far so good. I take a deep breath and type out the message I've been rehearsing. I back-track several times because I keep bungling it up.

me: Well, since I value your input so much, and I'm such a nice guy, I'm going to clear my schedule for Saturday night. U are a lucky, lucky grl!
em: Gee thanks :) but isn't it better to discuss during lunch time?
me: it can't wait till Monday, so let's do it Saturday night.
em: but lunchtime is more traditional for weather reports, no?
me: that doesn't matter, we will start a new tradition.
em: But why? No, seriously, I can't make it Sat. night.
me: oh…ru sure?
em: yup. bsy with friends.

Busy with friends? What does that mean? Seriously, we haven't been on an almost-date in ages, millennia even, and she still prefers to hang out with her friends? Who cancels the date of a lifetime for some lame friends? You hang out with friends during the week, if you really, really must, but you don't give up a perfectly good Saturday night for them!

me: I'm sure they'll understand
em: understand what?
me: that ur canceling for something more important.
em: :) hihi, fnny guy! no thanks, really looking forward to seeing my friends

I'm trembling. My heart pounds in my ears. I quickly lay down on my bed because I appear to be having some kind of attack.

me: fine, if that's more fun, then good luck. Gotto go. I am ill.

This may well be the big one: the heart attack. I probably won't even make it till morning. I can hardly hold my tablet long enough to check for messages. Which is just as well, as Emma declines to reply.

20

Observation:

Apparently there's something about shoe-shaped objects that activates the pleasure centers of the female brain.

Mom and I are out shoe shopping.

That's what's happening right now.

Fragile morning light filters through the glass ceiling as our footsteps echo around a deserted mall. Mom's up ahead, walking surprisingly fast for her age, and I trundle behind, my feet slowly killing me. We've covered six stores already and the day has yet to see its first 9 o'clock.

Strangely enough, the road to this shoe-shopping point in my life wasn't all that long and winding. In fact, the decision felt quite natural at the time. My shoes were wearing down, in need of replacing before further interaction with Emma, and Mom offered to help.

I'm completely hopeless at finding shoes. I wouldn't even know what kind of shoe shop to visit (assuming there are different kinds – it feels like there would be). So, once again, I find myself on the unpleasant path of least resistance.

"Come on," Mom says. "Stop dragging your feet."

"I'm not dragging my feet," I tell her. "I'm observing generally accepted pedestrian speeds."

"All I'm observing is generally unacceptable nonsense," Mom says. She picks up the pace even more.

"Where's the fire? That's all I want to know."

We pass the food court and my brain immediately offers images of life-giving burgers, mental health saving fries. Alas, my powers of persuasion are no match for Mom's current level of determination. She's treating this like some kind of Shoe Emergency.

A ShoeTastrophy.

"The stores will still be here in an hour," I call after her. "They'll still be here in a thousand years, long after society has collapsed and the New Cavemen take over. I think we can afford to stop sprinting for a second or two."

"Always complaining," Mom calls over her shoulder. "Hey, let's check here."

She disappears into a store I've never noticed before. I could swear it

111

appeared out of thin air mere moments ago.

I follow her inside.

At first traversing the mall and popping in and out of shoe stores made me feel like the good son, like I did on holiday. Once again I was donating my precious time to help my aging mother do something she loves more than life itself: shopping. But now, in this latest store, I'm starting to feel a little self-conscious. This place is huge – easily larger on the inside than on the out – and it's clearly divided into two sections: left for women's shoes, right for men's. Wandering deeper and deeper into the maze that is menswear, I can no longer kid myself. We're obviously here for me. There's no room for onlooker misinterpretation: Mom's about to pick out a pair of shoes for me like she did when I was still a distraught, gloomy, strange-looking-but-surprisingly-intelligent six year old.

Mom shows me a pair of sneaker-type shoes with wild streaks of purple and green marring its otherwise fine surface. The sole is thick with nonsense that has air and foam passing for *shoe technology*.

"Nice and modern," she says. "What do you think?"

"I think you are mistaking ugly for modern," I tell her.

"Just try them on, you might like them." She reads from the box, "They have Superior Airflow (tm) technology."

Exactly.

I tell her to find something else.

She practically skips along the aisle, placing the purple monstrosities back where she found them and examining their direct neighbors.

"You might as well skip this entire rack," I call after her. "All these shoes are entirely too, as you put it, modern."

Mom shrugs and moves out of sight.

I glance around furtively, half expecting to find my old high school crushes magically gathered behind me, shaking their heads.

Really? Shoe shopping with your mom?

But no one's noticed me. In fact, it dawns on me that shoe stores are very much the domain of the female – even the men's departments. Among racks of off-road boots and hiking gear, the few men I do spot are all accompanied by at least one female.

This, apparently, is how nature intended it.

I relax and check for messages from Emma.

There's nothing.

It's her day off, though, so she might be busy with friends. I hope she didn't take my last message too personal. It wasn't a snide remark, I just wanted her to realize how mean she was for preferring to spend time with people who are not me. And Saturday's a really long day. If she really wanted to see me, she could've easily re-allocated one or two of its twenty-four hours.

"How about these?"

Mom waves a pair of sturdy dress shoes in my face.

"They're black," I say, "so that's good." I look them over carefully. They're the right size and weight. They'd be perfect if it weren't for one little thing.

"Look at this tongue. It's gigantic. Almost size of the entire shoe."

"All shoes have tongues."

"Not this size they don't. It looks ridiculous. I really don't understand why you can't filter out these deal breakers yourself."

I send her away. She doesn't seem to mind.

It's definitely true that women derive extreme levels of pleasure from shoe shopping. And it's not just for the sake of replacing their own defunct footwear, no, their enjoyment extends to any kind of shopping involving footwear. I suppose the reasons for this could be twofold:

1. There's something about foot-shaped objects that activates the pleasure centers of their brains.
2. They need to approve the footwear appropriated by the men in their lives.

There could be a script in there somewhere.

I hear Mom ask a clerk about Superior Airflow(tm) technology and share a bored eye roll with a chubby guy down the aisle. He's wearing a Star Trek t-shirt with a suspicious stain above Lt. Data's left eyebrow. I decide to assume it's coffee.

Chubby is about my age and tags along behind an old woman wearing sweats. There's a great deal of resignation about his body language.

I immediately feel better about myself. This is obviously a very, very sad individual. He really *is* out shopping with his mom. I bet she still buys *all* his clothes. This isn't just a fluke happenstance for him, this is what his entire life looks like. He has no YouTube channel filled to the brim with wise-isms, no hoards of followers awakening to enlightenment and, most importantly, he has no *Emma;* his cell doesn't carry two-hundred-and-fifty messages sent by an angel.

He and I are nothing alike.

I offer him a dejected shrug so he can continue to delude himself with the idea that we're kindred spirits. He's just trying to survive, after all. There's no need to make things harder for him by setting him straight. He'll probably be okay, though. He'll go to a comic-con and meet an overweight chick with bad teeth and a stained Firefly backpack. They'll get married, have a bunch of kids with stained shorts and socks and they'll be happy. Eventually they may even learn to wash at higher temperatures.

Mom hovers closer. I decide to walk around.

It occurs to me I could save time by finding some shoes myself. The torture factor of the day could literally plummet. I browse the racks but it quickly transpires the situation is hopeless. I have no idea where to start. I don't even know how to figure out the sizes. And, grouped together, all these shoes look weird to me. It's a massive informational overload of leather and foam and I'd need some kind of high-powered app to help me filter out all the unnecessary details.

Perhaps moms are better equipped to work with this kind of unsorted data.

"How about this?" a familiar voice says. "It's got a weird nose. You like weird noses, don't you? I mean, why else would you have one yourself?"

I whirl round as my brain floods with happy signals. How strange to hear Emma so unexpectedly! How wonderful to be able to have a quick chat with her! I rush towards the sound of her voice but then stop dead in my tracks, struggling for breath. Still a rack away, I see the worst sight I've seen in years.

Emma's not here with friends, she's here with *leopold!*

And what's more, she's smiling at him.

And giggling.

And, and, worst of all, she showing him a pair of shoes.

That she's picked out.

For him!

I try to steady myself. Suddenly queasy and lightheaded I look for a place to sit. Of course, there's not a chair in sight. I end up dropping to the floor unceremoniously.

"It's okay," I hear leopold say. "If you like them, then I like them."

"Don't be silly," Emma says. "They're horrible. I was joking."

Their voices now seem to come from far, far away, sounding unreal, ghostly, and somewhat mean.

"But I'd love to see you in a pair of these. Will you try them on?"

There's a grunt from leopold, as if it's all too much for him. As if Emma picking out shoes for him isn't quite special enough.

I struggle for air. My body's being crushed under an enormous weight and it's shaking like a leaf. The Emma in my head tries to calm me down.

'*Don't worry,*' she says. '*I probably just ran into him on my way to see my friends. That's all this is.*'

There's a high-pitched ringing in my ears.

I'm probably dying.

'*Come on,*' Emma says. '*Don't be so dramatic. I'm just helping Leo because I feel sorry for him.*'

'*No way,*' I tell her. '*Listen to you, you're giggling!*'

114

'Yeah, that is true...' She thinks this over. '*Maybe I'm thinking of something you've said? I'm not laughing at Leo's jokes, I'm laughing at yours!*'

But I don't trust the Emma in my head anymore. Not one bit.

Especially when she goes on to suggest that I should just go over and say hello.

'*Don't worry,*' she tells me. '*It'll be fine. Just say Hi! and I'll take it from there. I'll pull you through this. We can get rid of leo together.*'

Mom appears at my feet, her arms full of shoes. "You're trying all of these and I'm not taking no for an answer," she announces. "Get up!"

She's insane. She's a shoe-monster. And, as I'm not quite well, I might also be a hallucination. But I can't take the chance that she's not. I have to get rid of her before Emma sees us. Luckily, I know the one remark that ensures the hasty retreat of a real, non-hallucinatory mom.

"I saw a nice pair of air-Clarks a few racks over," I say. "I think they might be on sale."

Mom disappears like a puff of smoke. Perhaps she wasn't real after all. But I needn't have worried, as I lift myself up, still somewhat unsteady, I see that Emma's way too busy with leopold to notice anyone else.

'*Of course I'm not! I'm just too bored to notice!*'

I reposition myself so I can hear them better. leopold doesn't say much. Which shouldn't surprise me. Apart from a few brilliant ECs stolen from yours truly, what does the guy actually have to say?

'*Exactly! Go save me before he bores me to death!*'

leopold and Emma babble on as I struggle to understand what she sees in him. Their conversation doesn't make much sense, and it's far from interesting, still, there's so much giggling, shoulder punching, and accidental touching, it drives me crazy.

Mom re-appears with a pair of air-Clarks. How did she do that?

I have to find a way out of this store unnoticed.

YouTube Script:

I've already talked about the need for dramatic storylines in relationships. I explained what they are for and where they come from. But the last word hasn't been said about this. Not by a long shot.

Consider this; there's a reason most viral books are written from the perspective of a female protagonist. The *Twilights* and *Shades* wouldn't really work if they'd been written from the perspective of the male character. The male in these stories needs to remain a mystery. His thoughts and feelings should be ambiguous at best. Whenever possible, he should be silent, especially at the most inconvenient moments. The heroine doesn't actually want to know what he's thinking, and neither do the female readers. It's more fun for them to wonder and worry and fret than it is to actually know. They are more interested in analyzing what *they think* he's feeling than what his feelings actually are. ~~This is why some girls accidentally fall for guys who don't have much to say. They mistake his uninteresting personality for an air of mystery!~~

As I've mentioned, there's a reason why romantic stories end at the point where the girl gets the guy. There's just no more mystery left, no more worrying. Unless, of course, there's a dramatic twist. Maybe a second guy shows up ~~(he could be a werewolf)~~, so now she can worry and wonder and fret all over again: What does she feel for this new guy? Can she possibly love two people at once? Was the first romance merely a test to see if she'd recognize her true love? Or is it the other way around and is the second romance a test to see if she'll stay with the first? And so on. And so forth. Ad infinitum.

[switch to cam #2]

This kind of logic does not hold up for guys, though. We're much more pragmatic. We *do* wonder and worry and fret. In fact, we tend to wonder for ages whether She even exists. Whether She's really out there. Whether that wonderful, intelligent, funny girl who'll like us for who we are has even been born. And if she has, whether she'll cross our path. And, if she does, whether she'll be too hung up on her placeholder boyfriend to even notice us.
But when we do finally find Her, when we win The One for ourselves, we are not disappointed that the drama is over. No, we are *relieved!* We're happy that the wondering and worrying and fretting part is done with. Because we really didn't care for that bit.

[back to cam #1]

For women, relationship dramas are delicious little problems they revel in and discuss with their friends. For guys they're annoying time wasters. We feel no need to artificially complicate matters any further.
Except that we really should, because we need to keep things complicated for *them*, because *they* want the drama. They need the fretting and worrying and wondering, so it is up to us to provide it.

Most importantly, we need to keep our thoughts to ourselves. We actually have to become the classic strong and silent guy. There has to be mystery surrounding everything we say and do. There's nothing interesting about a guy who completely and satisfactorily explains all his actions. He just ends up making himself predictable.

[sign off]

21

em: sorry I've been so quiet.
em: I've been really busy :p
em: u there?

em: u have time to chat?
em: Hello?
em: guess ur busy too :(

em: hey, just thought I'd try again...
em: miss u...

me: hey...
em: ah, ur there! Jipeee!!!!
me: what u been so busy with?
em: u know me; friends and stuff. u?
me: me? I've been buying shoes...
em: ok. R they nice?
me: nice enough, I suppose. so. how are your friends?
em: they're okay.
me: so have U bought any shoes lately?
em: actually have. and I have some great news too!!
me: I doubt it..
em: waht?
me: never mind. what's ur great news?

me: r u still there?
em: sorry, got interrupted. what were we talking about?
me: u had news.
em: yeah! get this: I have a boyfriend!! can you believe that? Me with
  an actual boyfriend?
me: well, you've said that before, remember?
em: Yeahyeah, but now it's actually true. isn't that cool?

em: hello?
em: u still there?
me: yeah, just had to go do something
me: hey, u know what would be great?
me: not really, no.
em: you should get a girlfriend (or maybe you have one?) so we can
  double date!
me: no thanks

em: :p funny guy. come on, it'd be sooo much fun!

em: r u there?
em: no?

em: Hello? you sleeping?

I write a string of scripts this week. Eight to be exact. A new personal record. I write and record one script each day and two on Sunday. But these aren't my usual, insightful, helpful scripts. These scripts are pure evil. They're laced with bad advice and are aimed directly at leopold. They're carefully crafted to help him destroy his relationship – it isn't really *his* relationship, anyway, it's *mine*, he *stole* it from me! I'm like an Evil Cyrano.

I vowed never to do this, but my reputation be damned. I'm unleashing the beast!

Without Emma there is no Leverage, and Leverage has to survive in order to save lives, so this is still for the greater good. True, there may be some collateral damage. Some of my fans, who happen not to be leopold, will get caught in the cross fire. They'll suffer and that's truly terrible. Unforgivable, almost. But sadly it cannot be helped.

> **em:** u there?
> **em:** ur so quiet these days…
> **em:** want to double date this firday?

I start out with a vid on *'Showing her how much you love her'*.

This vid explains in detail how you need to shower a girl with gifts and attention once she's officially your girlfriend. It explains that you no longer have to worry about her finding out that you like her more than she likes you. The rule doesn't actually apply to girlfriends. In fact, I warn that She may stop liking you if she doesn't think you like her *enough*. And I add enough made-up detail to make these crazy notions sound plausible. It turns out I'm actually really good at that.

I follow it with a vid on *'Keeping your girlfriend away from her friends'*. In this vid I mention that She shouldn't really need anyone else. You should be more than enough for her. And she certainly doesn't need her jealous girlfriends in her ear making her doubt her choice. She doesn't need them taking her out and introducing her to other males. Her girlfriends will only cause trouble. No matter what their intentions, their effects on your relationship are neutral at best and negative at worst. Keep them away.

It's not hard to make that kind of bad advice actually sound logical to the male brain.

And then I do a vid on *'Flirting with other women in front of her'*. Which is obviously a great way to re-assure her that she's bagged a highly desirable piece of man-meat. But I leave out the bits that explain just how to do this without looking tacky, without making her think you're unsatisfied with your current relationship. And I certainly don't warn about what will happen if you get shot down by other women in front of *Her*. How devastated she will be by that double whammy of disrespect and undesirability.

> em: hey! want to get a coffee with me and leo?
> em: i just know you'll like him.
> em: u guys have so much in common

Of course I miss Emma, but I can't talk to her until her so-called relationship starts showing some cracks and she stops inviting me on double-dates with the devil. So far, though, for all my vids and hard work, I've seen no change in her demeanor.

I really have to wonder whether leopold is giving it his best. If he's even paying attention. Am I not clear and destructive enough? Or has he stopped watching my vids altogether?

Meanwhile, I have these strange images running through my head. Sometimes I see the new 'couple' fighting, and leopold can barely hold on to my Emma. Their relationship is on the verge of collapse. Other times I think they're too busy sleeping together for leopold to watch my vids.

I quickly start on a new script before my brain implodes.

> em: did ur cell break? ;p talk to me!

The number of views on my last eight vids has shot up. I'm getting more followers every day. Sadly, I don't know if leopold is still among them. As long as he doesn't comment, he's invisible to me.

The number of comments has gone up as well, while the number of flamers stays relatively low. This should be good news, but I can't really interact with these new fans. I'm giving so much bad advice already. There's way more collateral damage than I'd anticipated. Men and boys are dropping like flies. I can't push this thing any further. I can't lie to them in comments sections as well. So even though it pains me, I have to ignore my new followers.

I watch the traffic on my channel rocket skyward for a couple more days, horrified as the collateral damage spreads like wild fire, then I finally break down and pull the plug.

No more Evil Cyrano vids. It's not working. I'll have to try something else.

me: Hey Em
me: srry I hvn't been in contact. soo bsy with my other friends.
em: hey you! Ur back! No prblm. Was pretty bsy myself ;)
me: Yeah, I just got so mch going on right now, it's insnae
em: cool :) ok, let's talk tomorrow then, gotto go

So much for making her jealous and having her miss me. Even subconsciously she refuses to notice how grey and boring her life is without me.

I wanted to wake her up and show her that the reason she feels so good now is not because of this so-called boyfriend, it's because she's got me in her life. Everything just seems better against the backdrop of our interactions. She's mixing up the signals in her head, attributing more than just my ECs to leopold.

It's just not working. I go back into my YouTube channel and take down my last eight posts.

YouTube Script:

It's important to remember that we're all connected. We're all expressions of universal energy. Down at the quantum level, we'll always be linked together. ~~So, even if you never ever see Her again, ever, you are still connected to her for all eternity.~~

120

Snag Yerself A Cool Guy!

A dating blog by Emma

There're still a few cool guys out there. Let's snag them up before the army of blonde bimbos gets its hooks into them, breaks their spirits, and turns them into wusses!!

Post #127: Follow your own advice

So I've been taking a dose of my own medicine, Grls. I mostly use this blog as a kind of brain-dump, so I can let you guys tell me I'm being stupid (and maybe you even soak up some really, really obvious advice :), but the last few weeks I've really been getting out there, and that's what I want to brain-dump about today.

A few weeks ago I started noticing this guy who's been coming to our store a lot. We goofed around with his orders and one day he asked me out to lunch. He's kind of different and interesting, if not your typical **Cool Guy**, so I said yes.

He was awkward and insecure at first, but just when I'd start to think he was just another creepy loser, he'd say something really funny. Something off beat that I'd never heard before, and that really made me think. Then I realized he wasn't being creepy, he was just *thinking* the whole time!! Doing his own little thing inside his head and not really caring whether I was even there or not. Which is kind of cool.

It's really strange how someone you see every day can suddenly turn out to be so interesting. I mean, I'm thinking about this guy a lot now and I don't even know why. It just sort of happens. Anyway, on our kind-of-date we talked about so many things, and it wasn't your typical date-talk, either. 'Where were you born, how many siblings do you have, where do you work?' We basically talked about all the little things that we really care about and that was really nice.

Oh, and get this, on my way home I ran into this other guy who comes to the store a lot. This guy always buys these weird peppered Brazil nuts that nobody likes. Anyway, he asked me to have a coffee with him and I said yes because, after the excitement of my kind-of-date, I didn't really feel like going home just yet and getting the third degree from Mom. ('Where have you been? Why don't you come straight home after work? There's rapists everywhere and you should be cleaning your room instead of making yourself available for rapists!'). So I got a coffee with

Brazil guy and, guess what? I had a good time with him as well!! He was really sweet and funny and we even exchanged numbers.

So, stop reading my silly blog and get out there, Grls!! You'll get your **Cool Guy** in no time and you'll make great friends along the way.

Let me know how it goes in the comments section. I read them all. Honest ;P

Go!!Go!!!Go!!!!

~Emma

So that was Part One of my story, Eric.

I hope you understand why I had no choice but to divert all mental resources away from 'attracting The One' and on to something much more important. After all, there's already so much information out there about finding someone and, in many cases, it happens completely accidentally anyway. All on its own, without you having to do anything (although that'll probably never happen to me). On top of this, I was starting to suspect that men should stop thinking altogether and just go at this purely on instinct.

So I got off the beaten path and refocused my efforts. I was going to scientifically determine a method for getting over someone with the highest degree of efficiency.

I'm not crazy, Eric. I don't think you'll ever read this, but it helps me to imagine you're here with me. That I'm telling you everything that's going on in my life.

So let me tell you what happened next. I'll call this part of my story...

PART TWO

Video #151 by *Leverage.* **Views: 1027**

Comments:

DissonantMelody: (11:27 pm) Where are you Lev? We miss you!!

OnMyWay: (15:19 pm) What's going on? Why no more posts for weeks? You have to tell me what to do next.

GomezP: (21:25 pm) In need of some help here, bro. At least warn us if you're going off-grid for so long.

OldMan1951: (16:23 pm) Did you get any of my messages? I can't tell if you can see these. I don't know if I'm doing this right. This world wide web stuff is complicated. If you want me to leave you alone, if that's what going on, then just let me know...

GaryXXX: (8:35 pm) All I have to say is, good riddance!

Voodood: (9:26 pm) He's finally realized how stupid his posts are!

DissonantMelody: (13:27 pm) Whatever's going on, take your time, Lev. We'll be right here when you get back.

22

I'm in this little diner on the other side of town trying to order my thoughts.

Across from me sits my dad, smiling amiably.

He looks older than I'd expected. More lines, less hair. And he simultaneously looks less like me than I'd hoped, yet also too much the same.

It's hard to explain.

"It was good of you to come," he says. He signals the waitress.

This doesn't feel real.

It feels like Christmas and an impeding fight behind the bike shed rolled into one. Am I supposed to be happy? Angry? Afraid?

I'm all over the place.

I should've taken more time to prepare. Sure, I had twenty years, but I didn't really think this was going to happen, so I never gave it any serious thought.

The waitress comes over and Dad orders two coffees. This makes me uncomfortable. I don't actually drink coffee so he'll have to drink both cups, or try to return one, or sell it to another table, which I'm not sure is entirely legal.

I take a deep breath and remind myself that the fate of the coffee isn't important right now.

"Why did you walk out on us?" I blurt out.

Let's just start with the big question, shall we?

Dad frowns, as if he hadn't expected that particular question. "Well," he says, "that's just the thing. I didn't *leave*. Not really." He searches for words. "In my mind, that's not what happened."

"And yet Mom and I have been living alone for twenty years."

We sit silently until the waitress returns. She places one of the cups in front of my dad, the other in front of me. Again I feel a twinge of panic. I remind myself I'm under no obligation to drink the coffee, cost be damned.

"I just didn't stop, that's all," Dad says, after the waitress leaves. He blows on his coffee before taking a cautious sip. "It was like I was on this road through life, you know? And then your mom decided to stop by the side of that road to have babies and settle down. But I wasn't at my destination yet, so I couldn't stop." He puts the cup down and attempts to give me a meaningful look. "It's more like your mom jumped off this train we were riding without ever consulting me."

I'm getting angry. He's not making any sense. "What the hell's that supposed to mean?"

Dad shrugs. "I wasn't ready. You have to realize that we never made a decision. There was never a point where we sat down and said, 'Okay, from here on in we're going to get boring jobs, stop traveling and slowly die in one place.' That wasn't the deal. The whole thing kind of crept up on me."

I stare at him.

"Look," he says, "she was always doing stuff like that, not including me in the big decisions. She changed everything, our whole lives, and I was just supposed to take it."

I look out the window. Life seems so much simpler outside. The people passing by all have easier lives than I do. The world is much nicer to them.

I wonder why that is.

"That doesn't make sense," I say, looking back at Dad. "You were still my dad. You didn't have to leave *me*. You could've just left Mom. What did I ever do to you?"

He shrugs, sips his coffee. I hate how little this seems to affect him, as if he's telling a story about something he hasn't thought about in years. A trivial little anecdote.

"You have to see it from my point of view," he says, after trying a sip of his second coffee. "You weren't really a person."

"Excuse me?"

"I mean, not yet, not at that time. You were just something that happened. I didn't actually leave *you*, I left the whole concept, you know? The *idea* of having a baby."

"But I *wasn't* a baby!" I almost yell at him. "I was ten years old. Of course I was a real person!"

He sighs as if I'm just not getting it. "It was nothing personal," he says. "You have to let that go. I just had the feeling that my life would be over and I had so much left to do."

"Oh, really?" I fight to keep my anger in check. "Then please enlighten me, Dad. What was this great thing that you went and did with your life?"

He gives me a look. It seems this question has never come up.

"Seriously," I say. "What did you do with your life that was so important that you couldn't even call me on my birthdays?"

He shakes his head. "Your Birthdays? You wanted me to call on your birthdays? What difference would that have made? What's the point of a few minutes of conversation here and there?"

"Are you really asking me this?"

"Yes. Wouldn't it have made things worse?" He tries another knowing smile. "Look, I don't know what you're getting so upset about.

You're talking about something that happened years ago, something we can't possibly change. You're smart enough to know this is a pointless conversation. We came here to talk about the future."

My head is spinning.

"I'm just saying, let it go. Leave it be. What I did was best for you, too. I mean, look at you now. You turned out great. You're not an addict, not a criminal, you have a good job, you even have your own TV channel, and on the World Wide Web no less!"

Words fail me – and I doubt the words even exist that can penetrate Dad's armor of kinked logic. Whatever I say will be dismissed. I'm just a child who doesn't see the big picture. With Dad, you either see it his way or you're simply not getting it yet.

I can only get up and leave.

No other action makes sense.

"Please don't say I turned out the way I did because of you," I tell him. "I turned out this way *in spite* of you!"

I leave the diner without looking back. And I almost don't seek out the waitress to pay for the second coffee.

Back out on the street something strange happens. At first I expect Dad to come running after me, to tell me he was joking, or that he's suddenly realized how much he loves me. But that doesn't happen. Of course it doesn't. What actually happens is that my feet get stuck in the sidewalk. I kid you not. The searing afternoon sun has turned the tarmac to gum. Try as I might, I can't move.

Meanwhile, further down the street, kids from my old high school have congregated. They laugh, taunting me. So I reach out to Charlie, the one who wasn't too mean to me back then, and I beg him to help get me, or to at least bring me some pants, because I seem to have forgotten mine. I'm stuck in the tarmac in my underwear. But Charlie doesn't budge. He laughs and sticks out his tongue.

Which is when I wake up, drenched in sweat.

I stare at the ceiling, perhaps for hours, wondering what all that meant. I do my best to unravel the mangled messages from my subconscious. What's it trying to tell me? Is it warning me, or making sure that I never, ever, get my hopes up?

Why must my brain torture me so?

23

Test:

Does every song on the radio remind you of her?*

*) If this is the case, snap out of it! You really think feeling this way is deep and meaningful? Think she'll somehow sense it if you wallow *deep* enough?

The account queues are filling up with the new round of quarterly reports. All hands are on deck and Questionable Deductions are put on hold. At least until Gharity feels we have the inflow of new work under control.

It appears there are slightly more companies looking for our services each quarter and slightly fewer accountants to deal with them. On top of this, it takes longer to do several small accounts than one large one, and we're seeing a shift towards smaller accounts.

So, right now, I'm staring at the reports for a furniture business. A start-up which we haven't represented before. Usually this gets my juices flowing, if only for the thrill of chasing down any and all mistakes made by their run-of-the-mill in-house accountant. But today I'm not feeling it. I'm not feeling anything.

It's 11 a.m. and my colleagues gravitate towards the coffee machines. The resulting noise is not unlike the buzzing of a beehive. These are the sounds of people trying to appear much happier than they really are. It's an over-compensatory thing that happens in the work-place: dumb jokes and boring stories are suddenly laughed at loudly. It's a malfunction deep within the human brain, part of a defunct survival mechanism.

I return my attention to my screen, clicking through inventory lists and expense descriptions. I can't get that work feeling to surface. I really *should* do something, I *want* to do something, but every second that passes just happens to be one of those seconds in which I didn't actually do anything.

It's odd how that happens.

I move my arm, just to make sure it's still in working order.

It appears to be fully functional.

I wriggle my fingers, shift my shoulders. There doesn't appear to be any mechanical problem. By all accounts I should be able to perform rudimentary tasks such as typing and mouse clicking.

(And can't the bulk of my professional existence be broken down into a series of mouse clicks and keyboard taps?)

(Actually, yes. Yes it can. Which is a chilling thought. Most of my adult life has been, in some form or other, about the moving of a mouse and the pressing of keys. So does this mean that my value as a human can be expressed in terms of how well I've clicked said mouse and banged away on said keyboard?)

(Apparently so.)

(Should this, then, end up on my headstone?)

Here lies Leverage, by God this man could click! We will miss him dearly, especially the way he managed to ctrl-s save his work without interrupting his typing.

I realize several more seconds have passed. And I've used them to no nothing but stare out the window at the grey, faceless buildings across the street. So now even the wasting of time has officially been wasted.

I'm slightly amazing that way.

"Welcome back!" Gharity's head appears above my cubicle wall. It's wearing a big grin – a grin way too big for the work place. "How was your holiday?"

I'm lost. "My holiday?"

"Yeah, where did you go?"

"You mean, where did I go three weeks ago?"

"What?" He frowns. "No, last week. You went to Paris, didn't you?"

I shake my head. "No, sir. I was right here, working on Questionable Deductions."

"You sure?"

"Pretty much, yes."

"Really?" Gharity thinks it over. "Didn't you send me an email about going to France?" He looks at me as if I might still come to my senses and remember my trip.

I shake my head.

"So why haven't you been at the belly-feeling meetings?"

"I've been to every single one."

"Nonsense." Gharity looks annoyed. "You weren't there yesterday."

"I was. I was standing next to you."

"You were?"

This is worrying. I can't have him thinking I've been slacking off. Not when my slacking off period is only just about to start. "I gave you the Cristmondale report, remember? You signed off on it, told me it was good work."

"That was you?" Gharity shakes his head. "I thought Quiton-James was on the Cristmondale account."

"Nope, it was me."

Gharity's not convinced. "Well," he says, "I'll have to talk to Quiton-James about that."

"Be my guest." I return my attention to my screen, where nothing much is going on. I could type a bit, to make it look like I'm busy, but there's nothing open to type into. No document, no spreadsheet, nothing. I'd type away but I have no idea what would happen.

Gharity turns to go, then, at the last second, turns back to give me a penetrating look. "So who went to Paris?"

I sigh inwardly. "I wouldn't know. I've been too busy working to pay attention to other people's holidays."

"Fine," Gharity says. "Have it your way. But you'll probably want to talk to human resources. Someone may have told them to adjust your pay. You know, to compensate for the five extra days off."

With that he heads in the direction of Quiton-James' cubicle.

I should probably tag along to make sure Quiton-James doesn't take credit for my Cristmodale report, but I can't move. I can't move because, apparently, I don't give a fuck.

My fuck-giving level fails to surpass the movement-requirement threshold, and thus I'm stuck in my chair.

The sad truth is, in a very real sense, nothing that happens in this building is of any importance. None of it ultimately matters.

Except, of course, for the scripts I secretly write.

Lately I've been thinking about a different kind of script. A script that is, dare I say it, even *more* helpful to an even *larger* part of the population than my scripts normally are. A script containing wise-isms which each of us will need during the unavoidable rough patches in our lives. I don't have it all worked out just yet, but I do have a title: *How to get over The One.*

Because, let's face it, it's only a matter of time before each of us will need this skill. It is the one and only truly meaningful life skill.

I'm hard pressed to even visualize the full power of such a script, how thoroughly it will raise the collective productivity of the human race, how deeply it will intensify the global feeling of wellbeing. With no one pining away for the elusive One ever again, our planet will reach previously unknown heights of productivity. A new Age of Man will be ushered in. If there is a surefire way to get over The One, and if that way can be harnessed, described, taught, optimized for speed and compatibility, then, well… then…

But, so far, I don't have a clue where to start. I'm not even convinced there *is* a cure, other than letting obscene amounts of time pass.

(Time that will, of course, be wasted.)

But one thing has occurred to me: it's your own brain making you miserable. Your brain is the one making you sad and lonely, the one forcing you to pine away for hours and days and weeks. And that doesn't make sense. After all, it's *your* brain. You don't just own the damn thing, you don't just control it, you *are* it. It only makes sense you should get a say in how it makes you feel.

It should be your fundamental right to pick and choose your own feelings.

I just need to figure out how to do this.

Or is it just me? Maybe my tragic flaw is that I'm an artist, a video philosopher, a knower of the human soul and psyche, whose brain is simply wired differently. It needs to be able to go places the average brain can't go, otherwise it wouldn't have anything to report back on. If it had no unique way of experiencing things, it couldn't create art that's new and surprising.

"Bring me any chocolate?"

My train of thought is brutally derailed by Wilson, one of our temps. I've only spoken to him once so I have to wonder why he thinks we're on 'bringing each other chocolate' terms.

"Chocolate?" I ask him.

"Yeah, isn't Paris famous for its chocolate?"

That again. Does the whole building think I've been on holiday? "No," I tell him, "I don't believe Paris is particularly famous for its chocolate, sorry."

Sometimes I wish there was something really annoying about me. Something so off-putting that my colleagues wouldn't try to socialize with me. Perhaps I could start wearing bits of spinach in my teeth?

"Clogs, then?"

"Clogs?" I shake my head. "Doesn't sound like France either."

Wilson seems confused. "How about windmills?"

I sigh. "If you're asking me if I brought you any windmills from France, then no, I didn't. Nor did I bring you anything else. Now, if you don't mind, I'm pretty busy."

"Gee." Wilson looks hurt. "For a guy just back from holiday you're not very relaxed."

"I wasn't on holiday!"

Wilson mulls this over. "Are you sure?"

"Yes, quite sure!"

"Gharity says you went to France… so…"

I stare at him a long time.

"Anyway," he mumbles, stepping back, "all I'm saying is, you may want to check with Gharity, just to make sure."

"I'll do that."

Wilson saunters off and I check my cell for messages.

There's nothing. It's like I don't even exist.

I look around at my colleagues. I cannot fathom how they manage to care about the things they're doing. What's the point of all the reports

131

and evaluations, of climbing the corporate ladder, getting promotions and obtaining a financial black-belt? These things are so inherently meaningless that it's downright scary.

Everything means exactly nothing when you don't have The One in your life.

It's like buying gas when you don't have a car. Like worrying about the best kind of tampon, when you're a guy. Like buying a really nice welcome mat, that's exactly the right size, the right material, the right price, when a tornado has just destroyed your home.

I look at all these people and wonder, why do they bother?

Why

Do

These

People

Bother?

YouTube script:

We (artists/mental facilitators/creators) suffer from a deeply tragic flaw. We feel everything much deeper than ordinary humans. Our pendulum of emotion swings back and forth between happy and sad just as it does with everyone, but ours tends to swing much higher at each extremity. The fun is brighter. The pain darker.

[hold up chart #1]

Here's a simple test to see if you're one of us. First, make a list of all the things going on in your life right now. Note down every relationship, every job, every hobby, every plan. Second, place an honest check mark behind each subject that, over the years, has given you slightly more grief than pleasure.

If you have any subjects left without check marks, congratulations, you're *not* an artist! You're one of the lucky ones. Go and live a rich, full life!

[sign off]

24

When I get home, Mom's in my ear right away.

I have no idea why, but it seems of paramount importance that I know about her friend's ingrown toenail and how badly she was treated by hospital staff except for this one nurse who was really sweet and turned out to be a post-op which just goes to show that people are people and do I realize how fast the price of bread is going up and where will it all end and why was the heating guy two hours late and still only able to do half a job because of some missing part and do I think he'll be late again tomorrow and how many parts can there really be and why not bring all the parts instead of letting decent folk wait around without heating in their bathrooms?

My brain starts to leak.

Bits of intelligent matter die off and seep out of my cranium.

Then Mom asks about Emma, or the shop girl, as she calls her.

"When's your next date?"

I shrug. "There are no definite plans."

Mom frowns. "Be careful, son. Don't let her cool off. You always have to have another date lined up."

"Okay, thanks Mom."

"Don't you *Thanks-Mom*'-me," she says. "A woman needs to know if she's a part of your ongoing plans or not."

Great. Dating advice from my mom. That's what's been missing from my life.

But I'm not about to tell her that making a date with Emma went from being extremely difficult to being completely impossible and more than a little pointless. And I'm also not going to explain how heavy my life has become, how tired and warn out I am.

"This is not back in the day, Mom," I say. "Women don't have dance cards. They don't sit around waiting for men to ask them out. Women are different now. They've *evolved*."

"Nonsense," Mom says. "Maybe they dress and talk differently, but on the inside these women are the same as your mom."

There's not enough time left in my life to debate this. I try a different track. "You don't understand," I tell her. "I'm an artist. A creator. If my work is to have any meaning, love must remain an obscure concept to me."

Mom rolls her eyes. "You're pretty obscure, alright. Why don't you give Betsy's niece a call?"

133

Oh no, not that again!

Apparently the ceasefire is over.

"I heard she just broke up with her new boyfriend." Mom gives me a wink. "You don't have to worry about her being too clingy, you'll just be a rebound guy. A pick-her-upper. You can use her for practice."

"Mom, stop it! I'm a deeply tragic figure! I suffer from a most tragic fatal flaw!"

"I know you do, honey." Mom raises her hand to pinch my cheek before she realizes I'm out of reach. "Your tragic fatal flaw is that you don't leave the house on weekends. And guess what, that's *my* tragic fatal flaw too. You need to get out more and leave the house to me and my knitting club."

I wave it away. "You just don't get it. I'm a tragic hero."

"Fine," she says, exasperated. "Be a tragic hero if you must, but please be the kind of tragic hero that has something to do this Friday from 7 p.m. till 10 p.m."

With that she finally lets me go. I sprint up to my room.

Mom doesn't understand. She has no idea what I'm going through.

It's as if I've been asleep for years, letting life pass me by, not really paying attention, simply living on autopilot. Then I meet Emma and I wake up. Suddenly I notice emotions and colors and that strange thing people call happiness. And, for the first time, I'm actually aware that I was sleeping.

And then leopold comes along and basically forces me to put myself to sleep again.

These are my choices: sleep or pain.

But I don't want to let go of all these wonderful new things that I almost had.

I don't want to go back to sleep.

I browse my tablet, researching heartache cures.

I find some folk tales about eating powdered willow bark and standing on your head. There's anecdotal support for journaling and talking to friends and cats (which should work almost as well as just letting time pass). There are stories about people who subscribe to rituals involving burning photos and mementoes. Others advocate travel, horseback riding, pondering the quantities of marine life found in the sea.

None of it seems overly helpful.

Through some inexplicable links and side-tracks I land on some pages that expand upon neurochemicals and the brain's pleasure centers. I discover heaps of data on curious compounds such as dopamine and serotonin, which may in fact be responsible for the way I'm feeling right now. But, even though it's mildly interesting, the only thing I can do is sigh. Right now, more than anything, I want to discuss all this with Emma.

'You know that I miss you too, right?' the Emma in my head says.

'No you don't,' I tell her.

A soft giggle. *'Of course I do, silly! How can you not know that?'*

'Well, for one thing, you haven't tried to contact me in ages.'

'I'm probably just waiting for you to send me a message. You haven't responded to any of my invitations, remember? What's a girl to think?'

'Invitations to spend time with you and your boyfriend...'

'Come on,' Emma says, *'that was a long time ago. We've probably broken up by now.'*

'It's been five days,' I tell her, and I immediately wonder why it seems so much longer.

'Come on,' she says, *'send me a message. You know you want to.'*

I put my tablet down. I can't concentrate. *'You have no idea what you did to me,'* I tell her.

'What did I do?'

'You woke me up! And now you're forcing me to go back to sleep!'

'Beg-pardon?'

'You didn't have to make me fall in love with you. Why did you do that?'

'How did I do that? You make me sound so evil. Maybe you just misunderstood me?'

'Misunderstood you? What about landing my plane on your building? What about all the accidental touching? What about the 250 messages you sent me?'

'Oh, that.'

'Yeah, that. What was all that about?'

Emma doesn't answer.

I think my mind may be imploding. I have to talk to someone, but I don't want to spend even more time with colleagues or relatives. Who else can I talk to? There really is no one. I'd have to find completely fresh, new people. People I don't even know exist yet. But how do you do this?

I think back to the last time I truly met anyone new. I guess that was Samantha Fox. I shudder. Not a good example. Before that, leopold. Also a bad example. Before that, I guess, well, Emma.

This is getting me nowhere.

I take out some paper and brainstorm. It's not easy for someone like me to meet new people. Sure, it's easy enough to bump into people, but actually *meeting* them is a whole different ballgame. You have to find a situation where it's not too weird for you to start talking to them. Where you can immediately find some common ground so the conversation doesn't die. And, even when you manage all that, you still need to find a way to set up a repeat meeting without looking creepy.

How do people manage all this?

I doodle on my brainstorm paper for a long time before it suddenly hits me.

In fact, the solution to my problem is so obvious, so simple, so elegant, I almost didn't think of it at all. It's been staring me in the face for so long that I forgot it was even there.

YouTube script:

A tip for getting out of a slump: Visit a funeral.

Okay, this sounds a little out there, but bear with me. Obliviously it shouldn't be the funeral of someone you know. Just find a random funeral, there's always one going down somewhere. Funerals give you a chance to mingle and talk to people ~~who are not your mom~~ and it will do wonders to lift your spirits. If you can manage it, sneak a peek at the casket. ~~Closed casket is okay, but open is better, as long as the deceased is not too old or mangled.~~ Walk right up to the casket and say to yourself: Hey, at least I'm not *that* guy.

Better yet, tell yourself: My time here is limited, sooner or later it's my turn, so I can't be scared to take a chance every now and then. We all go to the same place, the only difference is the amount of fun and love we experience along the way.

[Show clickable google-map location]

I have more tips. Many more. And I'm going to do something I've never done before. Something big. Something truly Monumental. I'm going to give you the opportunity to pick my brain in person. That's right: in person! So, if you feel like having a chat, meet me tomorrow at 5 p.m. at the clickable location on screen. Take advantage of this opportunity ~~before I come to my sense and change my mind~~!

[sign off]

25

Observation:

Make sure to keep busy, or life will seem increasingly meaningless.

"I can't believe you're doing this!"

"Yeah, you're a life saver!"

The guys sound happy. They look happy, too. The problem is, I'm not entirely sure what they're so happy about.

It's early in the evening and we've taken up position at the King's Bar and Grill. An impressive number of followers showed up, five in total. Three in their twenties, one in his thirties, and one in his early sixties.

They were easy enough to spot, greeting me with loud cheers from a table by the window when I came in. It appears I'm somewhat of a celebrity to them, an internet deity, if you will.

They ordered a round of beers and it took some doing to convince them alcohol doesn't agree with my finely tuned digestive system. In the end they relented and ordered me a Coke.

"So, when are you going out there?"

This is a guy called Eddy the Lizard. I'm not sure when we started with the weird handles, but this guy actually looks like a lizard, so maybe it's what his friends call him. His face is thin and angular with dry, flaky skin. He wears one of those obnoxious 'Female Body Inspector' t-shirts and his eyes dart around the room as if he's looking for prey – or worried something else might see *him* as prey. There's definitely something reptilian about him. In fact, when you first meet Eddy, you almost expect him to jump up on the table and make a grab for your wallet, with his tongue.

"How do you mean," I ask him. "Go out where?"

"You know..." he gestures around the bar, his movements sparse and efficient, lacertilian almost. "Out here."

I still don't get it.

"Yeah," Tony chimes in – he's asked me to refer to him as Agent Orange but I refuse to on general principle. "When do you start the demos?"

"What demos?"

I'm getting an uncomfortable feeling here. I'd feel a lot better with something in my hand. I signal the waitress again and she makes a

137

gesture that indicates she's only just now remembered my existence and the fact that I'm in need of refreshment.

Meanwhile, the Lizard's glaring at me. "You don't expect us to just go in and start picking up women without a good demo, do you?"

"Yes," says Antonov. This is the old guy. I'm not sure if his is a silly name or if it's his own. "Don't throw us into deep end," he says, annoyed. "You have to show us with example, Leverage!"

His spiky hair looks aggressive and his raspy voice is thick with some kind of accent. When I was first introduced to Antonov I had this knee jerk reaction, the one I always have when meeting guys his age. Without really wanting to, without consciously noticing, I checked out his features, a fleeing question whispering through my mind: *Are you him? Are you my dad?*

But, as soon as he spoke, that voice was silenced. Antonov's accent put all questions to rest.

Unless, of course, he's faking?

"Lead the way," Antonov barks. "We need to see how not to scare away females."

"How about her," the Lizard points out a woman across the bar, who is very obviously a model and quite possibly an Olympic gold medallist. By her demeanor, I'd say she's waiting for her agent to take her to a photo shoot likely followed by a cocaine-fuelled orgy. "Why don't you pick her up?" the Lizard suggests. "Should be easy for you, right Lev?"

The girl notices the Lizard pointing in her not-so-general direction and backs away to the safety of the bar.

"See?" Antonov barks triumphantly. "You need show how not scare female!"

I'm appalled.

"That's not what we're here for." I tell them.

"Of course it is," they say, almost in unison.

The Lizard: "You're going to give us hands-on experience, right?"

Tony: "Yeah, that's what we came here for."

Antonov: "Da!"

The extent of their misconception is painfully clear. I shudder. How did I not see this coming?

"I invited you for a drink," I tell them. "So we could talk. You know, shoot the breeze, discuss things."

"Discuss things?"

They glare at me.

"You can ask me questions," I explain. "Pick my brain. That kind of thing."

"Pick your brain?" Antonov almost knocks over his beers (he ordered multiple). "You need to paint us picture," he barks, "not tell us thousand words!"

Antonov is much louder than he needs to be, and the others seem upset too. What happened to all the smiles? Where did the love and admiration go? Am I not the same Leverage I was four minutes ago, when they still quietly adored me?

"You've seen my vids," I tell them. "You know that's not how I operate."

My statement is met with glazed looks and I suddenly understand how my grade school teachers must have felt, explaining a simple concept to a sea of dazed looking kids.

"I'm not a pick-up artist," I remind them. "I'm not here to show you how to pick up random chicks."

"You're not?" Antonov seems genuinely surprised. He's obviously missed the main point of every single one of my vids. Tony doesn't look too happy, either. The rest of them, well, they look stunned.

The waitress finally arrives with my Coke – perhaps she's been trying to work out the secret formula to brew a batch herself. I take a thankful sip. "Look," I say, "I wasn't teaching trickery and pickup lines, I was trying to explain how to go about getting The One. And as my The One isn't here, I wouldn't have approached any females tonight. But, as I was about to explain, I actually don't do that anymore. I'm re-dedicating my channel to a much higher goal."

The guys look dejected, then the Lizard pipes up. "Okay, okay," he says. "I guess we can appreciate that." His eyes dart about the bar, hungry, desperate. "You have your rules and such, but it'd still help us to get a little inside peek, see you in action. Why don't you think of it as performing a little play?" He scratches his cheek, dislodging some flakes of skin. "Just pretend that *she's* you're The One." He points out a girl who is very obviously having a drink with at least two of her boyfriends. "Just do a little role playing."

I suddenly feel very alone.

"Even if I were inclined to do that," I sigh, "it just wouldn't be fair. Not to her, not to me, and not to her boyfriends."

"He's got a point," Tony says. "We can't just make a girl fall in love with Leverage and then break her heart, just because we want a demo. It wouldn't be right." He thinks it over. "There's really only one solution. We need to get Lev's girl to come here. That way he can demonstrate on her."

The Lizard is immediately enthused. "Yeah!" he says. "That'd work, right, Lev? Can you ask her to come over?"

"What? No! Impossible!"

"Why not? You want *us* to call her? Make it a little less obvious?" He grabs my coat. "Where's your cell, I'll do it."

I bat away his flaky, lizardy hands. "Stop!" I say. "No one is calling my girl!"

"Why not?"

"You're just not! That's all there is to it."

The lizard looks crushed.

The rest of the group starts to argue among themselves.

'Come on,' Emma whispers into my brain. *'I gave you my number. Obviously I want you to call me...'*

'You know I can't do that,' I tell her.

'Of course you can. Don't you want to hear my voice?'

'I do. Very badly.'

'Then just call me, dummy!'

'It won't do any good. It'd just be awkward and painful.'

Emma scoffs, *'You don't know that. I could be sitting by the phone right now, waiting for your call.'*

'You could, yes. But you're not.'

The discussion between the guys becomes heated. I quickly signal the waitress for more drinks to stave off a full scale mutiny. Then I realize I wouldn't mind a mutiny. It'd get the attention away from me.

"Oh my," I say, glancing in the direction of the model-slash-coke-fiend.

"What?" the Lizard asks excitedly.

"Don't look now, guys," I mumble under my breath, "but I think the model just looked at Eddy."

"She did?"

The guys take turns trying to gaze at the girl inconspicuously.

Her evening is about to get so much worse.

"Yeah," I say. "Clear as day. She turned and looked straight at him."

For a moment the Lizard can't believe his ears, then a thick, syrupy wave of smugness washes over him. "Of course she's checking me out," he says. "She's no fool. She knows quality when she sees it."

"You sure?" Antonov frowns. "I don't see her move. I look at her whole time, she don't move."

"Yeah, she did." I speak directly to the Lizard. "When Antonov glanced at the bachelorette, the girl at the bar turned and looked right at you. Then she said something to the waitress. They were giggling."

Eddy trembles with excitement. I worry he might explode. He pulls at his FBI t-shirt. "Yeah! I mean, who can resist this?"

"It's classic reverse-desirability," I say, making up a fake concept as I go along. "By ignoring her, Eddy inadvertently triggered her value-seeking response."

"I did?" Eddy hangs on my every word.

"Of course. Her rejection filter was overruled by her desire to be desired. She simply cannot deal with the idea of not being wanted by someone as repulsive as Eddy. It makes no sense to her. She has no option but to assume that there's something about him she's not seeing.

Something very special."

"Go! Now!" Antonov barks at the Lizard. "Go get her, you crazy bastard!"

But the Lizard suddenly looks scared. He scratches at his face. "I probably *should* go talk to her," he says, "but maybe it's even better if I make her wait." He glances at me for support. "Make myself even more desirable, the illusion of scarcity and so on?"

"Oh no," I say, "it doesn't work that way. You have about three minutes before she moves on, decides that she's wrong about you." I look at my watch. "Get her before she disappears from your future forever."

I know it's cruel, but, in fairness, this is what the Lizard wanted. He came here to get a little push. Have someone nudge him into action and watch over him as he practised approaching girls. Plus, he's taking one for the team here. Without his sacrifice this evening will turn into an ugly mess of accusations and disappointment.

"Go!"

Eddy is shoved from his stool and he decides to approach the bar using a strange kind of flanking manoeuvre. I've never seen anything like it.

The guys cheer him on.

When he reaches the bar, the Lizard takes the seat next to the model and, for a long time, for a very, very long time, nothing else happens.

And nothing continues to happen for quite a while after.

Then Antonov bellows, "Talk to female, damn it!"

The Lizard flinches. He shoots us an angry look. But, perhaps under the threat of further embarrassing outbursts, he finally taps the model on her shoulder and says a few words to her.

Which she ignores.

Intensely.

In fact, she chooses that very moment to get up and leave the bar.

Mortified, Eddy slinks back to our table, but the guys receive him like a war hero. They cheer and Antonov even shares a generous number of his beers with him. Tony can't stop slapping him on the back.

Eddy quickly settles into his new role. He spends the rest of the evening telling ever taller tales of his encounter. We listen, rapt. After all, Eddy's the only one of us who's actually spoken to a real human female tonight.

Later, I head home tired but proud. For all its rollercoaster-like properties, I handled this evening well. I don't often spend this much time with humans in social situations so I was worried it'd prove too taxing, but I survived. In fact, I managed to adjust my inherent level of brilliance to my surroundings in such a manner as to make communication not only possible, but even somewhat pleasurable.

But now it's time to unwind. Unclutter ye olde mental processor from tasks and apps needed for social interaction. Switch off hosting mode and go back to being myself.

The cool night air ruffles my jacket, trying and tries to remove the smell of smoke and stale beer. There's a little chill that bites at the tip of my nose as I follow a series of streetlights back to my car.

"Hey, hold up!"

A scruffy looking man with a grey stubble pops out of the shadows and blocks my path. I assume he's homeless and struggle between brushing him off and giving him change. Or both. Or neither. Then I notice the look of distant recognition in his eyes and realize he must be another of my followers.

"Sorry, man," I say. "The meet-and-greet is over. You just missed it."

"That's okay," he says, "I just wanted a quick word with you."

"I understand completely. I would too, if I just ran into me. But it'll have to wait till next time. At which point you might try arriving a little earlier."

I brush past him but he repositions himself. "I actually wanted to talk to you alone," he says. He blows on his fingers. "I've been waiting out here for hours. Who knew you'd last that long in a social situation, right?"

Which is an odd thing to say to someone you've never met before.

"I'm sorry, but I have to go."

"Hold on a second, son."

He smiles amiably and it takes me a moment to understand his use of the word 'son'. Shocked, I look him over.

The one time I didn't wonder if a face in the crowd was my dad's. The one time I didn't search for familiar features (as seen in old photographs and in the mirror, during those precious few seconds before looking into your own eyes starts to feel weird and you have to look away).

I search for those features now. I look past the scruffiness, which is probably due to his oversized coat and greying stubble, and I do spot something. Around the eyes, around the mouth. Distant echoes of a mischievous smile, signs of high cheekbones and dormant intelligence.

This could be him.

This could be my dad.

"Sorry to ambush you like this," he says. "I'm sure it's strange for you, but, well, you didn't leave me much of a choice."

He looks so different from what he looked like to my little boy brain. In my imagination, Dad never aged. He didn't grow wrinkly and grey. He never stopped towering over me.

I stare at him a long time, still in shock.

I always wondered what I'd feel at this moment. How I'd handle it, what I'd say, but, even with decades of preparation, I still surprise myself with what I actually say next.

Video #152 by *Leverage*. **Views: 27**

Comments:

WhipCrck: (6:28 pm) Here's a question for ya: would you rather have a really fat wife who's very funny, or a sexy wife with who you'd never laugh again?

Agent12: (6:44 pm) How bout neither?

SchmidtAbout: (6:53 pm) <u>Date Nigerian Spam-Millionaires here!!!!!!!!!</u>

WhipCrck: (6:53 pm) Nope, you gotta choose.

Agent12: (6:54 pm) 'kay, then it has to be the hot wife. No contest.

Lovelost: (6:54 pm) Why?

Agent12: (6:55 pm) Simple: you can always laugh with your buddies, but you can't fuck them!

Lovelost: (6:55 pm) That's just SAD!

WhipCrck: (7:17 pm) It's not, it's valid socio-economical research!

DissonantMelody: (7:27 pm) Don't you mean 'with whom' and 'social' research…?

GaryXXX: (8:35 pm) What about a smoking hot embalmer, would you date her?

OnMyWay: (9:19 pm) There's no such thing as a smoking hot embalmer. Natural selection has bred them out of da species.

TheLizard: (1:11 am) Just back from my first outing with my main man, Leverage! The dude rocks even harder in real life! Case in point; I just talked to a super model!! She was totally into me!

AgentOrange: (1:11 am) Yeah, that was an amazing night! U have to do that again soon, Lev!!

AnnyTov: (1:12 am) Da! Females much less scared of us now. This is great!

26

Research topics:

Love and other sources of dopamine...

I always wondered what I'd feel if you'd come face to face with my dad. How I'd handle it, what I'd say, but, even with decades of preparation, I still surprise myself with what I actually say next.

Which is nothing.

Not a single word.

There are so many things that need saying that my brain can't hope to order them into coherent sentences. The task is too complex, too convoluted. Instead, it simply gives up.

"What, no hug for your old man?"

Dad doesn't lean in. He just stands there, waiting for me to make the next move.

I suddenly notice his stubble has some clear patches where his beard won't come in. I wonder if I'll get that. Then again, I've never let my beard grow out, so I may already have it and not even know.

I feel some rain on my face.

"So you're not dead," I finally manage.

"Certainly looks that way." He grins, but there are no laugh lines around his eyes.

"And it really was you in my comments section."

"Guilty as charged." Another awkward grin.

I gaze down the street. The rain's coming down harder now, cold, watery tendrils working their way down my collar. I shiver. I should get to my car.

"Now what," I say.

Dad frowns. He hasn't thought this far ahead, which is good, I suppose. At some level he understands this shouldn't go well. He can't just pop up and expect me to welcome him back into my life instantaneously. That wouldn't make sense. (And for all I know, he doesn't even *want* that!)

On the other hand, he could've prepared better. He's the only one who knew this was coming. He could've spent a little time considering the two main contingencies.

"We could get a coffee," he ventures.

"I suppose we could."

"There's a place down the road," Dad says.

There always is.

There's a whole world of places down the road.

It's what we've built society on.

"What do you say? Have a few minutes to spare for your old man?"

There's a crackle of distant thunder. My shirt is getting soaked. A few minutes isn't much to ask, not at all. It wouldn't put me out. It would give me a chance to dry out before the long drive home.

But it's not going to happen.

"Sorry," I tell him. "As I mentioned before, you're a little late."

I step past him and head to my car. And not one tiny part of me listens if his footsteps are following me.

I watch the rain run down the windshield, my brain awash with thoughts. My life has changed so much recently. Mere days ago there was no Dad but there was an Emma. Now one has been traded for the other, but I didn't get to choose. It was a trade made without my consent.

I take my tablet from my backpack. It's time to start on the first of my new scripts. I have more than enough data by now, and I can't keep my followers waiting.

Draft Script:

How to get over your crush:

1. Control your inner voice.

First of all, you have to realize that love isn't real. It's not an actual thing. Love is just a story your brain tells itself to give it a goal and keep it busy. Your brain chooses someone moderately compatible and convinces you that this is the love of your life. It does this to stop you from getting bored.
If you think about it, you never actually miss Her, not until your brain gets the time to remind you to. The truth is, with a breakup you don't actually lose some magical person, you lose a story.

Secondly, your inner voice really enjoys making you feel bad. Given half a chance it'll show you an endless stream of mental images to help keep you miserable; things you and her did together, things you could be doing, things you'd planned to do. But you have to remember that your inner voice is secretly against you. It will always try to make you love your crush more. Never mind the fact that she never saw your true value, that she never went out of her way to spend time with you, ~~or that she ran off with a guy with one green and one red eye~~! Your subconscious doesn't care about any of that. Again, nature is secretly stacking the deck against species survival, giving us one more hurdle so we can prove our worthiness.

You have no choice but to cut your inner voice off when it tries to make you believe that life without your crush is meaningless. ~~Even if, for a short period, it feels as if that's very, very true.~~ Studies show there's a simple chemical reason for all this. When you're in love, your body rewards you by flooding your system with neurotransmitters called dopamine and serotonin. These chemicals have a direct impact on the pleasure centers of your brain. In fact, these are the same feel-good chemicals your body releases when you use heroin or cocaine. The same chemicals that make people believe they actually enjoy exercise. This is powerful stuff.

However, after a dopamine rush the body quickly performs a clean-up action. It uses prolactin to flush all that nasty happiness from your system and return it to normal operating parameters. Prolactin is the chemical responsible for taking all the color out of the world after a breakup and making you mourn a life that will never be.

Prolactin was originally invented by the brain as a way to protect itself from an endless pursuit of pleasure. It prevents overstimulation of the brain's pleasure centers. For example, prolactin makes you stop wanting food after you've eaten an entire cake. It makes you stop wanting sex after you've had an orgasm. Without it, we might get stuck in an endless indulgence cycle. So prolactin is generally a good chemical. However, when you're coming off the dopamine high of a crush, the prolactin isn't all that helpful. The world

already looks dull and grey due to the sudden decline in dopamine, the prolactin just makes things worse.
The fact that your system floods with prolactin after you've been dumped is basically a design flaw.

So how does knowing about this chemical brain-soup actually help you? Well, it tells you that you need to keep busy, keep your mind pre-occupied so that your inner voice can't trick you into wallowing. And it tells you that you have to make a serious effort to beat what is essentially a dopamine addiction.

2. Interact with new females.

Talking to other women will give you small doses of dopamine. Nothing compared to spending time with your crush, but we're trying to kick our dopamine habit here, not fuel it. Small doses is exactly what we need.

In the not too distant future there will probably be a medical treatment for heartache. It'll be a matter of slowly waning you off the dopamine. A simple pill that'll help bring your system back to a stable dopamine cycle, one without crazy crush-induced spikes. And this pill will also help curb the initial flush of prolactin when you get dumped.

3. Find other sources of dopamine.

In the meantime, you'll have to find your own sources of dopamine. Natural dopamine is secreted during pleasurable moments, so go out and do things you love. Not just things you enjoy, but things you truly *love*! Go drive a race car. Take a flying lesson. Go scuba-diving. ~~Find the perfect graphic novel or hamburger.~~ You're allowed to indulge yourself a bit here, because it's the lesser of two evils.
~~I also suspect that if you don't get over your crush fast enough (if you wallow for months rather than weeks) there could be some actual neurological damage. Damage you may never fully recover from, so get busy with the healing!~~
At the same time, avoid places, activities, and objects that remind you of her, because these can give your subconscious a much stronger position of attack!

4. Let time pass.

[note to self: obviously this is the main point, but why is it so effective and how can these effects be intensified and sped up??
Idea: do some research on addiction and the three day rule.]

27

Observation:

Your brain is your worst enemy!

I re-read the first draft of my script a few times before putting my tablet away. It's not exactly brilliant, but it's a start. I'll work on it some more later. Meanwhile, the rain has slowed to a drizzle and the thunder's moved on. It seems we're all starting to calm down a bit here.

On my way home I make a detour past a somewhat shady little place that just happens to serve a killer burger. On the burger scale of things, I'd say they're probably number two in the world. Their subservience to the Ultra Burger may merely be down to the omission of the BBQ sauce. I park in a dark alley that serves as their parking lot – and that will see my tires go missing in the time it takes to eat two burgers – and head inside to order one burger. In my emotional state, I very nearly forget to bring my bottle of emergency BBQ sauce from the car.

I select a booth by a window overlooking the alley to keep an eye on my car. The neon light reflecting off puddles of muck and the sound of distant traffic tells me I'm way off the beaten path. I'm slumming it. I have no choice, though, you can't get an Ultra Burger this early in the morning.

There are only a few patrons in the place and half of them look homeless. The other half look like they expect to be homeless by Friday, latest.

My burger arrives and I open the bun to apply the BBQ sauce. I do this with near surgical precision, glancing intermittently at my car (no sign of trouble yet) and the patrons closest to me (no signs of begging yet).

I decide there's actually a kind of reverence to this place. Even the customers at the counter order in hushed tones. This is like our library. Our church. We are the Late-Nite people. The midnight dwellers. Those who can't face returning to dark, empty apartments. (Or to their moms, as the case may be.)

I like this kind of atmosphere. It's peaceful, respectful.

I look down and notice my burger's gone. I didn't even notice eating it. I spent the entire time thinking and forgot to enjoy even a single bite. So much for squeezing out a little burger-induced dopamine.

I clear my table and dump everything in the bin, including the BBQ sauce. It's been opened so I can't keep it in the car anymore. I'll have to get a new bottle in the morning and pray I don't suffer a BBQ sauce related emergency in the meantime.

Back in my car I notice that it's finally stopped raining. My jacket and pants are dry too. I dab at my eyes with a napkin anyway. For some reason they're still wet.

Sleep is restless and marred by convoluted dreams. Work the next day isn't much better. And when I finally return home, there's a stranger sitting in my living room.

Which is very upsetting.

The guy is about my age, I suppose, but he looks more defeated. His temples are grey and he has those weird guy-bags under his eyes.

I'm not sure what to do about him.

Mom's nowhere to be seen but he's sipping tea from one of her fine china cups – the set she uses for special occasions. So, unless he's part of a weird breed of burglar that breaks in to make something relaxing to drink, this guy appears to be mom-approved.

I take off my coat and linger in the hallway, weighing my options.

"Your mom went out for biscuits," the guy offers, smiling at me from the living room.

I consider ignoring him, but as we've just made eye-contact, I guess that's no longer an option. Instead I say, "Ah."

There's an awkward silence. I'm not entirely sure whose fault that is.

"Are you coming in?" He gestures at the couch. "Plenty of room to sit."

I shrug and enter the living room, more than a little annoyed at being invited into my own home.

"Your mom asked me over," he continues. "She said you wanted to talk to me."

"She did?"

I have no idea what crazy scheme Mom is hatching now. I can only hope she doesn't expect me to go on a date with this guy.

"It's been a long time," he says.

Which is a worrying remark. "What has been a long time?"

He frowns. "Don't you remember me?"

I shrug. I'm not in the habit of remembering people I've never met. I look at my watch and wonder how long I have to stay here to meet politeness requirements. Do I have to keep this guy company until Mom returns? I really hope not. Damn my social robot!

"I'm Tommy," he says. "We used to play together. We built Lego forts in your backyard when we were kids."

Ah!

This is my preschool pall, Tommy Moretti. The one who moved away when we were twelve. "It really has been a long time," I say.

He nods, nipping his tea.

I feel a little more at ease now, and slightly intrigued. "How did Mom find you?"

"Google, probably, or the phone book."

"And you came all the way here just to talk?"

He shrugs. "Why not, I didn't have much on my plate, and we only moved three streets over."

"You did?"

"Yeah."

"Three streets?"

"One and a half if you don't count the park."

"Oh. Somehow I remember you moving very, very far away."

"I guess three streets is a lot when you're a kid."

"I guess so."

"I always wondered why you never came over to play anymore."

I shrug.

Silence descends over the living room.

Tommy sips his tea. Whenever our eyes meet, we smile awkwardly. I really want to watch cartoons but something tells me we still haven't reached that point where that would be acceptable yet. Even though, technically, Tommy is not my guest, but Mom's.

I wonder why she keeps springing this kind of stuff of me. What makes her think I need help with my life? And how can I make it clear that there's really nothing to fix, that I like my life the way it is?

(Except for the bit where Emma's brain has a glitch that prevents her from seeing we belong together, and the bit where nobody at work really appreciates me, and the bit where Dad refuses to be dead, or, at the least, offer a really great explanation…)

Tommy stares at me. I might have been frowning at my own thoughts. "So," I say quickly, "how's the import/export business?"

Tommy finally puts down his cup. "What import/export business?"

I'm not entirely sure. "Weren't you doing business in Asia or something?"

"Oh, that." He waves it away. "That's what my mom keeps telling people. She makes such a big deal out of everything." He smiles apologetically. "A few months ago I ordered a case of special anti-dandruff shampoo from Singapore. The stuff turned out to burn my scalp so I put it up on eBay. Some guy in Sweden bought it." Tommy shrugs. "I guess that technically qualifies as import/export."

"Ah."

"But it's not my main thing, though," Tommy says.

"It's not? What's your main thing?"

"Well, mostly I'm unemployed."

"I see."

"Yeah." He smiles weakly. "It's pretty shit, actually. My wife left. She took the kids. And the dog. And most of my stuff."

"Well…" I say, but I'm not sure how to finish that thought.

I did put a lot of feeling into the 'well', so maybe it's still of comfort to him.

"I have a little money coming in, though."

"Good," I say.

"Yeah, I signed up for a drug trial. They give me pills and then I have to write down my experiences so they can search for side effects. It's not too dangerous. I think I may be in the placebo group."

"Good. That's really… good."

What kind of idiot enrolls in a drug trial?

"Placebos are good for you, aren't they?"

I shrug.

"Maybe they'll cure my adult onset acne."

It appears Mom went to get the biscuits in China. I glance at the TV. I can feel valuable content streaming away.

"So," Tommy says, "do you still do magic tricks?"

"Me? No, not really."

"Me neither… How about Legos? You still have those?"

"Of course not."

"Me neither. I mean, I have some special sets, I guess. You know, limited editions, but I don't open them. Unless it's a really cool set, then I buy two. One to build and one to keep unopened."

My cell buzzes. "Sorry," I tell Tommy, "I have to check something."

"Sure," he says.

em: hiya!

I stare at my screen, hating how happy I suddenly feel.

I really shouldn't feel as if life is now good and something special is about to happen – because it's not.

em: r u there?
me: sure, what u up to?
em: nothing much, just trying out some new makeup an stuff
me: why? u don't need makeup
em: course I do, silly! u know my credo: come for the looks, stay for the personality ;)
me: i like u just the way u are
em: U see? It's working! You're staying for the personality :P

Tommy looks curious. "Good news?"

I shrug. "It's really hard to say."

"Really? Why is that?"

"Because good news and bad news tend to look very similar these days."

"Ah." He nods sagely. "I know what you mean."

em: so why aren't you coming to the Shoppe anymore?

me: no reason, just busy

em: come on, 2 busy for me? Not possible ;P

me: i had some things to take care of

em: okok, but Rn't u running out of brazil nuts??

me: i might drop by for some. not sure when

em: ok, no sweat. anyway, leo said he'd love to do a double date with you. did i suggest that already? can't remember.

And that's precisely the problem.

While I've been waiting around, thinking about Emma, fighting the urge to contact her, she's been busy completely forgetting about me. She doesn't even realize we've been out of contact! And it's really annoying how easy it is for her to enjoy her Leverage-less life. How can she know such a large part of me, understand so much of me, and still not care about me?

I decide not to reply. Not right now. I stifle a painful sigh as I put my cell away. I suddenly feel like sleeping. And perhaps crying a little in my sleep.

"Look," I tell Tommy, "it's been kind of a weird day for me."

"Sure," he says, nodding.

We stare at each other silently.

I try again. "It's probably best if you go."

An hour or so later I hear Mom return. I'm sure she had a great time setting me up and going off to play knitting.

I'm in bed, trying to compose another script in my head and I it's not going well.

YouTube Script:

I want to talk a bit more about getting over a crush. I believe there are different levels to being over someone. The most dangerous of these is the level where you can get through an entire day without thinking about her. Where you can feel good, not too depressed, not constantly as if something is mis sing from your life, but then you'll suddenly find yourself doing something you'd want her to see and you're right back where you started. In this phase, you're more or less okay as long as you don't have any contact with her. As long as you don't run into her (or get a message or a phone call) you can actually keep thinking that you're over her. But if she contacts you, she'll suck you right back in. Without even trying. She just has to hint that your break up was a misunderstanding and you'd simply let her back into you r life.

28

Observation:

There are over 6 billion people on the planet.
That's 6 billion people, give or take a few, who don't like me.

Breakfast is a strained affair.

It's silent warfare.

With last night's ambush still fresh in my mind I'm unwilling to start up communications. For her part, Mom pretends nothing's happened, hoping it'll blow over. She makes sure she's too busy with breakfast to be the first to talk, because, as long as no one talks, the issue of whether or not we're fighting, and whose fault that is, can remain unaddressed. A social Schrödinger's-cat-in-the-box.

She slides a pancake onto my plate and smiles patiently. It seems it's up to me to break the silence.

"I can't believe you did that!"

Mom starts buttering my toast. "Did what, honey?"

"Tommy!"

Mom sets the toast down next to my pancake. "Tommy?" She gives me an innocent look. For a moment I can almost believe she has no idea we've been at war all morning, that she hasn't lain awake, going over this very conversation in her head, like I have. But the moment passes. No one can be that hurtful and simultaneously that clueless.

Mom beams. "So you two did meet!"

"Of course we did. The guy was sitting in my chair, in front of my TV, inviting me into my living room. It was very annoying."

"Annoying?" Mom tries to pinch my cheek. "Of course it wasn't annoying. You were a little shy at first, but then it turned out to be fun, didn't it?"

"It didn't!"

"Can you imagine he only moved three streets over?" Mom shakes her head in wonder. "I thought it'd take me years to find him, but, there he was, three streets over. Isn't that great?"

"I fail to see what's so great about it."

"Now you can play together again!"

"And you really do mean play, don't you? Should I go out and buy some Lego's? Get some little cars and decoder rings?"

155

She waves it away. "You know what I mean," she says. "You can," she searches for the right words, "*spend time together*. Do whatever it is that men of your generation do. Compare tube trenches, make collages, that kind of thing."

"I do hope you're not referring to my charts as collages. There is actual science behind them, it's not just silly pictures. I make use of a sophisticated blend of psychology, wrapped in reverse psychology, infused with deep insight into human nature."

"Of course you do," Mom says. She slides another pancake onto my plate. "And now that you've re-connected with Tommy, you can watch cartoons at his house on Saturday. How does that sound?" She smiles at the thought.

I push my plate away and get up. "Look," I say. "I have no desire to start up a relationship with this man. In a very real sense he is a complete stranger to me. There's no reason to believe that, just because we lived next to each other as kids, we'd have any more in common now than any two random strangers. And I'll thank you to stop making play dates for me!"

Mom suddenly turns stern. "You listen to me," she says, waving a bony finger in my face. "You need all the help you can get! The way you're headed, you're going to end up alone!"

I roll my eyes at her and get my coat. Breakfast, it appears, is beyond saving.

I get in my car and reverse out onto the road. And, for the first time in over a decade, I forgo the customary goodbye-beep of the horn. I'm just not feeling it today.

Mom really doesn't know what she's talking about. There is a huge difference between being *alone* and being *lonely*.

There's no problem with being alone. I find it quite enjoyable. Sure, there's no one around, but the people who are not around are simply elsewhere. They'll return at some point and until then you can go about your business undisturbed.

Being lonely, however, is being in the absence of a very specific person. Someone you'd really like to be around. Someone you may in fact never see again. Being lonely sucks big time.

Being alone is when you create great art and watch good TV and eat interesting food.

Being lonely is when the radio won't stop playing songs that make you cry.

Being alone is when you can burp and scratch your ass with impunity.

Being lonely is when every bit of you hurts and you realize the pain is actually there at cellular level.

Being alone is a temporary state that shortens with every passing minute, while being lonely seems to stretch out forever.

The solution to being alone is simply waiting for it to resolve itself, but the solution to being lonely is… well… I guess taking some kind of specific action. Perhaps on an emotional as well as on a physical level. You may even need some kind of brilliant, hi-tech list.

You can't just wing it and hope for the best.

At work the day refuses to improve in any way. I don't hear from Emma and I keep having useless thoughts about Dad. On top of that, Quiton-James and Gharity have an hour long discussion right next to my cubicle, their voices scrambling my mental processes like one of those sonic mouse traps. And, from time to time Gharity, even leans on my wall, shaking it and knocking my action figures off their perch.

'Who does this guy think he is?' Emma giggles. *'Does he even know how ridiculous he sounds?'*

I ignore her.

'He's one re-organization away from being homeless,' she continues. *'But, you're lucky, you don't work in a nut shop. You wouldn't believe the characters I deal with on a daily basis.'*

She's trying to give us a sense of shared experience, and she isn't even real. Damn my inner voice!

The morning continues its worrying decline.

John from Acquisitions wants me to update him on a new account.

Isha from reception is tallying people who prefer the new paper stock.

And Lenora from Human Resources wants me to help her find her cat.

She proposes I do this by letting her put up a flyer on my cubicle wall (what?), and a few around my neighborhood (why?), and, naturally, her flyer has to be one of those sad, last-century stencils featuring a faded black-and-white photo.

Try as I might, I can't get her to take my advice on turning it into a real eye catcher (using nothing but dried macaroni and crayons – MacGyver style).

By lunchtime my spirits are so low I actually fear for my mental health. So I check my getting-over-a-crush-list to see if I can squeeze out some brilliant wise-isms to keep my mind occupied.

'Please, pretty please get rid of that list,' Emma whines. *'You don't need to get over me. We'll be together soon.'*

'No, we won't.'

'Of course we will. We're just a bit preoccupied at the moment. It happens to all the great couples in history. We'll eventually end up together and tell our grandkids about this silly little intermezzo.'

I don't respond. I don't even allow my mind to envision us growing old together and sharing stories with our highly gifted offspring.

At least, I don't think I do.

Instead, I study my list. I might actually be failing at a few of my own bullet points. Especially the first one. If I'm ever going to get over Emma I can't keep talking to her like this. And I probably shouldn't be in contact with the real Emma, either. You don't heal wounds by constantly ripping them open.

I head over to the mall on my lunch break to replace my bottle of emergency BBQ sauce. I also order an Ultra Burger at Spaky's and decide to make a real effort to speak to a woman who isn't Emma. Through verbal communication with a lesser female I'll try to score a few droplets of dopamine. This should help me ease off the drug that is Emma.

I scan the crowd and choose a woman at the back who is, admittedly, a bit on the heavy side and who doesn't have a nice complexion in any traditional sense of the word – in fact, there may be no complexion to speak of, just a pitted landscape of despair.

I sit down opposite her and almost spill my drink. For some reason my tray shakes as if it's being held by a nervous person. I quickly steady my tray and say, "Mind if I sit here?"

The woman looks at me wearily. "Smoke drink pets?"

"Excuse me?"

"Smoke drink pets?"

Which is what I thought she'd said. The poor woman's probably gone bat-shit crazy from loneliness. After all, this world can be pretty cruel to those with brains that suffer a misalignment with reality. Especially a misalignment that causes them to believe there are people out there who enjoy smoking pets.

"Nice to meet you," I say, ready to duck at the first sign of actual physical craziness. "I have never smoked any pets, but I'm sure, for those who are into that kind of thing, it's a very rewarding experience."

The woman leers at me. "Fuck you, asshole. I was asking you if you smoke, drink, or have pets!"

"Oh."

"You're trying to pick me up, right?" She subconsciously shifts her bosom the way a more elegant female might flick a strand of hair from her face. "So I'll tell you right now; I don't do guys who smoke, drink, or have pets!"

"I…"

"Although drink is probably not so bad," she adds. "In moderation. A little social drinking I'll allow, but I don't want no alcoholic."

I have to stop her train of thought from derailing further. "I wasn't trying to pick you up."

"I'm sure you weren't," she balks.

"Not in the slightest."

"Well then you're a pretty weird guy." She gestures around. "All these empty tables, and you sit with me at a table for two. If you're not hitting on me, then what the hell are you up to?"

This isn't going well. In fact, this situation would have to improve drastically before I could even considered calling it 'going badly'.

This is disaster squared.

Still, I can't get up. It's the social robot, it doesn't want to have people staring at me, thinking that I've just been chased from my table. So I'll just have to prove to this woman that I'm being truthful and that my motives are far from ulterior.

"Well," I say. "We're both people, both humans, can't we just talk and have a meal together? It doesn't all have to be premeditated, does it?"

"Nonsense," she snorts. "No man sits down with a strange woman unless he wants something!"

"Perhaps. You could be right there. But what if that something is just be a nice, normal conversation?"

"Bullshit!" She leers at me. It's unclear whether she's angry at me for getting her hopes up or if she thinks she can force my hidden attraction for her to the surface. And it's also unclear what she's willing to do to resolve this ambiguity. Will she make a scene? Will she actually attack me?

This is Sam Fox all over again!

I start to perspire. My only hope here is to pass out. Get swallowed up by a gray mist and suddenly find myself at home, hours from now, wondering how I got there.

The woman gets up. "Fuck you!" she says, spitting out the words like venom. "I can do much better than you anyway!"

She leaves our table and suddenly the world becomes a little brighter, a little less oppressive. It's like cloud cover breaking and letting in warm, gentle sunlight.

I wipe my brow and take a few deep breaths. This wasn't exactly the effect I was going for, but perhaps a hearty dose of relief is as powerful as a drop of dopamine.

I take out my tablet and start scribbling wise-isms. Weird as it was, this encounter has actually given me some ideas about the fairness and purpose of physical attraction.

YouTube script:

Successful relationships have a good balance between physical and emotional attraction. Both ingredients have to be in the mix and at sufficient levels. It's easy to say that physical appearance shouldn't matter, or that you can always turn to a friend for good conversation, but that's doing the human organism a disservice. We're just not built that way.

Think back to that time you talked to a stunning female, one who is attractive beyond compare, but, as soon as she opened her mouth, nothing but a stream of platitudes came out. You were immediately turned off because no amount of beauty can compensate for a lack of personality. Talking to her was like being alone, only it was less interesting.

Logically the reverse must also be true. Oodles of personality won't make you attractive. And starting out a relationship without physical attraction would be an equally bad start to a long journey.

[chart# picture of beach – perhaps use google images instead of crayons?]

I see a long term relationship as a rock in the surf. A great big stone on the beach of life. It's strong, magnificent, tall. However, waves will be crashing into it relentlessly. It is going to wear down, microscopic bit by microscopic bit.

Now a huge rock will still have a lot of presence after twenty years. But a small pebble not so much.

So are you going to start out with a huge rock? Are you going to start a relationship with enormous amounts of emotional and physical attraction? ~~Or are you going to settle for someone with nothing more going for them than a pair of colored contacts and some stolen ear catchers?~~

[sign off]

29

Observation:

Never assume you're the only one courting a woman. Right now she's secretly talking to a couple of other guys to expand her options.

A chime from my tablet tells me I have a new comment. I follow the link and end up on a very old post. A quick check of the page tells me this is actually the very first vid I ever made, which was posted under my real name, on a forgotten YouTube channel.

This vid only ever received three hits, two of them probably being mine. In online terms it's less visible than a needle in a stack of needles in a warehouse filled with stacks of needles. The only way to find it is to search for it specifically, so who could have found it?

Before I can read the comment, though, a flock of loud teenagers descends upon the table next to mine and starts throwing fries at me.

This is neither warranted nor provoked.

It's also not the first time this has happened to me.

I have no idea how teenagers the world over instinctively know that I'm one of their targets. I can only assume it's one of those things the universe enjoys doing to me.

I calmly gather my stuff and get up. The joke is on them; they've only succeeded in having me abandon a table I was finished and starting my brain on the path to a previously unknown brilliant-ism. (Including, but not limited to, coining the term *brilliant-ism*).

For instance, right now I'm laying bare the intricate patterns behind optimal food-court table choice. (Not too close to other occupied tables, but not so far from the main crowd so as to attract attention.)

I'll have to write that down soon. Meanwhile, though, I head to the parking garage and try not to wonder what Emma is doing at this very moment. In fact, I detour all the way around the Shoppe so we can't accidentally meet.

Back in the car, I take out my tablet to read the mysterious comment.

From: OldMan1951
Hey kid!

I know I ambushed you the other night and that wasn't fair. You need time to think, I get that. You were always a big thinker. Even before you could walk, you'd crawl around the room with a big, solemn frown on your face. There was always some kind of war going on in your head.

But now you've had some time and maybe you decided you want to meet up. I'll be at the Dragon and Wolf in the old neighborhood around 7 tonight. You don't have to come, I won't hold it against you if you don't, but I'll be there just in case.

- Dad

I put my tablet away and start the car. Traffic is mild and I circumnavigate pensioners and housewives with ease, which isn't good, because it allows my mind to wander, letting ancient thoughts re-surface. They pop up like pieces of a giant puzzle that I could never finish. A puzzle that was missing its box lid so I never knew what the picture was supposed to look like.

Some of the puzzle-piece thoughts go like this: Unbeknownst to Mom and myself, Dad was a secret agent. Maybe not exactly like in the movies, he was never all that physical, or heroic, but then, life isn't like the movies. He could've had a desk job. Some clerical function with an agency that tracked people. Bad people. And some of those bad people tried to follow him home, so he had to go into hiding. He couldn't tell us because any communication would lead the bad people to us. He was keeping us safe by staying away.

Other puzzle-piece thoughts head off in a very different direction: The stacks of letters that Dad did actually send me, chronicling his life and exploits in great detail, were intercepted by Mom. Angry about the way he left she decided to sabotage our relationship. Eventually Dad stopped calling, too, because Mom would always tell him I didn't want to talk. It would take two decades and a neighbor explaining the internet to him for Dad to get around this roadblock.

And some of the puzzle-piece thoughts are far more vague: I may never know all details surrounding Dad's disappearance, but whatever the greater picture, some terrible mystery must certainly underlie it all.

I arrive at work and push the puzzle away. These thoughts were unbecoming for a child of my severe intelligence and I certainly have no business entertaining them now. It's strange, the more I tell myself the old man doesn't deserve my attention, the more resources my brain dedicates to him. Eventually the load might get so high I'll have no option but to hold Dad responsible, making him pay rent for the parts of my brain he's been squatting in all these years.

The day drones on in that senseless way it has and when I get home,

Mom greets me at the door in her bathrobe and curlers. I notice there's no hint of kilos of shredded letters about her.

There never is.

"I'm going to talk to Dad," I inform her.

She follows me into the living room without saying a word. When I turn on the TV she finally asks me one question; "Do you really think that's a good idea?"

"Of course not," I tell her. "It's a terrible idea. One of the worst I've had in years. But, I'm doing it anyway."

Mom considers this a moment, then gives me an almost invisible nod. "Okay," she says. "Then that's what you'll do."

The Dragon and Wolf is what you'd get if a British pub was raped by an American diner and its offspring was raised by Romanians. From the chic grade-F upholstery to the cheap laminated picture menus, this place is wrought with internal contradiction and crimes against style and consistency.

I enter knowing full well that Dad might not show – or, if he does, he's likely to be a few decades late. But, before claiming one of the partly upholstered, partly laminated booths, I still do a quick check, just to make sure Dad isn't already there.

Few things are as silly as two people waiting for each other at opposite sides of a diner.

I find Dad at the third booth in.

My cell buzzes as I sit down but I ignore it. I can't deal with more people right now, even partially virtual ones. In fact, I feel a bit woozy. This whole moment seems surreal, as if I'm watching some other son sit down with some other dad for some other long overdue conversation. And I can't help but wonder how they'll do.

It doesn't help that this whole situation reminds me of the nightmare I had about my dad a couple of night ago.

"I'm glad you came," Dad says. He shoots me a careful smile.

He looks different from the other night, but also the same. It's as if I'm seeing him for the first time in twenty years all over again. I try to recognize him from photos and overused memories. Scan his face for similarities with the one I see in the mirror every morning. I decide his is more angular, with sunken eyes that sit slightly closer together. The hair is lighter, an almost white kind of grey, and the millions of lines crossing his face make me think of parchment.

"I just have a couple of questions," I tell him.

It's strange how thin my voice sounds. It must be some weird acoustic feature of the diner.

"Of course," Dad says. "I didn't expect anything less."

Looking at him now, I already have one important answer.

All those faces I saw in the crowd, all those times I caught someone's gaze and wondered *'Are you him? Are you my dad?'* It never was. Not once. I haven't seen this guy in years.

I compose myself. "I'd appreciate some straight answers."

He nods. "Fire away."

Let's just start with the big question, shall we?

"Why did you walk out on us?"

Dad looks pained. "You don't believe in mincing words, do you," he says. "I don't suppose you'd prefer to start with something easier? Like, How's it going? What are you up to? That kind of thing?"

"Not really, no."

We've wasted decades already, let's not drag this out any further.

"I suppose not." He smiles ruefully. "You always were a determined kid. Very focused."

"I suppose I was."

"Okay, then." He blows on his coffee, ordering his thoughts. "It's not really that simple," he says. "I never actually made the decision to walk out on you."

"And yet Mom and I have been living alone for twenty years."

Dad nods thoughtfully. "True. But it wasn't like I just woke up one morning and decided to vanish. I'm not sure what your mom told you, but there were things that happened, over a long period of time, after which we found we'd re-established the whole way we approached the situation."

"What the hell's that supposed to mean?"

"Look at it this way: don't you agree that, in any given situation, you should do the very best you can? Find whatever scenario optimally fits everyone in that situation and try to approximate it?"

"Of course I do," I say. "That's the only way to approach life."

"Okay, well, sometimes finding the optimal solution is more of an organic thing. A complex process that needs to grow and change, go through a series of iterations before it settles on a final shape."

I look out the window. Life seems so much simpler outside. The people passing by the window all have easier lives than I do. The world is much nicer to them.

I swallow. I suddenly have this weird sense of déjà vu.

"And sometimes," Dad continues. "Sometimes you come across a situation that has no optimal answer. No solution that fits all the people involved. Maybe there isn't even a solution that fits anybody involved."

"Even *if* that made sense," I say, giving Dad a hard look. "And even if I understood a fraction of what you think you're saying, you were still my dad. You didn't have to leave *me*. You could've just left Mom. What did I ever do to you?"

Dad sips his coffee. He doesn't look at me. I'm suddenly reminded of the heartless bastard from my dream. The dad who denied that I was a real person. The one who let me get stuck in sidewalk gum. But I realize that this dad, the one in front of me, has at least one differentiating characteristic. The hand holding his coffee cup, it trembles ever so slightly. This guy is not unaffected. There's a lot going on inside him as well.

I decide to stay and hear him out.

He clears his throat. "I was broken," he says, still not looking at me. "There were just so many things I couldn't get right, no matter how hard I tried. I didn't know if I could be fixed and I didn't know how long it would take."

"You're still not making any sense," I mumble.

He tries again. "All I knew was that I didn't want my brokenness to break you two as well. A dad should be..." His voice catches. He takes a breath, then another sip. "A dad should never be a burden."

Part of my anger dissipates. Maybe I started out this conversation being angry at the dad from my dream. He was just so cold and distant. But this guy is different. Not better, necessarily, he still left us, he still didn't call me on my birthdays, but, well, he seems less deliberately guilty.

This guy is just... helpless.

"You were better off without me," he says. "Even though I didn't want to, I did the best thing I had the capacity to do, which was to not get in your way." He finally looks up at me. "If you only believe one thing I tell you today," he says, "believe that leaving you was the hardest thing I ever had to do."

Some time passes.

We both look in different directions at nothing in particular.

"Then why do it?" I finally manage.

Dad searches my face for a moment, trying to figure something out. "You really don't remember?"

I suddenly feel very cold.

"In your mind," he says, "when did I actually leave?"

"A long time ago. I was little, maybe ten."

"But what happened just before I left?"

"I don't know."

And I don't want to talk about it anyway. There's no point in sending my mind to that place.

Also, it's suddenly freezing in here.

The AC must be broken.

"Think back," Dad urges.

"No." I get up. "I have to go. I don't have time to listen to this nonsense. I have things to do."

"Already? But we still have so much to talk about." He reaches out to try and stop me, I stumble back.

"Look," he says. "It's terrible what happened to you, to me, to all of us, and we can't change how we got here, but we can choose to—"

"I can't," I blurt out. "I don't have the time."

I rush from the Dragon and Wolf, it's the only way to stop Dad talking.

Back in the car, I take out my tablet. I desperately need to write a script. I need a lightning rod or something uncool will happen to my brain. Things don't feel right, as if something's trying to dislodge itself, wriggle loose. I have to fill my head with thoughts that do not, in any way shape or form, include, or lead to, my dad, my past, or my Emma.

Luckily a topic has been fermenting at the back of my mind. A nice safe subject with many intriguing angles for me to ponder.

Ever since I went shoe shopping with Mom an annoying mystery involving the female brain has been nagging at me. From time to time little ideas have sprung up and insight has eventually developed. What's more, there's an important side effect to this mystery that all men should know about. Immediately. So this is what my mind should be working on right now. This and this alone.

30

Pitch perfect e.c:

I love your shoes. They're really cute!
I'm kidding, of course. I haven't looked at your feet all evening.

YouTube script:

Here's a conversation that has never taken place:

Man 1: Did you see that chick?
Man 2: You mean the one with the seriously fashionable Italian shoes?
Man 1: Of course I mean the one with the seriously fashionable Italian shoes! Who else?
Man 2: Damn right I saw her! You don't think I'd overlook shoes like that, do you?
Man 1: I'd love to date a girl with that kind of fashion sense!

Without having heard even a millionth of a millionth of the conversations that have taken place on this planet, I can say with certainty that this conversation has never, and will never, take place.

Ask any man to describe any pair of his girlfriend's shoes and he'll draw blanks. Men simply do not store that kind of information. It's not useful to us. It'd be an inefficient use of storage space. In fact, put a man on a beach in flip-flops for a week and ask him to describe his own shoes back home and he'll probably describe a pair he owned in high school. If he describes anything at all. More likely he'll just run away to find a ball or a monster truck. Shoes can't hold our attention (barring a few outliers with sneaker collections).

[hold up chart #1]

It's a universal truth that most guys own exactly three pairs of shoes:

1. His normal shoes.
2. His sports shoes.
3. His previous pair of normal shoes*

*) this pair isn't worn but he's afraid to throw them out. He'll need them if-and-when he loses his current shoes in a freak shoe-related incident. Or when he has to paint the house. This pair will be thrown out on the day a *new* new

pair is acquired. That's when his current pair becomes his previous pair – it'll be like a changing of the guards.

Women, on the other hand, have a secret mission. Subconsciously they feel the need to obtain a single pair of shoes for each day of the year. They may not realize this, but ask any woman who owns less than 365 pairs of shoes whether she has enough shoes, and you'll have your answer.

So where does this shoe-fetish come from? For guys the whole situation seems kind of random. Why shoes? Why not head bands? Or gloves? Or painted twigs for that matter? It's such an arbitrary choice of things to obsess over, and one that is not at all practical. For one thing, shoes are always far away, all the way down where the dirt and the dog shit is. That place we never really look, and where things can easily get covered up by a pant leg.
It's the first thing we take off when we get home because we don't want to get the carpet dirty, and it's the first thing we put on when we think there's glass on the floor. It's the fashion equivalent of a wet dog.

Furthermore, there isn't much room for improvement. There's no real future from a design standpoint. Shoes will always be either shaped roughly like a foot or they'll be mostly unusable. All you can really do is cover them with different colored bits that have no function.

But perhaps the most baffling thing is how all women everywhere have at least a mild shoe-fetish. What happened? Did they get together one day and make a unanimous pact to devote major time and financial resources to shoes? And since when can women make unanimous decisions anyway? Any why weren't we men invited? Don't we have a say in the matter? More importantly, was there any cake?

But what confuses men is why women bother. After all, haven't men made it painfully clear what they look at? Don't women know that list is very, very short?

[hold up chart #2]

Here it is, in order of importance:

1. Her eyes.
2. Her tits.
3. Her ass.*

*) notice the absence of shoes? That's because we're not aware of them. In fact, if you have nice enough eyes, we won't even notice if you've been going barefoot all evening.

So it's unlikely to have anything to do with us. Sadly, that doesn't mean we don't need to break our heads over it.

[hold up chart #3]

The important thing about shoes is this:

- She *will* pay attention to *your* shoes.
- Yes She will!
- She'll notice them right away.
- And she'll form an opinion of you, *based on your shoes*!

Yup.
So we'd better get with the program, find out what kind of impression our shoes are making on the women around us. Who knows what kind of secret message our current pair is sending out? It could be anything! Some decoding is needed here! We have an opportunity to send a very precisely calculated signal using just our shoes, if we manage to crack the shoe-code. Clearly men should pool their resources and get some scientists on this. In the meantime, though, it seems safe to assume that a clean, expensive looking pair is a good way to go.

[sign off]

Video #159 by *Leverage*. Views: 327

Comments:

LoveLost: (8:59 pm) You're so right! I just wear shoes that are comfortable. That's what they're for, right? To keep your feet off the cold, hard ground? You don't get Italian style hardhats do you? Coveralls that go out of style every 6 months? Can't we all just agree to stop looking at each other's shoes and evaluate each other based on our minds? It will save our country billions each year! That's enough to feed all hungry people *and* send them to the moon!

DissonantMelody: (9:27 pm) This post is hilarious, and so true!

Johnniesgrl: (9:36 pm) My boyfriend had this old broken smelly pair that I couldn't get him to throw out, not until I got him another pair!

2ForWendy: (9:39 pm) So funny! I had to move recently, total number of boxes of shoes: 5! I don't think I've even worn most of them in years, but I just couldn't throw them out! This guy is hilarious!!

SallyKnowsWorst: (9:41 pm) This is a really funny channel. I love these off-beat comedy channels!!

Leverage: (10:27 pm) This is not a comedy channel! This channel is the result of years of serious research!

2ForWendy: (10:28 pm) You're right SallyKnowsWorst, this guy is hilarious!! I just checked out some of his other posts, I love the one about Hair Pulling and the one about Visiting Funerals. Leverage, I don't know how you come up with this stuff, do you have a writing team? You should work for Comedy Mainstreet!

Arnie: (10:28 pm) The following question has been nagging at me for years and this seems like the perfect place to ask…
So we all know that when you have 3 empty urinals in a public restroom, you always take the one at the end. This way the next guy can take the urinal at the other end, leaving an empty urinal between you.
Never stand next to a peeing man if you don't have to.

But today I was confronted by a new combination in the urinal dilemma. Of the 3 urinals, no.1 was in use, no.2 was empty, and no.3 was flushing! And the guy who had just used no.3 was washing his hands. Ideally, I would of course take urinal no.3, keeping an empty urinal between me and the other peeing guy, but, as stated, that one was still 'warm' from its previous occupant.

Should I:
1) take clean, empty urinal no.2, but thus stand next to a peeing guy.
2) leave an empty urinal between me and the other guy, but stand at a urinal that is still flushing.

WhipCrck: (10:34 pm) You still take urinal 3, but you walk over really really slowly to give it time to stop flushing.

OnMyWay: (10:49 pm) Idiots! You stand in the corner and pee on the floor!

Leverage: (10:57 pm) Get off my channel, all of you!!!

Arnie: (10:57 pm) How about using the second wash basin. I think that, given the circumstances, the other guys would understand the necessity of putting it in play.

OnMyWay: (11:09 pm) Sure, if you're embarrassed about peeing on the floor, then just use the wash basin. But make sure to 'flush' with cold water, not hot. Because **that** would be gross :)

31

Observation:

Things that don't really matter take up about 90% of our time.

My week turns out to be strangely unproductive. Even though I have oodles of time, I can't concentrate enough to catch up on my gaming, graphic novel reading, or backup making. Luckily Mom doesn't ask me about my meet-up with Dad, and that suits me just fine.

I do come up with a wise-ism for a new vid. One that'll rebalance the forces of light and darkness on my channel, show my followers I'm not trying to create a comedy channel.

But by Saturday things start to deteriorate much more rapidly. It begins with my cell ringing with an unknown number.

"Hey you!" a chipper voice says. "How's it going?"

The voice is endlessly sexy without a hint of irony. I instantly recognize the mismatched vocal stylings of Samantha Fox, my nemesis.

"Hello Samantha," I say, turning to Mom to mouth silently: '*You gave her my mobile number?*'

To which Mom shrugs and mouths back: '*What else could I do? I can see when my boy is hurting. You're in a terrible slump and the sooner you get over that nut-girl the better off we'll all be.*'

Of course I might be paraphrasing here, lip reading isn't my strongest suit.

"So," Samantha says, "when are you picking me up?"

"Sorry?"

"You can't still be grounded, can you? Let's go out. You promised."

I shoot a desperate look at Mom, but she just smiles.

"You know," I say, trying to doggy paddle towards a different subject. "I heard you just broke up with your boyfriend."

"Oh, you did?"

"Yup."

"Well," Sam says, "we didn't really break up, because he wasn't really my *real* boyfriend. He was more of a guy friend. We kind-of, sort-of just stopped hanging out. That's all that was."

"Either way, let me give you some advice," I say. "What do you know about the Kübler-Ross grief cycle?"

"The Kirby-what?"

"The Kübler-Ross grief cycle is a psychological cycle which I've adapted for break ups. It could really help you."

"Great! Why don't you explain it to me over a cup of coffee?"

"No," I say. "It turns out that this particular adaptation of the cycle is best explained over the phone. In a very short conversation. After which it is best to hang up and spend some time thinking about it. Alone."

"Oh." Samantha sounds disappointed. "Are you sure you don't–"

"Here's the thing," I say. "When you break up with someone, you go through several stages of loss. Most people make the mistake of thinking they just need to get over one thing, one silly little person, but in reality there are three separate losses you need to deal with."

"That's not really–"

"First, of course, there's the most obvious loss; the loss of a specific person in your life. In this case your kind-of, sort-of boyfriend. You have to get over the fact that you won't be seeing him, listening to him, touching him, sharing thoughts and fantasies with him."

"Well, we only went on two dates so we didn't ha–"

"Then, when the sharpest memories of your time together start to fade, you still have to get over two more losses. That's where most people trip up. They forget they still need to get over 'not having an exciting new relationship in their lives'. This means not having any intimate little meetings to look forward to. Wonderful messages to fret over all day. They completely forget they have to accept that their days will go back to being long and boring, the way they were before."

"Oh, don't worry," Samantha breathes sexily. "I'm not bored at all. I have so many friends and hobbies and–"

"Then, if-and-when you manage all that, you still have the third and final loss to recover from. And this is the most difficult loss of all."

I pause for effect.

But not long enough for Sam to get a word in.

"You have to actively mourn 'the life that you thought you were going to have'. You have to mourn your planned future. No longer is it wrapped up nicely with this other person. It's now just a long empty stretch of time that you don't know what to do with. This huge vacuous thing that needs to be reassigned and which will make you feel superfluous until you do."

There's a heavy silence on the line.

I think I've actually reached her. If so, I've not only rescued myself from another bad date, I've also helped her move on to a much better, healthier place. I'm actually pretty cool.

The only thing that worries me is that Samantha hasn't hung up yet.

"You know," she finally says. "You're kind of a downer."

"Me?" Where is this coming from? I'm her savior! "I'm just helping you, that's all."

"Not really. You're depressing me."

"I—"

"On second thought, I don't think I *want* to see you again."

And with a sharp click Samantha Fox disappears from my life.

"Well?" Mom looks at me expectantly. She can barely stop herself hopping from foot to foot. "Tell me everything!"

"I just gave Samantha some advice," I say. "Now she needs to go and think about it."

I put my cell away and head up to my room.

"Wait," Mom calls after me. "When's the date? Do I need to do any ironing, or are you going to wear that nice tux jacket again?"

I slam my door to shut the world out. As lousy as I felt at breakfast, I actually feel worse now. Which makes no sense. Not only did I craftily manage to get out of a future date with Samantha, I'm pretty sure I got out of all future dates with Samantha.

It's actually pretty amazing, the way I made her believe that I'm a depressing downer of a guy. And I did it all subconsciously. Even when I'm not trying, I'm still a genius.

I should be feeling great.

Grey light filters through the blinds and washes the color from my room. It's probably going to rain all day.

I spend an hour or so browsing old vids, remembering the good old days when my viewers didn't think I was being ironic. I also find myself wondering if Dad is still following my vids, now that we've met up. He didn't mention them, so I have no idea what he thinks of my thoughts and wise-isms. Does he still think of me as a little kid with obvious little kid observations, or does he…

I push it away. I shouldn't be thinking about that. At least I wasn't thinking about Emma, though. In fact, I should congratulate myself for not thinking about Emma for a while. For days, actually. Apart, of course, from occasional moments like this one when I stop to congratulate myself for not thinking about her.

I close the tab with my channel and check my list, my heartache cure, just to see what else I could be doing. I really should try harder to keep myself pre-occupied, but that's easier said than done. I check my messages. A new private message has just popped up on my channel from Eddy the Lizard. He writes that he and Antonov are at the mall and need my help desperately. It's a matter of life-or-death. He's added his number.

I consider this for a long, dark moment.

It's not that I want to see them, it's more that I want to not see them even less.

Meeting up with the guys could actually be a bit like going to a funeral, I suppose. Or watching a sad movie. Or standing outside a hospital greeting sick people. Another reminder that, however bad life gets, there are always people doing worse, and therefore I should be grateful.

It'd be like mental slumming.

I decide to give it a go. I get dressed, tell Mom I'll be gone for a few hours, and head out.

It takes me a while to locate the guys, even though they send me a slew of messages in which Antonov gives me GPS coordinates (which I don't think are accurate) and Eddy passes on cryptic location descriptions (which I have no hope of deciphering). I have no idea why they do this until I accidentally run into them at the back of the North wing. Their outfits tell me the whole story. They're dressed entirely in black and have utility belts. Antonov even sports a pair of expensive looking night vision goggles.

They appear to be deep under cover.

Although I can't say that they don't stand out.

Eddy pulls me down behind the large potted plants they're using as a hiding place.

"What the hell are you guys doing?" I ask.

Eddy quickly peers over the plants before hissing, "Antonov, debrief him!"

Antonov huffs. "Don't you mean: *brief* him?"

"How so?"

Antonov shrugs. "De-brief you do after mission. Brief you do before mission."

"You sure?"

"Yes, very sure."

"Okay, so brief him already!"

Antonov turns to me. "Here is deal," he whispers. "We have group of selected females cornered at table. We follow them all morning, gathering intel."

"Yeah," the Lizard chimes in. "They've been to seventeen shoe stores, two delis, and threw some coins into the fountain." He thinks this over. "Our intel suggests it was approximately two dollars and seventy-nine cents."

"Da," Antonov continues. "And they visit bathroom. For very long time."

The lizard nods. "We have no reliable data on what goes on in there."

Antonov hands me his binoculars. "Now we are ready to move in for kill. We need your help." He points out over the plants. "It's group drinking coffee at table."

I refuse to use the binoculars but I nod as if I understand perfectly

174

who these lunatics are talking about.

"We need help initiating contact," Eddy says. His eyes dart around, scanning perhaps for mall security, wayward boyfriends, or enemy aircraft. I suddenly have very strong feelings about heading home. Simply running away and never contacting these guys again. And I would. I might even defy my social robot to do it, but then I'd just end up alone in my room doing nothing and, strangely enough, I'd rather stay here and see what happens next.

Eddy gives me a fierce look. He's started chewing some kind of dehydrated food from his utility belt. "How should we proceed, sir?"

Antonov moves his hand over what I hope is not a smoke grenade sticking out of his belt and adds, "We are 100% ready for action."

"Well," I say. "I guess one way to go about this would be to walk up to them and, you know, just start a conversation."

Eddy and Antonov share a look. Information passes between them silently, then Eddy nods. "Yes," he says. "It's so crazy it might actually work."

Antonov agrees. "Yeah, enemy will never see that coming."

Eddy puts his jerky back into his belt.

Then, for a long time, nothing happens.

"So," I say. "Do you want me to lead the way?"

Here's a sigh of relief. "Sure," Antonov says magnanimously. "You go, we cover you." He slaps me on the shoulder. "We got your back."

I step out from behind the plants and walk towards the girls. I don't think I've ever been so relieved to get away from people I know while moving towards people I don't know.

Context really is everything.

As I cross a busy mall intersection, I look back and see that Antonov and The Lizard still haven't moved. They're watching my approach intently. Eddy gives me a thumbs up, then ducks back behind the plants.

I reach the girls' table and do another quick check. The guys are finally on the move, but they appear to be making weird flanking maneuvers. Eddy's circling in from the east, keeping low while sneaking from cover to cover. Antonov is coming from the west, using the cover of incoming sunlight to hide his approach – which would be a smart move, if only it wasn't still raining.

Meanwhile, I'm acutely aware of the fact that I can still bail on them.

I can be in my car in less than five minutes.

However, I also notice how relaxed I feel. I guess it's much easier to approach women on someone else's behalf – women I'm not actively interested in. Maybe I'll just do a quick introduction for the guys. How hard could that really be? And any rejection I suffer won't even reflect on me.

I'm suddenly reminded of one of my old vids on intros.

YouTube script:

Make sure to show a girl that you're different from other guys. Show her the real you, ~~but in an interesting way~~. Don't get scared and edit everything you say to sound PG, because they hear PG all day, it's boring.

Let's take one of my ECs as an example: "I read somewhere that all girls pee in the shower."

As you say this, face her and give her a serious yet quizzical look. "Is this true?" She might be too shocked to respond, but don't make the mistake of back-tracking. That'll make you look weak. Just wait and see if she: 1) walks away (she's probably not for you) or: 2) responds (there's still hope for her). If she's funny (or tries to be), stick around. Otherwise, move on.

[pause for effect]

This last bit is actually very important. It's important because if you're the one walking away, then you can always approach her again later. You showed her that her response wasn't interesting enough and she lost your attention. But if *she's* the one walking away, then any new approach will just seem desperate. Her subconscious will shut you down, ~~no matter how unbelievably perfect you might be together.~~ Never miss an opportunity to leave women alone.

[sign off]

32

Observation:

Anyone can be forgotten. I'm quite sure of that.
The only trick is really wanting to.

"Hey girls, how's it going?"

There are five girls at the table. I'd put their ages between twenty-five and thirty-five. The two blondes, two dark haired girls, and the redhead are all stylishly dressed and fairly pretty. One has an unfortunate nose-shape, another somewhat uneven ears. They look interesting. They sip lattés and appear to be in a nice, non-hostile mood.

"We're pretty good," one of the blondes says. She has greenish eyes and freckles. The other girls don't respond, they just share a look among themselves and giggle.

I take out a little notebook that I keep on my person for emergency info gathering and write all this down. There could be some valuable information in here for future vids. Meanwhile, I remember to smile and look somewhat mysterious, while simultaneous exuding a general air of general confidence.

The girls don't offer anything further by way of conversation but they do appear curious about what I'll say next.

Which I am too.

"My name is Leverage," I venture. "You may know me from my YouTube channel."

"Oh, are you going to interview us?" the blonde asks. She seems pleased. I make a note of this.

"Not really," I tell her. "Why do you ask?"

"Are you going to a funeral?" One of the dark haired girls wants to know.

I make a note of this too, and put an asterisk next to it. I'll have to find out more about girls' fascination with funerals. (If they're unfamiliar with my channel, then it's unlikely to be related to my vid on re-affirming life, so something else is going on here, and I want to know what it is.)

"I'm here to introduce you to a couple of very interesting guys," I tell them in the meantime.

"Really?" The girls look around. "Where are they?"

"Well, they might be making flanking maneuvers at the moment, it's difficult to say, but they should be here soon."

"It's not those weird guys with the binoculars who've been following us, is it?"

"Eh… I wouldn't know about that."

Eddy finally arrives. He takes up position next to me and gives me a nod.

"This is Eddy," I tell the girls. I think about adding something about his background and interests, but realize that all I know about him is his handle, 'The Lizard,' and I don't think that'd help his case. So, instead, I decide to go rogue.

"Eddy's a total freak," I tell the girls.

Eddy gasps.

"You wouldn't believe the things he gets up to."

One of the girls looks at Eddy disapprovingly, but the rest sit up. "Really?" the redhead asks. "Is he more freaky than me?"

"No one is more freaky than you," one of the other girls says.

They all start giggling. I'm not sure why. It may be a private joke. I make a note in my little book and briefly consider correcting the redhead's grammar, then decide it can probably wait.

Antonov arrives. "I am here," he announces.

The girls look at him with interest, but Antonov adds nothing more. He merely smiles at them, mysteriously.

I have taught him well.

"I can't really tell you anything about Antonov," I tell the girls. "Whatever I'd divulge would probably be highly classified. If you're lucky he'll tell you some things about himself, but they'll either be total lies or very dangerous facts."

Only one girl shakes her head at this, the rest seem at least mildly intrigued. They invite us to join them. Chairs are pulled up, tea and coffee is ordered, and the girls introduce themselves. There's an Adina, a Sue, two Rebeccas, and a Claire.

My guys soon fall into a groove. Whenever they're at a loss for words, or get a difficult question, they just smile mysteriously. This works even better than I'd imagined, weeks ago, when I made it up in my dark, empty room.

"That's an interesting belt," Claire says to Eddy. She runs a finger over his jerky and smiles approvingly.

I can't really tell whether her interest is genuine, and, if it is, if this is the kind of interest she reserves for potential mates, or for unexpected road accidents. Either way, Eddy's ecstatic.

"It's pretty cool, right?"

"Yeah," Adina nods. "I should get one of those to keep my lipsticks in."

"That is XR-15 utility belt!" Antonov barks. "Military issue! Is not for lipstick!"

"But it could be, right?" Adina smiles innocently.

"Well, yes. Technically could be," Antonov concedes. "But is not."

"And this compartment would be great for my compact mirror."

Antonov considers this. "Mirror would be good," he says. "Perhaps with telescopic handle, adjustable neck, rotating bezel. I think is good plan."

"You talk weird," one of the Rebeccas laughs. "Are you from Spain or something?"

"My heart belongs to mother Russia!"

"What about you," Sue asks me. "Did you say you're a tuber?"

"I'm more than a tuber," I tell her. "I'm a student of the human soul and psyche."

For some mysterious reason, Sue decides to roll her eyes at this, but Adina is interested. "What does that mean?" she asks.

"It means I observe humans and draw extrapolated conclusions which I report on on my channel so other humans can improve their lives without having to extrapolate for themselves."

Adina nods knowingly. "Yeah, I have the same thing," she says. "Like, I can totally tell when one of my friends is cheating on her boyfriend. They don't even have to tell me, I just *know*. It freaks them out."

Sue's started talking to one of the Rebeccas. I'm still trying to decode her eye-roll message which is difficult because she won't make eye-contact with me, no matter how hard I stare at her. Whatever she was trying to signal me, it's obviously something highly secretive.

The conversations bubble on for about an hour or so, with only the occasional awkward silence, but when the girls decide to take off, neither Eddy nor Antonov has the presence of mind to ask for a number. I'm not convinced there's a The One for them in this bunch, though, so I let it slide this time.

I never do find out what Sue wanted to signal me.

When I return home, Mom has vanished. Perhaps on another biscuit run. I hang my coat and head up the stairs. Before I reach the landing, though, my breath catches. There are clear signs that my inner sanctum has been compromised.

Someone's been in my room!

First of all, even though it's Saturday, there are no stacks of ironed laundry waiting outside my door – they must be inside already! Second, there's no vacuum cleaner with note attached stating by which insane deadline dust should be removed from my carpet. And third, my door's wide open. The lock has been brutalized beyond recognition!

Holding on to the banister, I keep climbing, reminding myself to breathe. When I reach my room, I notice that there *is* a note, but it's tacked to the inside of my door. It lets me know in no uncertain terms that now that I've taken to locking my door, I should expect to spend at least an hour a week repairing said lock, and, as my room is part of the main property, I'm liable for any and all damages incurred during access by the main occupant. Mom's added some docket numbers, which look frightfully real.

It appears she's finally retained legal counsel.

Our silent war has escalated, and I may need to acquire some shark-toothed counsel of my own.

I drop onto my bed and spot the final piece of evidence showing that the shrine to my nerdhood was desecrated: on my chart-building desk stands a foreign object. It's wrapped in purple wrapping paper.

My curiosity is peaked, for a moment I even forget that I'll have to follow an online course in lock-smith-ery – and perhaps acquire intimate knowledge of metallurgy – to restore my lock to its original splendor. I get up and weigh the foreign object in my hand.

It's light for its size, and feels fragile. There doesn't appear to be a note, but I decide its location implies I'm well within my rights to open it.

The wrapping paper flies off and the emerging item has me stunned. Not only because of its value, but also due to its high level of obscurity. I don't believe more than a handful of humans know what this is, or understand its rarity.

I hold it up to the light to make sure it's not an imitation. Or a copy. Or a reproduction of an imitated copy. Because this, honestly, cannot be real.

I can't find any fault. This really does appear to be a vintage Kenner Jawa figure from 1979, original and mint on card!

For the second time today I remind myself to keep breathing.

Turning it over and over, I find no signs that it's been doctored, reopened, or retrofitted. This is the real deal. Moreover, it's the version with the *plastic cloak*.

I've heard of these, but I've never actually seen one.

Some might say that the second edition of this figure, the one with the fabric cloak, looked better, more expensive. In fact, the fabric was added because the figure was so small, Kenner worried people would think it was overpriced. But, as only a few were ever produced with the original plastic cloak, it's this early version that has become highly collectible.

The plastic cloak Jawa is somewhat of a myth. These days, when you find one on an auction site, it's almost always a figure with a retrofitted cloak. A home brew made by a fan who Frankensteined a plastic cloak from a much less rare Obi-One figure.

Inside the wrapping paper I notice a folded note. It reads:

Dear son,

I know life's always seemed so difficult for you. Even when you were little, you had so much trouble connecting. It was just hard for people to understand how different you were, so they didn't always tread carefully. And I know you've been hurting lately. It breaks my heart to see you finally go out there and open up, only to get trampled.

There's nothing a mom can say to make that feeling go away, but I hope you won't give up. I hope you'll find a way to get past this and keep on going. You were doing so well!

I found this toy at a yard sale and I remembered you had a picture of it above your bed. Maybe it can lift your spirits, remind you that, however bad it gets, there are always people around who love you,

Mom

I fold the note away and place the Jawa on a special shelf, then go online to find a course on lock smithery. Perhaps I can get this lock fixed before Mom comes home. She'd like that.

I understand what happened here, of course. I'm not completely blind to the undercurrents that move the world. Obviously some poor guy moved out of his parent's house and they wasted no time putting his collectables up for sale. They may even surprise him with a couple of bucks on his next visit. *'Look what we got for your silly little toys,'* they'll say. After which he'll probably have a heart attack.

So I should feel guilty. I should go find this collector and reunite him with part of his treasure. But fair's fair; he abandoned it. He left it in the dangerous hands of his parents and thus this Jawa deserves a better home, a safer home. I'll hold on to it for now.

Plus, I wouldn't want to hurt Mom's feelings.

YouTube script:

Without wanting to sound overly dramatic, here's a very good reason you shouldn't kill yourself.

Let's skip over the beautiful flowers and sunsets and people who love you, shall we? As true as all that is, it obviously hasn't stopped anyone really devoted to their cause. This is because, secretly, we all know that life is inherently meaningless. Of course it is. We've just collectively decided to deploy a sophisticated set of filters to help us ignore that every single thing we assume has meaning is really just something we do to keep busy.

You think your hobby matters? Try not doing it for a day and see if the world ends. You think your business matters? Try shutting it down and see if anyone notices. ~~You think your significant other matters? Try introducing her to a guy with weird eyes and you'll see how fast she'll get over you.~~

Nothing you do, by definition, has any real meaning. It's all nonsense.

So you might as well end it, right? Especially if it's not that much fun to begin with. ~~If life seems more like an endless series of annoying trials than a hot pocket of wonderful opportunities.~~ In fact, you could end it tonight. Why not? And since you now only have a few precious hours left, why not spend them doing something really fun? Something you really love? Go out and have a really great, fun time!
Come to think of it, why not postpone it a little longer, and have *even more* fun? Why not postpone it, say, another fifty or sixty years? Or let nature do the deed for you? Just spend the rest of your limited time not worrying and go enjoy yourself.

[signoff]

33

Observation:

Not cool to say at work: I'm going to the toilet, you guys need anything?

The next morning I don a random selection of clothes and head down for breakfast. Mom's busy preparing pancakes. I take a plate and sit at the table.

"Sleep well?" she asks.

"I don't really recall," I tell her. "I wasn't consciously participating."

Mom nods. She scoops the first batch of pancakes onto my plate and I realize there hasn't been much complaining lately. Nor have we found reasons to start new arguments. This is a weird time for us.

I haven't mentioned the present she left in my room and she hasn't thanked me for the expert job I did repairing my lock. I think we're on the same page here, though, it's just that neither of us is good at saying 'thank you.' We've had so little practice that saying it now would feel awkward. Forced. So we don't. And we're the same about saying 'sorry'. Our way of letting each other know that we're sorry is to simply drop an issue and move on.

We're kind of cool that way.

The toast pops up and Mom brings me my portion, then returns to the counter to do more mom-ing.

"So," she says over her shoulder, "how did it go with your dad?"

Oh.

Are we doing this? Right now?

"Well," I say, gathering my thoughts, "he wasn't dead, that's one thing." I prod the toast. "I guess it's fair to say that your reports on that matter were greatly misleading."

"Did he look okay?" Mom continues, still not turning around. "Healthy and everything?"

"I suppose." She doesn't sound as casual as she thinks she does, there's a definite edge to her voice. "He looked normal," I tell her. "You know, from what I could tell. Just a regular guy."

"Did he say anything... problematic?"

"Like what?"

Mom pauses for a second, then says, "Did he want to talk about the past?"

183

"The past? Like Columbus and ancient Rome? Not really, no. Somehow it failed to come up."

"You know what I mean," she says. "Did he talk about what happened before he left?"

I feel a sudden chill.

"I don't want to talk about it, Mom."

"Neither do I," she sighs.

I realize she's not actually doing anything. She's not mom-ing at all, she's just moving plates back and forth between two stacks on the counter.

"Good," I say. "I'm glad we've cleared that up–"

"But," she says, "I think we *should* talk about it, don't you?"

I don't. In fact, I suddenly want to get the hell out of here.

"We could never agree on how to handle it," Mom says, her voice small now. "Your dad and I had very different ideas on what to tell you and what not to."

"I really don't have time for this. I have to go."

"No, you should listen." She clears her throat. "I think… I think maybe I made a mistake. A very big mistake–"

"You didn't," I cut her off. "Whatever you did, it was fine. I'm okay. Everything is okay. So let's just finish breakfast and forget about this."

Mom shakes her head. "We can't go on like this."

"Yes we can. Whatever it is you want to tell me, you don't need to. I'm fine with the way things are. Just let it be."

"But you're *not* fine," she says, her voice trembling. "And *I'm* not fine. And your father…"

"He didn't say anything, okay? He didn't mention anything bad, so we don't have to talk about this, whatever it is."

"Your father was right," she pushes on, still facing the wall. "I never should have tried to shield you from this. I shouldn't have locked away our old stuff…"

I look at the door. It's really close.

"I just thought this way would be easier for you."

Luckily, she still hasn't turned around. I don't think I could stand her looking at me right now.

"All I wanted," she says, "all I tried to do, was to stop your pain. I never thought what I did would end up hurting you more."

I send panicked commands to my legs: start moving already!

"I'm so sorry," Mom whispers. "I really hope you know… I hope you understand… it wasn't your fault. None of it was your fault." She clears her throat. "It wasn't anybody's fault."

With herculean effort I get my robot body moving. Slowly at first, but picking up speed along the way. Mom goes on talking, I can't stop her, but I can preoccupy my mind while I drag myself from the room. I can

184

stop my brain from absorbing whatever it is she's saying.

At work I struggle to keep my mind in check. It won't listen to reason, though. Something is trying to drag my thoughts towards darkness.

It's almost as if the more I try not to think about what Mom was saying, the more I do.

Thankfully, crazy Lenora pops up out of nowhere to distract me.

"I found her!"

She stands on tip-toes to peer over my cubicle wall. She looks insanely happy.

"Who?" I ask.

Lenora waves her cell by way of explanation. The display shows a selfie of her holding a distraught looking pet.

"My cat! Can you imagine?"

I tell her I'm not sure, I've never tried.

"How many times have you heard of that actually happening? How many times have you heard of a cat going missing and then being found again?"

I have no idea. "Almost never?"

"That's exactly right! It almost never happens!" She claps her hands excitedly – which I feel, even given the circumstances, is still a bit much.

"I'm very happy for you," I tell her. "And please feel free to take this opportunity to remove all your flyers." I point at my cubicle wall, where she's stuck quite a number of her pleas for help.

"Of course!" she beams. "Oh! Sandy! Have you heard the great news? I found my cat!"

Sandy's vicarious excitement is so immediate, so intense, I fear she might faint. Luckily she leads Lenora away to share the good news with the rest of the department. Happy times all round.

Of course this means my cubicle wall remains helplessly marred by impromptu cat literature.

Almost instantly my dark thoughts try to return. My inner voice wants to analyze that thing Mom and Dad are trying to dredge up. But I can't let that happen. I never want my mind to go to that place again so I dig up one of my old YouTube scripts and start reading. I examine all the brilliant-isms while I remind myself that, no matter how badly Mom and Dad think it affected me, there really is nothing wrong with my beautiful little brain.

34

YouTube Script:

Always be mindful of the three minute rule!

When you meet a woman for the first time you have exactly three minutes to make her feel attracted to you. If you don't do anything in the first three minutes to show her that you're different, that you're special, she'll subconsciously put you in the Friend Zone. And guys in the friend zone have as much chance of marrying a girl as her brother does, or her Nigerian pen pal.

I repeat: once you're in the Friend Zone, it's impossible to get out.
Greater men than you have tried, greater men than you have failed.
To even have a chance of getting out, you'd have to do something HUGE, like save her cat, and her grandma, from a burning tree, that's falling off a cliff. And even then I'd say your chances were slim.

Here's the mistake most guys make. They have a good time with a girl, laughing, talking about all the things they have in common, and they think they're 'in'. There is such a strong connection, it must be going well, right?

Wrong. A girl can think you're the funniest guy in the world, hang on your every word, and still turn around and sleep with someone she meets a minute later. She can make all those connections with you without ever feeling any kind of emotion other than just 'having fun'. Similarly, she can think a guy is only kind of funny and mildly interesting and still be attracted to him.

[change to cam 2]

It all depends on your friend zone status. Once her subconscious has decided you're in the friend zone, the part of her brain that looks for potential mates gets switched off with regards to you. You are now simply a person, an amorphous mass of bio-matter, no longer a man in any functional way. You could turn into George Clooney overnight – with the looks, the money, the personality – and she still wouldn't notice. She now has an active blind spot that covers you completely.

Of course, this is contrary to popular belief, as TV and cinema have tried to teach us since the late 80s that a girl's best friend can become her lover. That it's inevitable, in fact. That, as long as you show her how much you care in some cool, publicly embarrassing way, she'll fall for you. But this is a lie. These shows were written by guys who were stuck in the friend zone themselves. They just wanted to wake girls up and destroy the friend zone in the process. Sadly, all they did was actually increase our chances of falling into the friend zone trap.

[back to cam#1]

But perhaps the opposite also holds true. If you ever find yourself in a situation where you worry about attracting an incompatible female, simply refrain from following any of my advice during the first three minutes of interaction.
You should be safe.

[sign off]

35

Mom avoids me for the next couple of days.

It's nothing too obvious, she doesn't actively ignore me or hide out in her room, she just happens to find things to do. I discover my dinner on the table with a note mentioning some vague knitting tournament. I find my breakfast with a note about sleeping in or buying biscuits. And when I watch TV, she just happens to need to clean another room.

Which suits me fine. I'm still trying to re-rail my brain. Get it back on track. Let it know it's working just fine and that it is in no way in need of new and scary information.

So the week passes more or less uneventfully until Friday, when I find a message from my dad on my channel. He asks if I've had time to get used to the idea of seeing him again and if I'm free for lunch.

I guess he really is serious about getting back in touch. Honestly, I half expected him to disappear again, having satisfied whatever small amount of curiosity made him look me up. But, maybe – just maybe – there's some truth to what he said. Maybe the bit about not wanting to leave but feeling he had to, maybe some of that wasn't an outright lie.

I wonder how I feel about that.

"Hey!" Quiton-James peers over my cubicle wall, grinning broadly. "How's it going, man?"

My heart sinks. I was hoping for some quiet time but it appears I'll be battling my office rival instead.

I quickly hit the send button to let my dad know what I think of his plan to meet, and, as I do, I experience this flash of trepidation. I really hope I didn't just make a big mistake.

Quiton-James waits impatiently. I'm sure he wants to tell me how unfair it is that Gharity now knows that most of his wins were actually mine. Or maybe he wants to trick me into doing something to make me look bad and him look good.

"Hello, Quiton-James," I say, making sure I sound appropriately exasperated. "It's a bit early for you, isn't it? Aren't you supposed to be sleeping in as per usual?"

Whatever trick he has up his sleeve, he can't get to me if I don't take the bait. And he can't bait me if he's too busy defending himself.

He shrugs. "Fair enough," he says. "I guess I've been a bit tardy lately."

"Don't worry," I tell him. "I understand perfectly. After all, there isn't much point coming in before we've done enough work for you to steal."

He reaches over and tries to pat me on the back but his stubby arms won't reach over my cubicle wall. "Yeah, sorry about that," he says. "For some reason Gharity assumed I was responsible for the Cristmodale report. I was going to set him straight but he just steamrolled over me. Gave me all this extra work. You know how he is."

"Sure."

"I guess I could've brought it up again another time," he continues, "but, well, it didn't seem all that important."

"I bet it didn't."

"Yeah. I mean, we're all on the same team, right? Any good report makes all of us look good."

"Yet some better than others."

He waves it away. "You know Gharity," he says. "He can't tell any of us apart." He chuckles conspiratorially. "To him this department is just an amorphous mass of financial-problem-solving matter."

He laughs at his own joke.

Given his casual demeanor, coupled with the Gharity-isms that do corroborate his story, one could be forgiven for believing him. But I don't fall for it. Nope. And it's definitely time for Quinton-James to leave. Right now.

"Well," I say, sidestepping his stream of generic conversational nonsense, "I'm sure you didn't come in early just to apologize to me. So, better get cracking."

"Oh, I'm in no hurry," he says. "I just wanted to punch in early so I can leave before five." He lowers his voice. "You see, I have a hot date tonight!"

"Of course you do."

"Yeah, I thought you'd want to know."

Now he's rubbing his social life in my face? Isn't making my workday a living hell enough for him?

He taps the side of his nose. "I need time to prepare. I'm sure you know what I mean."

"I'm sure I don't."

"Don't worry," he says, trying to pat me on the back again, really straining this time, and almost succeeding. "Your secret's safe with me." He taps his nose one more time, like an old-school super villain. "Got to go," he says. "Got to work on my ECs!" He winks and leaves.

It takes me a moment to realize what's just happened. Then I stare after him, not sure if I'm still supposed to hate him or not.

Life can be complicated.

"I'm glad you came."

Dad smiles encouragingly.

Again he looks different. I just can't get used to seeing him like this.

The little boy inside me still expects the man from the photographs. The guy with the big hair, that weird moustache, the orange shirts. But that guy no longer exists. It's a sharp reminder that no matter what we do from here on in, no matter how we decide to re-structure our lives, we can never get back what we lost. There are no do-overs. That little boy, he will never get his dad back.

I sit and order tea.

"I was worried I'd seen the last of you," Dad says.

I shrug. I wasn't sure I should come. There's real danger in being here. But I couldn't really stay away, either. After all, this is my dad. So, as long as we stay away from that one dark subject, I think it might be okay.

"So, does your mother know we're... talking?"

"She knows."

"And she's fine with it?"

"I wouldn't go that far."

"But she tolerates it?"

"I wouldn't go that far, either. Let's just say she's aware."

Dad nods. I notice he has two cups of coffee in front of him again. I wonder if he orders them for himself.

"Well," he says, giving me a long look. "How are you holding up?"

"I'm okay," I tell him. "Just battling the futility of existence on a day to day basis like the rest of humanity."

Dad smiles as if I've said something funny. "You always had a flair for the dramatic," he says. He smiles, remembering. "You had this strange, interesting way of looking at things. Your ideas always seemed so alien, so counter intuitive, but then you'd explain them to us, this little boy holding miniature lectures in the living room for his mom and dad, and suddenly it'd be impossible for us not to see the world through your eyes."

I shrug. "I have that kind of effect on people, I guess."

I sound pretty casual, but inside something's happening. Something warm and sticky. I'm not sure I like it. It doesn't feel entirely natural.

"Which explains why they gave you your own TV channel," Dad says.

"My what?"

He searches for words. "You know, your dating show."

"That's not a dating show, and it's not on TV. It's a YouTube channel chronicling my exploits in charting out the human condition."

"Sorry," Dad says. "You're on computer-TV. My neighbor explained it to me. Computer-TV is global. You're on every computer in the world."

"That's one way of looking at it."

"Don't sell yourself short," he says. "Don't you ever do that." He takes a breath. "I've read the comments," he says. "You're making a real

190

difference in people's lives. You're helping them through painful times. Not many people do that for others." He looks away. "You turned out so well, I don't think I can ever fully express how proud I am."

I suddenly feel very uncomfortable.

"I always was," he continues, his voice starting to crack. "I always knew you'd become someone special. I couldn't wait to see what you'd–"

He catches himself, takes a sip of one of his coffees.

The waitress takes forever to bring my tea. Perhaps she's off hand selecting the leaves somewhere in rural China.

Dad recovers. "That's why I couldn't risk my problems damaging you," he says. "I couldn't take the chance of you not becoming the person I knew you could be–"

I try to signal the waitress. Any old chemically processed leaves will be fine.

"So," dad says, clearing his throat. "I guess we should talk about what happened before I left."

I get that cold feeling again. "Maybe we shouldn't," I say. "You can't go back and fix it, Dad. You missed out and we can never get that time back. The only thing we can do is decide where we go from here."

He shakes his head. "When I left I knew your mom would handle it *her* way. And I knew that wasn't going to work... I should've pushed more."

"But you didn't."

"I didn't, but it's not over." He looks pained. "It's not like we passed that station and now it doesn't matter anymore."

"But it doesn't."

The waitress finally brings my tea. I blow on it and take a sip.

"There's this guy," my dad says. "A professional. He helped me a lot. It took me a while to find him, all the other guys were no good, or at least, they weren't right for me." He thinks it over. "It's a bit like your wise-isms," he says. "You really understand that most solutions are more about finding the right way of looking at a problem than anything else. Once you look at a problem the right way, the rest falls into place. So I got to thinking, this guy I'm talking to is more like you than anyone else I know. Maybe it would be good for you to talk to him too. He could, you know, help you adjust your way of looking at things."

Dad's rambling.

I don't need any help.

"We should've been seeing him together," Dad says, "but I only found him recently, and I had no idea he was going to be good. But, now that I know..."

He slides a card across the table.

The way leopold did.

191

Centuries ago.

I think back to the things I've gone through lately. Trying to find the right way to approach Emma. Setting up my channel to decode the intricate male-female interactions. Helping leopold with my vids and seeing him misconstrue all my advice and still end up with the girl – *my* girl! Starting my list. Putting myself out there with my followers. Actually making friends. Starting to re-connecting with my dad. And I find myself wondering how much easier all that might have been, how much faster it could've gone, if I didn't have to work out every single detail for myself.

I could've used someone smart and insightful to guide me, give *me* some leverage for a change.

I pick up the card, flip it over. I feel the texture of it, the density. Something about this doesn't necessarily feel completely wrong. I guess. Even if it doesn't exactly feel right, either.

"It's just a guy," my dad says. "All he does is talk. And there's nothing scary about talking, is there? You can do that."

That's true. I am a good talker.

"Who knows," he says, "you may end up helping him more than he helps you. You have that kind of effect on people."

36

Back at work my screen is overrun with numbers that tell me my computer has crashed. For no quantifiable reason, while it was doing nothing but sleep until my return, it still managed to execute a command so thoroughly confusing it had no option but to commit temporary suicide.

I restart while I go back over my conversation with Dad. He made a few good points, I suppose, but that doesn't mean I should just overlook ye olde adage: *let sleeping dogs lie*. That's ancient wisdom, after all. Probably saved millions of lives over the centuries. You don't just throw that out over a quick lunch conversation.

My computer reboots but then hangs. It shows a progress bar that isn't progressing. Not even very, very slowly. I peer at it for a long time to make sure, but it's definitely not going anywhere.

I sigh. If this were my own computer I'd restore a previous disc image and be done, but my work computer is completely locked off. I can't make any changes to its configuration. If it doesn't boot on its own someone from IT has to come fiddle with it and they may or may not discover a giant collection of scripts that someone wrote during office hours.

Not a fun prospect.

Desperately, I switch my computer off completely. Even pull the cord from the wall and let it sit for a full minute. Then I start feeling silly and ancient and I plug it back in.

Mercifully, it starts up this time. I watch the start-up screens, feeling a giant wave of relief wash over me. Of course the thing declines to give any indication of what was wrong, or why it's suddenly being so compliant, but, well, at least my scripts are safe.

After the boot I make sure I have all my scripts back-up-ed online, then I erase them from my work computer completely.

When I get home there's only a hint of mom-ness about the house.

There are vague traces of her perfume, distant sounds of vacuum-related activities, wisps of echoes of indications of her trek through the domicile, but it's all very ethereal, very subtle.

I decide not to look for her. It isn't easy for Mom to not jump on my case the moment I get home, so she must be working at top capacity to try and stay at the very fringes of my perception. Moreover, I have bigger problems to deal with right now. I have the very real and very solid manifestation of Tommy Moretti, my wayward childhood friend, to manage. He greets me in my doorway, gesturing for my coat.

"Hey, man," he says. "Welcome home. Let me take that for you."

I hand him my coat and consider running back to my car, then driving around the block until he either dies or goes home.

"I thought I'd pop over," he says. He brushes a crease from my coat and hangs it up. "You know, see how you're doing. What you're up to."

"You could've just emailed," I tell him.

"True," he says, "but, you know, we live pretty close..."

"Or sent me a message. Or commented on my vlog. Or just imagined how I was and then left it at that."

He smiles as if none of those were actually viable options.

"I brought Legos," he says. "Just in case."

I eye him suspiciously. "Legos as in to play with? Or Legos as in collector's items that need to be admired from a distance without opening the box?"

"Legos as in collector's items that need to be admired from a distance without opening the box," he says quickly.

I nod approvingly. Short of him announcing his immediate departure that was probably the best thing he could've said.

"I'd offer you some tea," I tell him, moving past him into my hallway, "but Mom seems to be fringing at the moment, so there's no way."

"Fringing?" Tommy gives me a look.

"It's a new thing we're developing. I'd explain but it's all rather complicated. The only immediate impact, however, is that there is no tea."

"That's okay," he says. "I brought juice boxes."

I stare at him. He starts to laugh.

"It's a joke," he says, which I don't feel is entirely accurate.

We sit on the couch and admire his unopened box of vintage Legos.

I have nothing with Legos myself but I understand what this object means to Tommy. It's all about reconnecting with the past and preserving stuff for future You-s. Strangely enough, Tommy moves the conversation to a different topic all together: his personal problems.

"So I finally decided to go out again," he tells me. "I mean, I'm not looking for anyone new, not really, but I need to get out of the house and talk to people, you know? Talk to women."

"Of course," I say. "Dopamine must flow, however small the trickle."

Tommy frowns a moment, then continues. "But just when I've set up a profile on a dating site, my ex suddenly starts dropping by. Can you imagine? She brings me food, offers to help with my laundry. What do you suppose that's all about?"

I ponder this for a moment. It's very odd indeed. Not just the fact that Tommy feels he's within his rights to unload on me like this – unless he knows about Leverage? No, impossible, there's been no other sign of that – but also that, somewhere out there, there's a woman who successfully got away from Tommy and is now trying to claw her way back in. It seems unnatural.

"Is it possible she found out about your profile?"

Tommy shrugs. "Maybe," he says, "but why would that matter? She's moved on, right? Now she suddenly wants me back? It makes no sense."

He turns the box of Legos over so we can admire the back. "I don't know if I should delete my profile and ask her out or if I should just ignore her."

"Well," I say, "let me ask you this: why are you waiting for her to make a decision?"

"How do you mean?"

"Just make your own decision. Stop wondering what she may or may not be thinking and concentrate on carving out your own future, separate from hers."

"I suppose I could," he says. "But it'd just be so much easier if she wanted me back, you know? Because of the kids and the house and all that."

"Of course it'd be easier," I tell him. "But even if she did want you back, how long do you think that would last? How long before all the little things she secretly hates about you started nagging at her again? How long before she'd start contemplating other options? You'd just be living on borrowed time, walking and sleeping on egg shells. How much fun would that be?"

Tommy plays with the box for a while. "You know what?" he finally says. "You're right. You're absolutely right. I really don't need any of that." He looks around the room, contemplating something, then comes to a decision. "So," he says, his voice a sigh, "you want to open this and build something?"

I shrug. "Sure, why not."

It's dark out before Tommy finally decides to go. I make some notes to leave around the house warning Mom never to let in Tommy, or any other street wanderers, while I'm away. I'm really not a fan of this whole ambush thing.

At the same time, though, this particular Tommy-interaction got me thinking again about how much easier things could be if you manage to find the right kind of help.

37

So this guy blowing his nose and surreptitiously checking the results before putting his handkerchief away, he isn't the therapist.

He's just the guy who ushers you into the room, asks you if you need anything (something to drink, maybe?), and then busies himself with the therapist's tablet.

I wait impatiently for the real therapist to arrive while this guy goes through the intake questions. It takes a long time, though, and the questions get oddly specific (what are some of the things you'd like to work on, when would you say was the last time you were really happy?)

I shrug and tell him I'll reserve my answers for the real therapist. Which awards me an odd look. The guy writes it down nonetheless, and continues with the intake, which has been going on for almost twenty minutes now.

How long does this session even last? At this rate there won't be any time left for the real therapist to go through these drivel questions – and my somewhat evasive answers – form a correct and sound opinion, and say the magic words to fix this last tiny part of me so I can go away and be happy forever.

Or whatever it is I'm doing here.

"What is it you'd like to get out of these sessions as a short term goal?"

I don't know, I'm still waiting for the real therapist.

"And what makes you feel that I am, as you put it, not a 'real' therapist?"

Probably the fact that he doesn't look very therapist-y. The fact that he doesn't talk very therapisty. And, perhaps most importantly, the fact that he doesn't have the least bit of therapisty air about him. In short, he doesn't inspire any kind of therap-i-ness.

I tell him so.

He nods and writes down 'therapiness', probably thinking about stealing it. No doubt he plans to claim it as his own and utilize it to become a real therapist (although I'm unclear on the exact mechanics that would facilitate this).

"Do you ever feel you tend to overanalyze things? Maybe as a way of evading certain issues or thoughts?"

"How so," I ask.

"Well, for one thing, you've looked at my shoes more than you've looked at my face. Why do you think that is?"

Because those are not therapisty shoes, damnit! Those are the kind of shoes you use to keep your feet warm while you're trying to decide whether you're going out for a run in the mud or are going to paint the house.

Those are backup shoes if I ever saw a pair!

"Why do you suppose it's so important to you that the 'real' therapy session, as you call it, hasn't started yet?"

Actually, that's a good question. The irony isn't lost on me. I feel hostile towards this man even though he isn't the therapist. I should be relieved, but I'm not. Perhaps it's the hypocrisy of the situation. The whole pretense of him pushing for me to accidently mistake him for the therapist. It's like someone asking you how old they look. They want you to be wrong by at least ten years and you can feel that pressure from the moment they smile coyly at you and say, 'So how–'.

But perhaps it'll be easier to talk to this guy. He might be less judgy, less formal. He won't have the answers any more than I do, so it'll be like talking to a regular guy.

Just another almost-person like me.

"You know I've been talking to your father for a while."

"I don't think you're supposed to mention that in any way, shape, or form."

"So are you calling me a therapist now?" He smiles a gotcha-smile, but it fades and his face softens. "I can, actually. I just can't give you any specific details about your father's sessions. But he has filled me in on your family history."

"Good," I say, immediately feeling worried. When do we get to the part where I'm helping him more than he's helping me? The bit where he realizes how insightful I am and that *he* should be asking *me* for advice?

That's the only bit I'm really looking forward to.

I guess it comes later.

"Can we talk about your family?" He turns up the air-conditioning, without even moving. The temperature just drops. Maybe the damn thing is on a timer.

I hug my jumper and say, "There's nothing to tell, really."

"You live with your mom, right?"

"That's completely incorrect," I huff. "She lives with me."

"In her house."

"Well, I suppose, if you are desperate to be historically accurate, then yes, it's her house."

"And your dad was absent for a large part of your childhood?"

"He has… issues."

"Does anybody else have issues?"

I shrug. "Most people on this planet have issues, I believe. It appears to be a very common theme."

"Okay. How about your mom. Does she have issues?"

"It's hard to say."

"Why is that?"

"It's just hard to tell where the issues end and my mom begins."

"Okay." He smiles. "I could see that. Anybody else we should talk about?"

"Me?" I glare at him. "No. I don't have issues."

"Alright, let's park that for the moment. Anybody else?"

I feel a bit dizzy, maybe I should've asked for something to drink after all.

"Any other close family members you'd like to mention?"

"I don't think so."

I suddenly have a glass of water in my hand. The non-therapist sits back in his chair. I take a sip, not entirely sure how I lost that bit of time.

The guy waits for me to put the glass down, then asks if I'm okay. I nod and he checks back over his notes. "Let's talk about your older brother, shall we?"

Again the temperature drops. It almost makes me gasp.

"Your dad told me you and your brother were great friends, very close."

I feel angry. Betrayed. Panicky. Is this guy really going there? In the very first hour of the very first session, straight to the place I swore I'd never go again? What kind of crap non-therapist is this?

Doesn't he know I'm alone?

Always have been, always will be?

There is no brother, there is only Leverage.

"He was a year older, wasn't he? Almost to the day?" The non-therapist smiles at me as if we're actually going to have this conversation. Right now. "He was ten and you were nine?"

"I don't– Maybe..."

"That's what your father told me."

I shrug.

"What was his name?"

I take another sip of water. I feel even more dizzy now, lightheaded, as if I'm about to float away – a little puff of Leverage-consciousness taking a stroll outside itself.

"Eric," I hear my body say. "My brother's name was Eric." The voice comes from far away.

"Good." The non-therapist makes a note. "Do you remember what Eric looked like?"

I haven't seen a photo in years. I don't remember ever seeing a photo, actually. When I think of him – which I haven't, not for a long time – I get more of a feeling than a picture. There was friendliness, caring,

198

protection. There was lots of explaining, planning stuff, building things. Always together, always looking out for each other. There are some images, at the back of my mind somewhere, but they're muddled and hazy. They're of long ago summers, walking in the woods. A flash of blond hair, a red jumper. Lugging around a fallen tree to build a fort, swimming in a creek.

It's all mixed up, nothing in chronological order.

"Do you miss Eric?"

I'm suddenly back in the room, anger welling up inside. "He was supposed to do this with me!" I blurt out. "He wasn't supposed to leave me here on my own! This is a crazy fucked up place and he swore we'd figure it out together!"

"Are you angry that he left you the way he did?"

"Damn right I am!"

"That's good. It's okay to be angry. It wasn't fair. You didn't deserve it and neither did he."

"We were supposed to go through this together..."

"But it didn't work out that way."

"No." My water is gone. The therapist gets up and pours me some more. "Sadly," he says, "that's the way the world works sometimes. We don't always get 'fair', no matter what we do or how good we are. We just get what we get."

"Yet another bug in reality," I manage.

"Perhaps," he says. "But it's up to us to figure out how to carry on, how to deal with things."

I finish the water, ask for more.

"There are many different ways of dealing with things." He pours out the last of the water. "And you had to figure one out on your own."

"I did."

"And you were only nine years old at the time. Seems like a pretty tall order for a nine-year-old kid, doesn't it?"

I can't argue with that. Even though I've been amazing on several unexpected levels for quite some time, it does seem like a lot for little Leverage to deal with.

"I'm sure you did the best you could back then, but maybe we can come up with something even better now." He gives me a long look. "What do you think, could we try to find something a little more comfortable for you?"

To be honest, that doesn't sound all bad. But I have no idea how that would work. "I'm not sure what you mean."

"Well," he says. "I think it's time you started talking to Eric again, don't you?"

"Talk to him?"

The therapist smiles. "Yes. Here's what I want you to do…"

Video #161 by *Leverage*. **Views: 476**

Comments:

WhipCrck: (6:14 pm) What happened to leverage?

LeopoldGreenEye: (7:04 pm) No vid in weeks, something's wrong guys!

TommyBoy07: (9:18 pm) Biggest gap since he started. I don't lik it.

AnnyTov: (9:21 pm) Lev, I have big problem. Please respond.

Chckmeout: (10:02 pm) Who cares? After all his endless rambling vlogs, he's never hit upon the most fundamental of all truths anyway, which is that girls never really grow out of playing with dolls. They just grow taller and continue playing dress up with themselves. In a way, they become their own dolls. Check out my vlog, it beats Lev's!!

TommyBoy07: (10:19 pm) U got it the wrong way round man. The dolls are just practice.

LeopoldGreenEye: (10:54 pm) No, women are like horses: you should never look nervous around them, it scares them off. They have to feel you're in control of the situation and know exactly what you're doing. That they're safe around you. That's why you always need to exude confidence. It has to ooze from every pore.

Chckmeout: (10:55 pm) That's more like it. Check out my blog Leo, you'll love it!!!

TommyBoy07: (10:55 pm) Stop trying ot poach Levs followers. Ur like a vulture, we don't even know hwat happened! This could be very serious

AnnyTov: (10:56 pm) I have life or death situation, Lev! Please respond to my pms!

Arnie: (11:19 pm) Where did you go, Lev? Don't make us wait so long!

DissonantMelody: (11:27 pm) We know you believe in the illusion of scarcity, allowing people to miss you and all that, but, come on, have a heart Lev ;(

38

Lost snippet on dating conversation:

> Gauge her level of interest in you by using awkward pauses to see if she'll keep the conversation going.
> If she does, immediately cut her off. Never let her talk too much, her subconscious won't respect you for listening to everything little thing she says. Keep cutting her off and before you know it she'll actually think she likes you. From there on in it's an uphill battle: you and her against her subconscious.

I'm not necessarily a connoisseur of silences – they're awkward and use up valuable time – but I've come to understand the need for a good silence now and then, and there's definitely a need now, so I'm not opposed to this one. However, the current silence has been going on for such a long time that the question arises whether this is a silence at all, or whether all communication simply ended a while ago.

I check my cell for messages, just to have something to do.

There's nothing.

I get up and pace the room, pretending to look for something, then sit back down. "So," I say, feeling I've shown ample respect for the 'good silence' window. "I'm glad you came here today. I'm proud, even." I give them each an encouraging nod. "And I'm even more proud that you're still here."

Silence.

"I know this isn't easy," I continue. "It can't be easy, so you should be proud of yourselves too."

I'm met with yet more silence. Somehow, though, I feel that this is the same silence from before. Even though I've just spoken, the silence between the two of them is still fully intact. I haven't succeeded in breaking it, or even putting a dent in its outer walls.

The last couple of days have been rough on all of us. It started with my first therapisty visit, which had my brain reeling, trying to piece together a coherent way of looking at things, and it continued with the exercise the almost-therapist gave me, and several more exercises that I gave myself.

But there were some highlights, too. For one thing, Gharity somehow figured out that many of the brilliant reports he attributed to my coworkers actually came from me. Which was a nice surprise. Although I don't need his approval, or even appreciate it all that much, it can't hurt to have my geniusness recognized from time to time, and so work has been slightly less of a bare-ass trip down the cheese grater lately.

And my YouTube channel is finally recovering. The comments from my real followers are starting to outweigh those of the comedy hunters again. Although I'm not sure I'll ever fully recoup my reputation as a serious video blogger, things do seem to be looking up.

I haven't made any new vids, though. I'm too busy with the therapisty exercises.

True, at first the almost-therapist's idea seemed very silly. And when I thought about it a bit longer, it seemed only marginally less silly. But I made somewhat of a start, just to prove how silly the idea was, and, low and behold, it just took off. My brain took to the task like a horse to water and it's been going strong ever since.

Right now, however, I'm working on a different exercise. One of my own design.

"You look like... yourself," Mom says, finally shattering the silence.

I'm not exactly sure what she means, and neither does Dad, but he nods and says "Yeah, you too."

Which is a start. I breathe a sigh of relief.

Mom was rather upset about coming home and finding Dad on our couch. I guess the reverse-ambush isn't fun, either. But it serves a higher purpose, so I'm okay with doing this to her.

"So," Mom says, "this is where we live now."

"It's nice."

"No it's not, but thank you for saying so."

Another silence, and I fear the worst, but Dad says, "I've been here before, actually. Well, not here in this house, but I've been in the street, outside."

Mom considers this, "You should've just come inside."

Dad looks at me for a moment, then back at her. "Really?"

Mom shrugs. She's not sure.

They handled Eric's departure very differently. I don't think either of them was right in the way they went about it, but I don't necessarily think they were wrong either. It's just what happened at the time. What the people dealing with the situation naturally gravitated towards. And in some ways the decisions they made damaged me; Mom burying the past, pretending Eric never existed, Dad running away, giving us room for whatever he thought was going to happen without him, but what we're doing here right now is not about dwelling on the past, or placing blame. It's about trying something else. Something different.

This is a reset.

"Dad, why don't you tell Mom some of the things you've been doing lately?"

Dad raises an eyebrow, then starts talking.

I'm no fool, I know we're not coming out of this a happy family. Dad is not going to move in. Mom is not going to forget he left. And no one is going to ignore all the years that were lost. But I think things are going to change from here on in. Maybe in big ways, probably just in small ways, but they're going to change for sure.

I head to the kitchen to brew Mom some tea and Dad two coffees.

There's a weird kind of full-circleness to this situation. Before I was the little kid holding mini lectures in the living room, surprising his parents in little ways with his strange thoughts and almost-insights, and now I've grown into my thoughts, grown into my brain, and we're back here, with me actually trying to fix them.

I feel very…. real.

I bring them their drinks, happy to see that they're still talking, if somewhat cryptic and haphazardly. I decide to leave them to it. This next part has nothing to do with me, after all. And I have my own work to do, my own journey to concentrate on. I take my coat and head out to the mall.

39

I'm about to enter an electronics store when I hear a familiar female voice.

"Hey! It's about time we ran into each other!"

I cross several possibilities off a mental list as I turn around: this voice isn't sexy enough to be Samantha's, not old enough to be one of Mom's friends', and far too familiar to be that of a random fan. I work out who it is before I've fully turned to greet the one person I really like but whom I don't want to see anymore.

She's wearing a summer dress with a rose pattern around which she's wrapped some kind of shawl as a belt. There seems to be a sparkle in her eyes when she focusses on me, but I could just be imagining that.

"Haven't you run out of Brazils yet?"

"Hey, Emma," I say. "No, I still have some."

I feel like I haven't seen her in an eternity. Forever squared. I'm reminded of the feeling of running into a minor celebrity; someone who's instantly familiar but somehow strange and otherworldly.

It's also like running into someone from my distant past.

Emma smiles, moving a strand of hair from her eyes. "Are you sure? You used to get a couple of bags a week."

I feel strange. I'm so used to having to plan ahead to meet her, and having time to work out what to say, that I feel a little lost. I remind myself that I have no feelings for this girl – other than, perhaps, some slight animosity.

"You used to come to the Shoppe all the time." She touches my arm. "Remember?"

Animosity for getting me to waste so much of my time.

"I remember," I say, "I just decided to cut back a little."

"No problem," she says. "I always thought they were pretty disgusting, to be honest."

"Well, they're supposed to be very healthy."

My voice sounds small. Must be all that animosity.

"They'd have to be," Emma laughs. "Anything that disgusting would have to be really, really healthy, right?"

I shrug. "Sure."

But why does animosity make my heart beat a little faster when she smiles?

"Anyway, you should come to the Shoppe soon," she says, giving me a nudge. "We switched importers so we have a lot of new choices."

"That's good," I say. "I'll keep that in mind."

"Yeah. We have some really horrible nuts, so maybe there's something in there for you."

Another big smile.

"I might drop by sometime," I say, "but I'm not sure when."

Emma holds me in place with her gaze. "Come on," she says. "You have to come. I *miss* you!"

Which is what I wanted her to say for so long.

But I don't anymore. Do I?

Either way, she's not fooling me. I know that by *'I miss you'* she means, *'I've noticed you haven't been around'*. Which is a bit late in the game and doesn't really mean that much.

Emma checks her watch. "Hey, let's get a coffee, I'm really thirsty. We can talk about your plane and my building. It'll be fun."

"I'd love to," I say, "but I really should get going. I have to work out an exercise, make some backups…"

"Come on," Emma says. "You don't want me to think you're mad at me, do you?"

She makes a pouty face and I'm surprised how little it affects me.

"Don't worry," I say. "It's not that. I just have things to do."

And if I did say yes, would you take out your cell and invite leopold along? Are you two still together?

But, no, that doesn't actually matter.

"No problem," she says. "But promise you'll send me a message when you have time, okay? I miss our little chats."

I promise and Emma leans in to kiss me on the cheek, then reconsiders and touches my arm instead.

As I watch her go, I feel somewhat empty. But it's not the emptiness I used to feel when we parted. That feeling of an invisible cord stretching out between us, fighting to snap us back together. There's just the dim sense of a conversation being over. And I suddenly realize how happy that makes me feel. How liberating it is. I actually feel as if I've been released from some evil spell. Like I'm an ex-prisoner, soaking up sunlight for the first time in years.

I'm free!

I'm finally, completely free!

I head back to my car, ecstatic that I don't have to go home and spend hours pining over Emma, obsessively analyzing everything she's said, planning our next interaction to the detail. And this is great. It saves so much time and energy. In fact, I'm so happy, this calls for a celebratory Ultra burger detour!

I'm enjoying my food when I suddenly feel watched. It's an unfamiliar sensation as I usually feel invisible. I try to shrug it off but fail. For some reason I'm absolutely sure someone, somewhere, is staring at me.

I scan the food court. At first glance, no one stands out. It takes me another two careful scans to notice another mostly invisible person who is giving me a look. It's a woman with unruly hair and a very unfortunate complexion. It takes me four full moments to recognize her: it's the dopamine lady. The woman I sat with before who asked me if I smoked and drank cats. I give her a friendly nod.

She gives me the finger, then leaves.

I smile. I'm going to be okay, and so is she.

As I eat, I marvel at the hidden debilitating properties of being in love. How it can easily consume all your time and energy, hold your thoughts hostage.

Of course you only notice this once you pop out the other end. When you stop waiting for your crush to grant you a few moments of her time. I feel kind of silly now for having been that guy. The guy who was debilitatingly in love with Emma.

I'm still not sure what I'm going to do with the rest of my life. I still want to find someone to share it with, but at least now I'm free to choose. It doesn't have to be Emma. In fact, I don't *want* it to be Emma.

I take a moment to let that thought settle.

I really don't want it to be Emma.

I bite into my burger and decide that this could actually mean that I've successfully completed my own list…

I finish my burger and head home to create the greatest vid ever.

YouTube script:

Here's another thing about getting over your crush.
At some point, when you least expect it, when your life is almost back on track, she'll try to pull you back in.
Yes she will.
Escaped prisoners are always hunted down!

[splice in gfx #1]

She'll give you that smile you fell in love with. Remind you of all the fun you had together. She'll give you long looks that appear accidental while still originating from deep seeded desire. She'll twirl her hair and be flirty, even if she wasn't very flirty before.

~~Again this is something she may even do subconsciously, but always for the same reason. And this reason is not that she suddenly realizes how wonderful you are. It's not that she just needed to miss you to understand how perfect you'd be together.~~
~~Of course not.~~

She does this just to see if she *can*.
She wants to know that she still has the power to pull you back in. She's like a child losing their least favorite toy. She may not like that toy all that much, but it's hers. No one else is allowed to have it. And she subconsciously knows how nice it is to have someone pining over her. It's a great confidence booster. She wants you to make her feel special and loved, without her having to do much in return. And when that feeling disappears, she misses IT. But that doesn't mean she misses YOU.

The only thing she actually has on offer is for you to come back into her life in a very small way. She wants you back in your old painful role, purely for her own benefit.

And make no mistake, if you let her, she'll keep this up for years. No time limit to this has ever been recorded. Look at it from her point of view; what a great payoff for just a smile and a kind word every six weeks. The ROI – Return On Investment – is amazing. It runs into the thousand percent range!

So what can you, as a guy using my list to get over her, actually do about this? Well, think of this as a test. Your final exam, if you will.

[splice in gfx #2]

When she re-appears and gives you that seductive smile, just know that every bit of it is part of your exam. And how can you be sure you've passed this exam? For starters, you're not actually over someone until you stop secretly wanting them back. You're not over her until she could give you a perfectly reasonable explanation for your 'break-up', show that it was all just an innocent misunderstanding and that she still 'loves' you, and you still wouldn't take her back.

Anything less than that and you're still kidding yourself...

When you no longer need her (or anyone else) to fix your life for you, when you can be happy on your own, then you're ready. So, tell me, are you going to graduate today, or are you going to cave and take her whole damn course over again?

[sign off]

So I finally passed my exam, Eric.

Maybe not with flying colors. Maybe not with any great lengths to spare, but I did it. Yes I did. She tried to pull me back in but my trusted list and I deflected her hooks and spears. We fought valiantly until we were free. And I don't mind telling you, I'm more than a little proud of myself.

Yes, sir.

Of course, at this point I had no idea what I was going to do next with my channel, with the oceans of time ahead of me, or even with my dad. But, well, that's just life. There's never a single point where all your problems are solved. There's always ongoing stuff, like this new journey I'm been on, working on the therapist's exercise.

So I hope you'll stick around, Eric. There's probably more to come.

Epilogue

I meet Antonov at a restaurant on the pier. He's sent me a string of urgent PMs about a life and death situation. Of course, with Antonov this could mean just about anything, but I'm not one to take chances with the lives of my followers. I have no choice but to show up and save the day.

I find him in the back, tearing up a coaster. Despite his age, he literally jumps out of his seat and rounds the table to pull up another chair. "Lev!" he beams. "You came!"

I nestle in while Antonov stares at me, rapt. "It's been very long time," he says. "I was worried you disappear forever. No update for weeks, no meet-ups. What is happening?"

It *has* been a long time. I've been busy with my new journey and I haven't had time for vids or even reading messages. I didn't think my followers would notice, or make such a fuss. I fully expected them to disappear quietly. After all, the net is a big place and there are more than enough people willing to dish out free advice.

"I've been writing," I tell Antonov.

"More scripts?"

"No, I'm writing a book of sorts."

"This is great news!" Antonov's eyes sparkle. "Book from the great Leverage! This is exactly what we need. When can we read?"

"It's not that kind of book." I try to temper his enthusiasm. It's important he understand I'm taking this particular journey alone. Or mostly alone. I do get some training-wheel-like guidance from a therapist, and I've had some surprisingly candid talks with my parents.

"It's more of an exercise," I tell Antonov.

"Oh?"

"A *personal* exercise," I add quickly. "I'm writing to my brother. I'm telling him about all the things he's missed out on. Why I set up my channel, how it kind of backfired and moved me to work on the greatest of all human problems... that kind of thing." I think a moment, then add, "I even mention how I met you and the Lizard."

Antonov's elated. "Really? I am in secret book by Leverage? Great!"

"Well it is great, in a way. For me. It's very cathartic, makes me feel like my brother's on this journey with me, you know?"

"Da," Antonov looks away a moment. "I also had brother," he says. "We were good in beginning, but then I move here and we almost lose touch. We make visit not long ago. It was just in time." He looks back.

210

"It's good to keep in contact, Lev," he says. "Any way you can."

"Yeah. It took me a while to figure that out."

Antonov examines my face. "You know, your brother has every reason to be proud of you. You are good person."

I shrug, not sure where to look. Thankfully a waitress decides to come and take our order. I ask her to bring me some tea along with Antonov's collection of beers.

"Any-of-way," Antonov says, "I have also news. And I have many, many life-or-death questions."

"So I gathered."

"You will not believe," he says, "but I meet wonderful American female on thing called facebook." He pauses. "Have you heard of it? Facebook?"

"I'm familiar with it," I tell him. "I think most breathing humans are."

"Okay, well, is new for me," he says. "I am getting good with Tube, but I did not hear of facebook. My neighbor set up account for me. Is really cool."

"Good for you."

"Any-of-way, I was minding my business, clicking 'like' on picture of cat, then, suddenly, there is Stacy, asking to be friend." He shakes his head in remembered amazement. "Can you imagine? We become friends through internet! I mean, how often that happens?"

I shrug. "I'd say just about all the time."

Antonov's enthusiasm falters. "Why do you say that?"

"Because it doesn't mean much to be someone's friend on Facebook. It's like... winning a paper medal, which was left out in the rain, and has someone else's name on it."

Antonov frowns. "You're probably thinking of some other internet-book, Lev. Stacy and I are very serious about our relationship."

"Your *relationship*? Antonov, how many friends do you have on Facebook?"

Antonov is shocked. "One, of course. Just Stacy. I am not insensitive American playboy!"

"Just one? Okay, well, most women have hundreds of friends. Some have thousands. It doesn't really mean anything."

"No, no. We have something special," Antonov insists. "She even find out how to make pictures appear on my computer. She's really smart."

"That happens automatically. That's what Facebook does."

"I don't think so."

I take out my cell, ask for Stacy's full name. It takes me only seconds to find her. "Is this her? She looks pretty young."

Antonov checks my cell. "Da, that's her," he says, excited. "She is great, don't you think? She's much older than she looks, that's not very

211

good picture. She just turned seventeen."

"Seventeen? I don't even think that's legal."

"I think it is, Lev."

"I'm pretty sure you're not even supposed to call her a woman, technically."

Antonov waves it away. "Look," he says, "this is whole new age. Generation X is very progressive, they don't care about artificial boundaries like age and heritage. And Stacy sends me messages all day. She tells me everything she does. She doesn't go to store without telling Antonov. She doesn't brush teeth without telling Antonov. And when she writes, she gets so excited she has no time to use even vowels!"

I click on Stacy's profile. "Generation X was over thirty years ago," I tell him, "and those messages are probably from twitter." I show him my cell again. "Did you check her personal details?"

Antonov looks appalled. "Of course not! I am not insensitive American stalker!"

"You should *always* check profile details. They're public, see? Even *I* can access them. See this number here?"

Reluctantly, Antonov glances at my cell.

"Number 1687?"

"Yes. That's her number of friends."

Antonov is confused. "How you mean?"

"I mean, you are 1 of 1687."

"Can't be," he huffs. "Your phone is not doing that right. You're supposed to do that on computer."

I suppress a sigh. "Fine," I say. "Let's assume that the number got mangled somewhere. Look at her Relationship Status, it says she's dating someone."

"It does?" Antonov pipes up. "You think she means me?"

"No, Antonov. I don't think she means you. In fact, I'd say that any time you have to ask that question, the answer is invariably 'No'."

Antonov slumps back. "Well," he says, "she could be sending me hint…"

"She could," I agree, "but let's just pretend we live in reality for a moment, shall we?"

Antonov shrugs.

"I honestly think this Stacy thing is a dead end, buddy. I'm really sorry."

"But are you sure? Isn't there, how you say, small chance?"

"Sorry. Even if she knows you exist, then you're just a friend to her. And an internet friend at that."

Antonov sighs. Something finally seems to click into place. The poor guy. I didn't like doing that, but it had to be done. And the sooner the better.

I signal the waitress to bring us some stronger drinks. We're going to be here for a while and my Russian friend is way too sober to start any kind of healing process. I look at him – I can almost see him descend into that deep dark hole, that moment where he realizes he's lost the life he planned for himself.

"What can I do, Lev?" he asks me.

"Don't worry," I tell him. "I'm here and I know exactly what to do."

In fact, I've created a killer list for just this kind of situation.

Snag Yerself A Cool Guy!

A dating blog by Emma

There are still a few cool guys out there. Let's snag them up before the army of blonde bimbos gets its hooks into them, breaks their spirits, and turns them into wusses!!

Post #132: hail to placeholders.

It's been a while. I know, I know I should blog more, but I've been crazy busy!! You won't believe the stuff that's going on in my life right now! But I read all your comments (honest!! ;p) and I know the exercises are giving some of you trouble, so this post will serve a double purpose.

First, I need to tell you grls not to give up, ever-ever-ever. It *can* and *does* happen. (If *I* can do it, so can you.) There are still **Cool Guys** out there and if you play your cards right you don't have to settle for a wuss just because he's the only guy who remembers your name. We all deserve a **Cool Guy**, someone who can make us laugh, who's not too pushy, and who is maybe not handsome in the traditional sense but who attracts us in mysterious ways. The kind of guy that always (always!!) seems to get scooped up by another girl just before we meet him. Well... not anymore.

Second, I want to talk some more about something that played a much bigger role in my success than I actually realized. I always told you it was possible for anyone to get a **Cool Guy** because I believed that, with a little work, it *should* be possible. But at the same time I didn't really believe it. Does that make sense? But today I actually *have* a **Cool Guy**!!! He's funny and tall and sexy and when I'm with him I never know what's going to happen next!!

So, what's this post about?
Let's call it a *placeholder* (I don't have a better word right now). It's your kinda cool friend. That fun, interesting guy who's into same things you are but who just isn't romantically interested in you. He'd be perfect boyfriend material because you connect on so many levels. He reads your mind, laughs at your jokes, likes the same movies (even the chick flicks!!), and he'd never leave you at a party with no-one to talk to. But, for some reason, he just isn't interested in making a move on you.

I loooove lists, don't you? So here's one I whipped up. Three good reasons for getting yourself a placeholder:

1. He'll give you insight into what guys are actually thinking.
2. He'll take you places where **Cool Guy**s hang out.
3. He'll let you test things out on him (outfits/hair tosses/that cute smile you've been practicing in the mirror). It's like having an instant hot-or-not test without having to put pics up on the net.

Believe me, grls, this stuff is *battle-tested*. Before I landed my **Cool Guy** I spent a lot of time with my own placeholder. (At one point we were messaging each over fifty times a day!) He really boosted my confidence. And even if he never wanted to make a move on me, he still showed me I was interesting and that a guy could have fun hanging out with me.

So try this out. Just get one (or more??) guys in your life that you can practice on. Talk to them, hang out with them. You'll learn a lot and it'll be totally safe!

Go!!Go!!!Go!!!!

~Emma

Early note: "Remember, if all else fails, instead of losing her forever, try getting a bit of Her DNA (a hair, some skin cells, a tooth). After all, it's only a matter of time before we'll be able to clone Her for you."

Dedications:

Emma:
I dedicate my dating blog to that one Cool Guy.
You know who you are.
Keep surprising me with your weird questions and your green eyes, from now until we're eighty years old.

Leopold:
I'd like to thank my guru and master, Leverage.
You made possible something I never dreamed of.
You have my undying gratitude.
I will always be your student.

Gomez Porter:
This whole ride was somewhat of a disappointment.
It seems we're forever getting closer, but we never arrive.
It sucks!

Melody:
I'd like to thank Emma, without her blog I wouldn't have the courage to go out and try to catch my own Cool Guy.
I just know we're going to get together and create thousands of wise-ism and brilliant-isms together!

Leverage:
I dedicate my video legacy to Eric. We were supposed to work out this whole complicated life-thing together, but fate had different plans. Wherever you are, though, I know you're still busy figuring things out, paving the way for when I get there.

em: Hey ;)

em: Are you there?
em: Miss you… We haven't talked for a while…

em: Okay :(I guess ur busy…

I'd like to thank you, the reader, for going on this journey with me. It was fun, albeit in a weird, dark way, to live in Leverage's skin for a while and see the world being warped and shaped through his eyes. If you managed to enjoy any of this, on any level, as well, then please consider leaving a review. Without reviews the Leverages and Gomezes simply turn invisible and fade away.

Regs,

Graham

Printed in Great Britain
by Amazon